# SAVING HEART & HOME

## NIKKI BERGSTRESSER
— AND —
## DENISE JADEN

SAVING HEART & HOME
Copyright © 2021 by Nikki Bergstresser & Denise Jaden

ISBN: 978-1-953735-32-4

Published by Satin Romance
An Imprint of Melange Books, LLC
White Bear Lake, MN 55110
www.satinromance.com

Names, characters, and incidents depicted in this book are products of the author's imagination or are used fictitiously. Any resemblance to actual events, locales, organizations, or persons, living or dead, is entirely coincidental and beyond the intent of the author or the publisher. No part of this book may be reproduced or transmitted in any form or by any means, electronic or mechanical, including photocopying, recording, or by any information storage and retrieval system, without permission in writing from the publisher except for the use of brief quotations in a book review or scholarly journal.

Published in the United States of America.

Cover Design by Caroline Andrus

*Wayne and Lorraine,*
*Fifty years, since "I do".*
*Hearts entwined, love that's true.*
*Forever your daughter.*
*Love,*
*Nikki*

*Roy and Marj*
*Who taught me about lasting love,*
*and following my dreams.*

*Love,*
*Denise*

# 1

## EMMA

Some people dreaded Washington's grey skies and rain. Not Emma Hathaway. She appreciated everything about a rainy day. Lifting her head up to the skies, she paused and closed her eyes, breathing it all in. The aroma of cedar filled her lungs, and a sense of calm eased her soul. She could feel her heart rate slow as peace took over her mind. To Emma, the small town in which she lived looked almost storybook-like with its tall fir trees lining the road leading into the heart of the town. Walking to work was one of her morning rituals she had grown to cherish since moving to Juniper Falls.

Emma always tried to arrive at work earlier than ten o'clock, when her shift began. It was her time to connect with some of the elderly residents at Heart & Home without the responsibilities that came with being an on-the-clock nurse of an assisted living facility. Today she had an extra skip in her step as she looked forward to spending time knitting with Mrs. Rothstein.

A wet nose nudged at her hand and she was brought back to the realization that she also had another purpose for her morning walk to work.

"Sorry Charlie, didn't mean to slow you down." Emma reached down and ruffled the dewy fur on her loyal companion's head. The yellow lab responded with a shake of his body, sending a shower of droplets in all directions. He proceeded to guide his owner along the pathway, occasionally stopping as he became tempted by an unknown scent or the perfect-sized stick to carry along on his journey.

Emma paused by the local coffee shop to consider picking up a treat for her knitting partner. Mrs. Rothstein loved tea lattes: skim milk, half sweet. However, peering in through the window, she noticed a long line of patrons waiting for their caffeine fix and a rather flustered looking barista. A young woman opened the door attempting to balance a drink carrier with two cups in her arms. Emma reached out to lend a hand as the one cup began to teeter.

"Thanks! That could have been a real mess!" The woman readjusted her load so she had a better grasp on the tray.

"No problem. Why the long line-up today?"

"2-for-1 special for the first." Emma must have looked confused, for the woman explained, "You know, February, the month of *love*, and all." She moved past Emma and down the street, calling, "Thanks again!" as she went.

Emma was left still holding the door, which allowed a wafting of freshly-roasted beans to greet her nose. Knowing she was already pressed for time, she decided her kind gesture would have to wait for another day.

As they left the coffee shop and continued on their walk, Charlie began to pull on the leash frantically, almost knocking Emma off balance as another dog out on a morning walk approached. Tail wagging and always eager to greet a new friend, Charlie pulled ahead so he could get face to face with the black cocker spaniel. The dog was dressed for the weather in a hot pink rain slicker complete with matching booties. Emma was amused by how a few articles of clothing could create such an air of pretentiousness from a dog. However, Charlie was not dissuaded from giving his full attention to his new friend.

"Fiona is rather cautious of larger dogs. Aren't you baby?" The owner bent down and scooped up his dog, while accidentally dropping one of the pink booties in a puddle. He looked annoyed at this inconvenient meeting of pooches. Emma wondered if Fiona was cautious or her owner simply overprotective. She smiled at the man as Charlie scooped up the drenched bootie in his mouth and lifted his face up to the man, waiting for him to retrieve the lost item. The owner did not make a move toward Charlie's offering.

"It's okay. Charlie's just helpful. He's really friendly. Honest." Emma put her hand out and Charlie dropped the bootie into it. She handed it over to the other owner who still looked distrustful. However, he accepted the item from Emma and put it back onto his dog who seemed eager to get down.

"Thank you." Fiona's owner grasped her tighter, and Emma felt badly for the poor little dog. "Fiona is a purebred and I just can't have her associating with *every* dog she comes across. You know how disastrous that could be."

Emma did not know and did not feel like waiting around to hear more. "No worries. Come on, Charlie, let's go." Emma tried to coerce her dog away from the cocker spaniel and arrogant owner, but Charlie was smitten. As her owner finally set her down, Fiona pranced away and poor Charlie pulled to follow along as his love interest disappeared around the corner.

Emma just shook her head in disbelief. Unrequited love. Charlie looked up at her with a pitiful look in his eyes as if to say, "I can't help myself."

It began to drizzle again, so Emma opened up her favorite umbrella, a bright yellow one with a happy face at the base of the handle and managed to convince Charlie to move on with a little help from a dog treat she had stashed in her bag. Rounding the corner by the bookstore, a new display in the window caught Emma's eye. Book titles such as *It's Never Too Late*, *Finding Mr. Right at the Wrong Time,* and *Love By Moonlight's Glow* were displayed for the hopeless romantics at heart, or those desperately seeking. Emma was contentedly neither. For the first time in her life, she felt satisfied with her life. Since her last failed relationship, she had worked hard to repair her heart and she was not willing to throw it all away on some romanticized ideal. Maybe she just wasn't meant for that kind of love. Some might call it cautious—her sister called it avoidance—but Emma just called it being realistic. Why search after something you don't even know if you actually want in the first place? What Emma wanted most was to get through this "month of love" without having it thrown in her face at every turn.

Emma and Charlie continued on their walk and soon approached the gardens of Heart & Home. Trails meandered through the gardens and benches dotted the pathways for those needing to stop and rest or admire the blossoming flowers during spring and summer months. It was a tranquil place with a small koi pond and numerous bird feeders, giving the residents some wildlife entertainment on their daily walks.

But as serene as it was, Charlie was done with exploring. His friends were now close enough that all he could think of was them. Emma let Charlie off his leash, and he rushed on ahead where the automatic doors at the front opened to let him in from the drizzle. Emma lowered her umbrella and shook off the excess water before closing it. She was relieved to know that for the next eight hours she could lose herself in her job, enjoy time with the residents, and not have to think about anything the least bit romantic.

# 2

## JAKE

Fog blanketed the valley like a suffocating covering. Jake navigated his Lexus effortlessly around the winding turns, descending into the town. The near-constant rain that was all too familiar this time of year on the West Coast had finally slowed to a fine mist. Approaching the worn wooden sign welcoming visitors to the small town, caused Jake's heart rate to increase as a flood of emotions took over.

*Juniper Falls.* He knew this trip was inevitable and consoled himself solely with the possibility of it being one of the last times he would make the drive from Seattle. To a visitor, the town may look quaint, but to Jake it was stifling. His body sensed the emotional discomfort and the memories nagging at the edges of his mind, making him tense. Just being in Juniper Falls seemed to cause the hardened exterior he'd built around his heart over the past ten years to begin to crack. But he wouldn't allow that. His foot pressed more heavily on the accelerator. The rain picked up along with his Lexus, making Jake's frustration with this trip rise even further.

A siren and flashing lights in the rear-view mirror snapped him back to the present. Jake heaved out a resigned breath and pulled over to the side of the street. Curious eyes of those passing on the sidewalk focussed on the law-breaking stranger in town. Great. Now he was the local entertainment.

"You've got to be kidding me," he muttered. Small towns: it was like living in a goldfish bowl. And everyone knew what happened to goldfish eventually—belly up and flushed. Yes, that would have been his fate if he hadn't made his escape when he did. Jake reached for his identification from the wallet lying on the passenger's seat. The uniformed officer approached and tapped on his window.

"License and registration, please, sir."

Without saying a word, and barely looking up, Jake produced the required documents, wondering if this day could get any worse. Before he could answer his own question, the officer beat him to it.

"Well if it isn't Jake Rothstein, gracing us with his big city presence." And here it was. All Jake wanted was to get in and out of Juniper Falls without much notice.

"Look, I was speeding. I get it." Jake looked up at the officer. "Now can you just give me my ticket so I can be on my way?"

Smirking. The guy was seriously *smirking* at him. Jake's hands tightened on the steering wheel and the rise of a sarcastic comment came up his throat and balanced on the verge of escaping his pursed lips. It was then he noticed the familiar grin. The face and eyes, too, were a few years older, but those eyes still held the same glint of mischief. After escaping into the city when he graduated from Juniper Falls High, Jake had deliberately cut most ties with people from his past and the small town. But there was one friend who had tried to practically force him to keep contact with him over the years: Paul Sanders.

It made sense, was almost expected, for Paul to now be in law enforcement. Both his father and grandfather had been police chiefs in the past. Their family was held in high regard in the community, and from the looks of things, Paul had grown into his ears just fine. There had been times when Jake had landed himself in hot water, being a teen with a chip on his shoulder, yet Paul had come to his rescue on several occasions, interceding on his behalf. Chief Sanders always treated him fairly. He never let Jake get away with things, but he also was reasonable, especially compared to some of the other officers around town that seemed to have it out for Jake. When he thought about it, Jake was still amazed the Sanders family had even allowed Paul to be friends with him at times during their youth.

A small part of him felt a sense of comfort at seeing his old friend, but his guilt overshadowed it. He had tried to bury many of his bad memories from the past. Jake had not returned phone calls or email messages from Paul over the years, and eventually they became less and less frequent until they stopped completely. But now, here was his childhood friend in the flesh, with that big, stupid heartfelt grin.

"Sorry, Paul. I didn't recognize you. Good to see you again."

"It's been a while, Jake." Paul's face still bore a smirk, but now Jake saw it as the good-natured expression it was. "You look great! How long are you in town for?"

"Just a quick visit. Hoping to be out of here in a couple of days. Or less."

Paul pulled out a pad of paper and began to write. "Well, if you have time for a coffee or beer, just let me know. It would be great to catch up." He tore off the paper, handing it to Jake. Expecting to see a hefty fine for his speeding, Jake was pleasantly surprised to find Paul had simply scrawled his phone number across the page.

Jake was torn, because he knew he should make time for his old friend after this gesture of kindness. But he opened his mouth to say what he had to in order to get through this trip as painlessly as possible: "Not sure if it will work this time, but I will keep in touch. Thanks, Paul," Jake said, even while questioning himself on the sincerity of his promise. He doubted that he would actually call Paul, even if he could find any time. It wasn't that he didn't *want* to connect with his old friend again. It was just that the friendship was long ago, in the past. Jake was sure they would have nothing in common now. It probably wouldn't be worth the time.

Paul began to walk back to his squad car, but turned around to add with a chuckle, "And Jake? Keep the speed down a little.

You might be surprised with what you see around you when you take the time."

Giving a wave, Jake put his car into gear and drove down the road to his destination, eager to wrap up his business in Juniper Falls sooner rather than later.

The one positive thing about Juniper Falls was it only took a few minutes to get from one end of the town to the other. Of course, that also meant there was nowhere to hide.

As he pulled into the cul-de-sac where his grandmother had been staying for the last year, Jake Rothstein felt a nostalgic sense of displacement. He had not been to see her once since moving her from the house he grew up in over to the assisted living facility of Heart & Home. For the second time today, he felt a twinge of guilt. But, he reminded himself, to his credit, he talked to her every Sunday evening and listened dutifully to her stories about knitting projects, sing-songs around the piano, and card games she participated in with the other residents. Still, Jake couldn't ignore the fact that she was also lonely for family. He was all she had left now that his grandfather was gone, and losing him had softened her. He knew she missed her husband. After all, they had been married for sixty years. Jake couldn't even imagine being with someone that long. But he had a plan to make her life less lonely and take away a little of the guilt weighing on him. She wouldn't be in this place much longer, and he called the new facility to reassure himself of it.

"Yes, I'll give them notice today, and my hope is to have her settled in your facility by the end of the month," Jake told the case worker. He felt pressure to make sure this went according to plan and he did not want anything standing in the way of what would be best for his grandmother.

The visitor parking lot for the nursing home was across a small garden from the main entrance. While Jake was not about to take any time to explore the gardens and pathways surrounding the place, he consoled himself that this temporary residence at least hadn't been the worst place for his grandmother to settle while he had been busy in the city.

The rain had grown heavier, but he only planned to be a few

minutes, so he pulled up the drive to the front doors and parked along the curb as the lady on the other end of his phone call went on about application requirements. He switched from speakerphone and beeped on his car alarm as he got out.

"Sure, I'll have the deposit couriered to you to hold her spot. I can do that by day's end," he said into his phone.

As Jake listened to a lengthy explanation of facility policies, an attractive nurse shook out a bright yellow umbrella from a few feet away, near the automatic doors. He continued to nod into his phone, but at the same time followed the nurse's gaze to his car. A shot of pride at the Lexus he'd saved for the last two years to buy moved through him, but when the nurse's eyes continued to linger behind him, that's when he noticed she wasn't actually looking at his car. Her eyes were on the No Parking sign, just inches in front of his Lexus. He'd been so busy on his call he hadn't noticed it.

The nurse shook her head disapprovingly and didn't offer Jake another glance as she continued on her way through the doors. Phone pressed to his ear, he couldn't very well call out and explain his short visit to her.

He looked back at his car and surveyed the area. There did not seem to be any security, and he really wouldn't be long, Jake rationalized again to himself. He'd be back out and sitting in his car before it would be in anyone's way. So he hung back to finish his phone conversation under the overhang of the entrance and he kept an eye out for anyone else being put out by his poor parking job.

"That all sounds great," he said into his phone. "I'm really looking forward to moving her into a facility that will provide the proper care she deserves. Thanks for all your help in speeding up this process."

He hung up, then glanced back at his car, considering moving it one more time. But better to get in to see his grandmother as soon as possible and tell her the good news.

He strode through the automatic doors and up to the front administration area, which was flanked by a long pink counter. On the wall above, a sign read: HEART & HOME ASSISTED

LIVING - HOME IS WHERE THE HEART IS, which felt like a contradiction somehow.

The pretty nurse had disappeared. Jake glanced at the nametag of the woman manning the front counter. Pam. He'd once had a personal trainer named Pam. To say she'd made his life uncomfortable and painful was an understatement. This Pam didn't look like she spent much time in the gym, but her no-nonsense face and tight bun suggested she could wreak just as much havoc on his life.

"Yes, can I help you?" Pam asked, and her voice sounded friendlier than he expected, but this information didn't make it to his brain before he opened his mouth.

"My grandmother has been accepted into Lexington Manor in the city so I'll need to sign any necessary forms to have her released by the end of the month." Without his permission, Jake's voice seemed to get more clipped, the more he spoke. "You provide transfer to the new home, I assume? There's no way her wheelchair will fit in my car. I will gladly pay for the extra service."

"I'm sorry, sir, and what is this regarding?"

He was doing it again. Slow it down, Jake, he reminded himself. Sometimes he tended to be a bull in a china shop with his efficient business approach. He expected everyone to keep up with the speed that he lived his life. Jake took a deep, calming breath, and started again.

"Jake. Rothstein. Meredith Rothstein is my grandmother. She's been on the waiting list at Lexington for the last eight months and a spot has finally become available. I'm sure she'll be thrilled to hear about it," he said in an attempt to smooth over his brash first impression, but he heard his own voice and it sounded more like bragging than making nice. He was confident in the city. Why was it as soon as he entered the town limits of Juniper Falls, he felt so insecure? It was as if he had to prove himself, prove his success, every time he opened his mouth. He came across just as flawed and as fractured as the road leading into the small town.

"Oh, I see." Pam had a concerned look about her, and her

forehead pulled together in a way that made the bun in her hair appear tighter. "Has Mrs. Rothstein been unhappy with her stay here at Heart & Home? We love having her here and would hate to see her leave."

Jake could see the disappointment in Pam's eyes. He tried again. "I just want the best. I'm not saying that where she is here currently isn't adequate. I'm sure it suits some residents just fine. But from what I hear, Lexington Manor prides itself on the latest and most advanced care for their clients." More unintentional bragging, and he was about to open his mouth and retract or at least apologize for it, when Pam interrupted in an argumentative tone.

"Lexington Manor, sir. I mean, I hate to talk negatively about other senior homes, but it is rather institutional. Have you dropped in to see their facilities?"

This was not what he came here for. "I can tell from their website that my grandmother would find the best therapeutic care with them." He motioned to the lounge behind him. "Ping pong tables and hot tubs are great for college dorms, but not exactly necessities for senior citizens, wouldn't you agree?"

That got her. Pam moved papers around on her desk to avoid answering. Red crept up her neck and Jake was not sure if it was from the awkwardness of the conversation or a pride in the facility where she worked, but she was clearly trying to control her frustration at his comments.

"Now if you'd be so kind as to get started on the paperwork..."

Pam took in a breath and let it out slowly. When she looked back up at Jake, she had regained her composure and the friendliness returned, as though it was a costume she simply had to slip over her head. "Before we fill out any papers, I would need confirmation from our resident to begin the transfer. She should be in her room."

He followed Pam's lead and tried to be equally pleasant. "I will go talk to her now, thank you." He turned on his heels, eager to leave this conversation but then a fact dawned on him and with slight embarrassment he turned back to her. "Um, could you please remind me which way I'm going to find her?"

Pam didn't let the smile go for a second, and in fact, it was so static that this alone gave away the falseness of it. "Follow the west hallway to the end." Jake began walking and had to once more turn around, but before he got any words out of his mouth, Pam had anticipated his next question. "Room 112. It will be on your right."

Jake forced his best smile back to her, but this time it was his neck he felt go red from embarrassment. He should certainly know his own grandmother's room number. "I appreciate it," he said. But Pam had instigated a niggling of doubt in him, and as he walked away, he murmured to himself, "Now all I have to do is convince Grandma."

He'd only walked a few feet, still slightly frazzled from his previous conversation, when he almost tripped into an elderly man shuffling faster than Jake would have thought possible with a walker. The blue plaid shirt and pleated pants pulled up high with suspenders reminded him of his grandfather and made him chuckle. Jake could only imagine where the old fellow was off to with such determination. He was trailed by a nurse.

"Gotta get outta here," the elderly man said, and at first Jake thought he was talking to him. But as the man brushed by with his eyes straight ahead, Jake realized his words were directed only to the air around him.

"Time for your meds, Mr. Wilson." The nurse fell farther behind the racing old man, and she called him again, "Mr. Wilson!" The nurse stopped and put her hands firmly on her hips. She rolled her eyes at Jake, as if he was somehow in cahoots about this, and then called out, "Geezer?" to the old man.

Jake was taken aback by the rudeness, which would probably go unnoticed in Seattle, but here in Juniper Falls, it felt out of place.

Surprisingly, though, the old man turned with a twinkle in his eye and innocently asked, "Yes? What can I do for you?"

"It's time for your meds, Geezer."

At this, the old man smirked at the nurse. Then he spun back around, took off a split second later, and said, "Only if you catch me!" The exasperated nurse followed in pursuit.

Jake shook his head as he proceeded past the unusual interchange and tried to remember where he could find his grandmother's room, because there was no way he would go back to the tight-bunned receptionist at the front desk asking for directions again.

# 3

## EMMA

Emma had completely forgotten about the self-important man who'd parked his fancy car right in the way of the entrance by the time she'd completed her first slip stitch on her new scarf. There was something soothing about knitting in the sunroom. The fireplace was going, and it felt cozy here just doing what she loved and enjoying the company of the residents. A purple ball of yarn rested in her lap as her knitting needles rhythmically clicked together. Emma hoped she could complete this project for her sister's birthday in a few weeks. It was an ambitious goal for someone new to knitting, but Emma loved challenges and knew how her sister would appreciate her efforts, even if there was an occasional knot in her labor of love. Her shift would soon be starting so she was glad she had made it in time for a few rows of stitches despite the unusual morning distractions on her way to Heart and Home. The residents here were what mattered to Emma. After all, they had become more like her friends since she began working here three years ago.

Glancing over at Meredith—Mrs. Rothstein insisted Emma call her by her first name—Emma noticed the elderly woman was much farther along on her project than herself, but that was because Meredith could take in whatever TV program they were watching, keep up on her end of the conversation, *and* somehow make progress on her knitting without making constant mistakes.

Emma laughed at the Seinfeld rerun they were watching today and took notice of how well Meredith laughed along, while seamlessly continuing her purl one, knit two as if she did it in her sleep.

Emma had just gotten back to her knitting when a cleared throat made her look up once more. An attractive man stood in the doorway of the nearly empty activity room. He was all cheekbones and eyelashes—ones she could see from clear across the room. But then his forehead buckled, and recognition struck. It was the man from the driveway, and he did not look any happier than when Emma had seen him earlier.

"Knitting?" He murmured under his breath, but not quite low enough to make it past Emma's tuned in ears. "This is what I'm paying for?"

Emma was about to ask him who he was, and if she could help him find something or someone, but he strode straight for Meredith before she had a chance.

He kissed her cheek and said, "Hi, Grandma."

Emma's mouth opened in astonishment.

Another cleared throat, and then, "The receptionist said you were in your room. Took me forever to find you in here." He cast his eyes to the knitting, "Looks like you're having fun." He said the words, and yet to Emma, this man did not look like he would know the definition of fun.

"Why Jake, this is such a surprise!" The elderly woman grabbed hold of his hand with such intent, looking as if she were afraid if she let go, he would be gone at any moment.

Emma kept opening her mouth in surprise, like a guppy, but then closing it again, not knowing if this could be real. Sweet Meredith was the grandmother of this brash man? And if they were related, why hadn't Emma seen him here before? He must live quite a distance away to not be a regular visitor. Emma adored her daily time spent with Meredith and couldn't imagine someone not wanting to be around her every moment they could. Mind you, she knew from experience that there were many residents at Heart & Home whose families simply neglected to make the time for regular visiting outside of Christmas and Easter.

Just as she thought this, he turned to her. "Can you give us a minute?" The tone wasn't any less brash, and it wasn't directed as a question. She was hesitant to leave Meredith with this man. The elderly woman lay her knitting needles down on her ball of yarn. She gave Emma a small smile and nod as if to say it was alright, she could go.

Emma popped out of her chair, letting her ball of yarn fall to the floor, and headed for the door. She didn't need to be told twice if one of the residents needed something. "Sure. My shift is starting soon anyways. Come on, Charlie," she called. "Let's go get you a treat."

Charlie, who had been enjoying a snooze, crawled out from under the table. She scratched at his yellow, furry head, still damp from the rain. He dropped an extra ball of yarn onto Meredith's lap, and then trailed Emma to the door. But Emma couldn't shake her distrust of the man and stood close around the corner.

"Seriously? A dog?" The man told Meredith. "I can't even begin to imagine the health code violations."

"It's lovely to see you, Jake, but you could be a little friendlier to Nurse Hathaway. And Charlie is part of our family here at Heart & Home."

Emma smiled. Meredith, while kind, had always seemed like the type of grandma who would put children in their place. She'd heard Meredith had raised her grandson, and in only ten seconds, it was obvious that Emma had been spot-on in her assessment.

"Sorry, Grandma," the man—Jake—said. "I just want the best for you, and it bothers me how people around here are getting paid to knit when they have a job to do."

It was all Emma could do to keep her indignant thoughts to herself. It didn't matter, though, because it seemed Meredith had plenty of indignant thoughts of her own.

"Sometimes, Jake, I wish you would see the bigger picture. It does an old lady like me good to have company, I get lonely. Nurse Hathaway is kind and cares about all the residents here. If you must know, she often comes in before her shift or stays later just to spend time with us. We are not just a job to her."

Emma smiled at that. It's exactly how she felt, and she was glad it came across to the residents.

"Well, that's neither here nor there." Jake's voice was all-business now. "I came into town to meet with the realtor. Turns out we're going to have to drop the price again on the house. That'll mean almost no profit, but it'll be good to finally sell it after being on the market almost a year."

"It's too bad. I loved that house." Emma could hear the nostalgia in Meredith's voice.

"Sure, but you can't live there alone, especially with the stairs. That's why you moved in here. It's really just storage now. It's an old house, Grandma. We all know how much work will need to be done on it eventually. The cost for maintaining it, plus having someone come in to cook and clean for you does not make any financial sense. Which brings me to another reason for my visit…"

He trailed off, and Emma wasn't sure she wanted to hear any more about what had brought this man to town, but obviously Meredith did, because after a second, he went on.

"I just got word that there's a place for you at a care facility in the city."

Emma sucked in a gulp of air at his words, which made her cough. Charlie was immediately concerned, nudging at her legs and her hand, until she bent down and shushed him. "I'm fine, boy. I just…I guess I couldn't believe what I heard."

Apparently, Meredith was having the same problem. She sputtered out several half-questions before landing on, "What are you suggesting, Jake?"

"We've talked about this, Grandma. I know Grandpa picked this place for you, but it was always supposed to be temporary. It's time to be near family and Lexington Manor is right around the corner from my place. This would be the perfect fit."

Emma had heard of Lexington Manor, right downtown Seattle. They kept care of over two hundred residents. She'd never been inside the place, but its brick exterior made her think of high-rise offices more than somewhere to call home.

"Lexington Manor?" Meredith said. "Sounds like some staunch, pretentious place."

"I've got some photos from their website to show you."

A silence passed, and Emma chanced a peek around the edge of the door frame.

Jake had proceeded to turn his phone around to face his grandmother, but Meredith had busied herself with her knitting needles again, apparently not interested in looking at photos off of his phone. When he held his phone in front of her knitting needles, she brushed his hand away.

"Grandma, I want you to have top quality care."

"What's that supposed to mean?" Meredith asked, as though she could read Emma's mind. Good for you, keep challenging him, Meredith, Emma thought. Don't let him just decide what is best for you.

"There are better doctors and better facilities, not like this here, where people, probably without any medical training, spend all day knitting with you, rather than taking care of your needs."

Charlie, feeding off of Emma's agitation, started pacing around her. Emma had to hold him by the collar to keep him from running in and probably barking at Jake in order to protect Emma and Meredith.

"And this would mean you'll visit more?" Meredith's question surprised Emma. She couldn't actually be considering this.

"Well, I certainly intend to, but you know I'm busy now that I'm trying to make partner at the advertising firm. That doesn't come without hard work and sacrifice. But I'd be only a phone call away in case you needed anything, and it would be much easier to take a short walk around the corner than drive all this way."

It suddenly made so much sense why Emma hadn't seen him around before.

"I'll think about it," Meredith said, and Emma couldn't tell without seeing her face whether or not she meant it.

Jake, on the other hand, didn't seem to want to take a

moment to read his grandmother's feelings. Emma sensed this was a man who did not deal with feelings, only facts. "Grandma, we really have to move on this opportunity. I told them I'd send a deposit by the end of the day to hold your spot. I have to stay in Juniper Falls for a few days to pack up the rest of the house and see if we can get a bite on it. I really need you to be on board with this, Grandma. Once you have some time to think about it, I'm sure you'll see things my way."

"Not if I have anything to say about it," Emma murmured to herself and Charlie. She had seen too many times when families just started making decisions for their elderly relatives, not even taking into consideration what their loved one might want or truly need. So many decisions were based solely on convenience.

"I don't know about that," Meredith said, "but I promise I will think about it."

Emma wondered by her soft tone if Meredith truly was having a change of heart toward moving from Heart & Home. As curious and concerned as she was for the elderly woman, though, Emma no longer felt good about eavesdropping, and it was only making her angrier toward Meredith's grandson. She led Charlie down the hall, where she met up with Patrick, one of the town's paramedics, as he was heading toward the lobby.

"I'm happy to report Mr. Wilson is doing just fine," Patrick said. The strikingly handsome paramedic was one of the residents' favorite visitors and it seemed to Emma that his visits to Heart & Home had been increasing lately.

"Another false alarm?" Emma asked.

Patrick nodded. "He tried to convince me that his heart was racing out of control. He even wanted me to take him to the ambulance to double-check, but I hooked up a monitor and there was no sign of distress."

Emma sighed. "I think it's only a matter of him trying to get out of the building again. We take him out to get some fresh air each day, but it's not enough for him. He always wants to stray farther. He's always talking about setting sail out of here. It used to be a joke, but I don't know anymore. Now that he's getting us to call you in, it seems like it could be more serious. I'm so sorry we dragged you out for this."

They reached the large double doors of the main entrance, and Emma followed him outside, instructing Charlie to head to the nearby field to relieve himself. The yellow lab bounded across the garden with the energy of a pup. Emma had rescued Charlie from a shelter almost three years ago, when she'd moved out of Seattle, but truth be told, it was Charlie who had rescued Emma during a lonely time in her life. Now he was bringing joy to all the residents of Heart & Home.

"Not to worry," Patrick said. "I'm always happy to help, and better safe than sorry."

Emma stopped by his ambulance door as he got inside. "I appreciate your understanding, Patrick. Really." Now here was a man who cared about people, not like that Jake Rothstein who only seemed to care for what made life easier for himself. Emma could not stand self-centered people and he had definitely given off that vibe. He was the complete opposite of the paramedic that stood beside her now.

"Not at all." He smiled and reassuringly touched her arm. "Just let me know if there's anything else I can do." No wonder the residents love him, she thought. He had such a warm and comforting approach.

Patrick glanced away as the doors opened behind Emma. She took a quick glance sideways, but soon realized it was only Meredith's grandson, with whom she had no desire to make eye contact. Emma's sudden discomfort had not gone unnoticed by the attentive paramedic. Patrick raised his eyebrows in question of her response toward the sharply dressed man.

"He's from the city, where apparently they can't read parking signs. But don't even get me started." Emma shook off her brief encounter with Jake. She thanked Patrick again, and headed back into the lobby.

Seeing Pam, she stopped at the front counter before she began her shift.

"I feel just awful. We're calling Patrick out all the time, and it turned out to be another false alarm."

Pam looked up at Emma with a smirk. "I don't think Patrick minds stopping by to see you one little bit." Pam was old enough to be Emma's mother, but she often teased her like an older sister.

Emma nudged Pam's arm playfully. "What's that supposed to mean?" When Pam only raised an eyebrow in response, Emma decided to get serious. "Still, it costs the home money every time we call."

Pam nodded solemnly. "True. I was looking over the incoming bills, and we definitely don't have any to spare. I'm just glad that Jake Rothstein is gone."

"Meredith's grandson? He caught me knitting and joking around with her, and he was not impressed. Seems like a stuffed shirt if you ask me. Just another one of those city guys, cut from the same cloth."

"Oh, Emma." Pam tilted her head. "How many times have I told you, you need to be more professional with the residents, especially if you're vying for that head day nurse job? There's a fine line in getting too close to the residents, and I think this might be another instance where you've crossed it. That Jake Rothstein looks like the type who would have a hot-shot lawyer in the city and enjoys getting people fired. I'd watch my step around him. He's wanting to pull his grandmother out of here, you know? That's all we need, losing another resident."

Emma looked away, not wanting to let on that she'd been eavesdropping. "Because we were knitting? That's not enough reason to take Meredith away from here. Is it? And how can he even get an accurate account of Meredith's time with us here when he is never even *here*?"

Geezer, having suddenly recovered from the racing heart problems they had called Patrick in for, passed with his walker. "'Bout time somebody broke *me* outta this place. I don't want to be here either."

Pam shook her head at Geezer, pressing a call button for the duty nurse to come and assist the wandering patient. In the day room, the other residents would soon be gathering for mid-morning teatime. Pam turned back to Emma. "I would hope that's not it, but he sounded to be in quite a hurry about it. And from the looks of him, he expects high quality. Did you notice the suit he was wearing? Seems like he's got caviar tastes in life and we serve the comfort of meatloaf living here at Heart & Home."

"I'd choose meatloaf any day." Emma's agitation returned, and suddenly she didn't care if Pam knew she'd been eavesdropping. This was too important. "Doesn't he care about his grandmother at all? She loves it here, and she is such a sweet lady."

"She may be sweet, but I can't say I'm surprised that Mrs. Rothstein has a grandson like him. Since her husband passed, she rarely gets a visitor. It's a shame her own grandson visits so seldom that he doesn't even know where to find her room."

Emma's inner protective streak seemed to grow with her frustration. "Meredith Rothstein spent her life in Juniper Falls with her late husband. He had made arrangements for a spot for her here in case of his passing. If home is where the heart is, then her home is definitely here with us. For someone to take their grandmother away from her home...I'd say he doesn't know what it means to have a home. Or he doesn't have a heart. He's even pushing her to sell her home in town as quickly as he can!"

"But in the end, Emma, we're just the caregivers. It's not up to us. Please don't blur the boundaries. It will only make things harder for you and for the residents." Pam tried to meet Emma's eyes, but Emma kept hers firmly set on the counter in front of her.

"Maybe. But I'm on Mrs. Rothstein's side with this one, and I'm not letting her go without a fight. Someone needs to advocate for her. Maybe I need to have a word with young Mr. Rothstein next time he's here."

"Just watch your step," Pam said. "Don't do anything that will jeopardize your chance at that promotion. Remember the saying, 'You get more flies with honey?'" Pam tried to meet Emma's eyes with a pointed look, but she didn't want to think about honey or sweetness when it came to Jake Rothstein.

Pam went on. "Look, I know how much you've been wanting to move out of your sister's place, and I just don't want to see your chances hurt. You've got a caring heart, Emma, but don't let it cloud your perspective."

Emma knew Pam was right. She enjoyed living above the garage of her sister and brother-in-law's house. It allowed her the opportunity to spend moments with her nieces and occasionally have someone else cook for her. However, lately she began to dream of owning her own home and had been saving toward a down payment.

"If residents keep moving from Heart & Home to larger facilities, there won't be a head day nurse job for me." With every word, Emma felt her determination rising. "I have to at least try to help Meredith." It would be beneficial for everyone.

It was settled. Emma made up her mind to muster enough courage and talk to Jake Rothstein about this the next time he came in, whether it put any future promotions for her in jeopardy or not.

# 4

## JAKE

Jake was glad that difficult conversation with his grandmother was over. She would come to realize he had her best interests at heart eventually. Turning the street corner toward his childhood house, he passed the park. He hadn't been there in a long time. Too many memories of his grandfather. But something made him slow down. Jake pulled over, putting the car into park, just letting the engine idle. He sat there, not moving. Everything looked just as it did when he left.

A little boy stood on the steps leading up to the gate surrounding a pond. Scattered around the edges of the pond were lily pads and bulrushes. At the centre of the pond, a large fountain burst with water. In his hands, the boy held a remote control, and with the help of an elderly gentleman, he guided a sailboat carefully around the pond to avoid running into any of nature's objects in the water. So proud of his accomplishment, the boy smiled up at the man, waiting for acknowledgement of his success. The man put his arm around him, bending down to whisper something that made the boy's face beam. Jake remembered that place all too well. However, in his memory, his grandfather was never leaning down to make him smile. There was always something or some way he could have done better.

After such a long absence from the town, Jake had a clearer perspective of exactly why he had left. That feeling of constant nagging inadequacy was the catalyst that changed everything and led Jake down the long road to bitterness toward family and life in Juniper Falls. Jake put the car into gear and pulled away. He had to remind himself why he was here, and not let the past draw him into reliving the painful memories. He called the realtor on Bluetooth.

The realtor seemed pleasant enough, but not the go-getter that Jake felt was needed to move the house at the price and speed he had hoped for. However, realtors weren't overly abundant in Juniper Falls or the surrounding townships, and his choices were limited.

"I'm pressed for time, Leanne. Why can't we get this house off the market? I've already lowered the price twice," he said, as he pulled up to the two-story house he'd grown up in.

It was explained for the fiftieth time that the market was far from booming in Juniper Falls. "We could try an Open House this weekend, if you're up for it," she offered.

"Open House? For *this* weekend?" It would mean moving at least three meetings back in Seattle, but he was desperate to sell this house. "I'll see what I can do. There's a lot still to pack. It may need to be during the following week. But if it means getting it sold, I'll do what it takes."

Jake now looked up at the house for the first time since pulling into the drive and he sighed. "Listen, I just got to the house. I'll work through the night and see how much I can get done. Keep that slot free for now and I'll let you know in the morning."

"Sounds great!" the agent said in her all-too-peppy voice and hung up.

Jake walked up the front stairs, trying with each step not to feel a sense of nostalgia. "It's just a house," he murmured to himself under his breath. "The sooner we get rid of it, the better off we'll both be." He rattled the key in the lock in the familiar way he could do in his sleep—his grandpa always claimed he was going to fix the thing—and seconds later, he was inside.

He'd been back a few times since his grandpa's death, mostly to meet with the realtor, but today, for some reason, the place felt emptier. Perhaps because he finally had a plan to get both his grandmother and himself out of this town for good.

Jake sighed again and strode for the upstairs bedrooms. He'd almost packed up his grandparent's room and the bathroom. All that remained was his room, which he had been putting off.

Most people, he imagined, walked into their childhood rooms to a line of trophies or wall certificates or trinkets that stirred up positive memories. For Jake, he'd hung nothing on his walls. Once he'd tried to hang a poster of a rock band, and his grandmother had asked him why he listened to rock music in the first place because you couldn't understand anything they were singing about. She'd always had a way of making him feel like whatever he was doing was wrong. He'd seen a hint of her criticism today, but how could she out-and-out argue when he was about to spend money on the best assisted-living home money could buy?

His grandparents hadn't remodeled his room or used it for anything else since he moved out a decade ago, as if they expected him to fail at whatever it was he chose to piddle his time away with and come running home. Jake had been determined not to do that. Even though the advertising agency still didn't exactly fit him like a glove, and he still felt like a little kid in his play clothes walking into a room of businessmen, he had been determined to excel. And he had.

The latest bonus he'd received for landing the coffee account went toward the down payment on his car. He had been eyeing that steel blue Lexus for the last three years and nothing made him prouder than to walk into the dealership ready to make the deal. Jake had worked tirelessly on the ad campaign and knew this was a huge step in convincing his boss he could handle the larger accounts. After all, he could work the long hours that many of his associates could not, since he didn't have a spouse and children waiting for him at home. Jake had undivided attention for work. Well, he had his grandmother, but once the house was sold and she was settled into her new place, it would be smooth sailing.

*Sailing.*

He glanced at the remote-controlled sailboat collecting dust in the corner of his room and made a mental note to find a box for the items he planned on donating.

Jake grabbed a blue recycle bag and began tossing papers left over from when he had lived here. He knelt down to clean under the bed and pulled out a shoebox from the back corner. It was crammed with baseball cards, his once-cherished collection. He had completely forgotten about his obsession with baseball during the elementary years. The Mariners were his team. At one time, Jake could recite every stat on each player and knew the history backward and forward of the team. He had dreamed of playing in the big leagues one day, even watching recordings of old Mariner games while muting the sound and pretending to be the sports broadcaster announcing the plays. One day Jake had been downstairs re-watching the old 1995 division championship where his beloved Mariners played the New York Giants. It was game five and the eleventh inning, where Edgar Martinez or "Papi" as his fans called him, drove home Ken Griffy Jr., defeating the New York Yankees.

Jake's grandfather had entered the room and chuckled. "Great game, but not one World Series win to their name. Such a shame."

"Just wait until I play for them, Grandpa!" A ten-year-old Jake had pretended to take the pitching mound, which consisted of a cushion from the floral loveseat, and wound up his arm to pitch the imaginary fast ball. Suddenly, his grandfather got that no-nonsense look in his eyes that Jake knew all too well. "Jake, don't hitch your star to the impossible dreams. Hard work, son. That is what will get you far. Keep both feet firmly planted to the ground, don't dream your life away." And with those words of warning from his grandfather, the young Jake stuffed his cards away in the box, along with his dream.

Once again closing the box, Jake tossed it into the pile of things destined for the pawn shop in the morning. He didn't need to remember any of that. He'd moved on.

## 5

## EMMA

Emma sat around her sister's dinner table, feeling perfectly at home, almost too much like part of their family. Amy and the kids usually started eating before Emma got home from work, but today, she was there in time to help bring the food to the table. Amy had made a roast tonight and it smelled fantastic. And at least it wasn't caviar. Emma chuckled to herself, thinking of her conversation with Pam. Both Amy and Emma had learned to cook from their aunt at an early age. The love of cooking never really took with Emma. Amy was the cook and baker in the family. She loved taking recipes, tweaking them, and adding her own special touch. At any school events or church potlucks, it was Amy's food creations that received the rave reviews. Now that her girls were older and more independent, Amy had a passion to start her own catering business. Emma was less ambitious—she was more than happy to lend a helping hand to Amy and wanted to be the fun aunt who kept her two nieces occupied and out of her sister's hair if she was preparing for an event.

Connor had just come in from the clinic and was upstairs washing up. As a doctor's wife, Amy never let the late hours Connor worked fluster or frustrate her. She just went with the flow. They'd start supper without him, just as the family started without Emma many evenings. It was reassuring to her that she and Connor both had unpredictable schedules yet they both fit into the family perfectly.

Emma carried the mashed potatoes, while Amy reached for a bowl of veggies and was quickly on her heels. Ever since they had started setting the table for dinner that evening, it had been like Amy had been chasing her with her pointed conversation.

"All I'm saying is that you should get out and have some fun once in a while. All you do is work, Emma." Amy set the veggies close to her twin daughters at the far end of the table, as though they might decide to eat more of them simply due to proximity.

"Auntie Emma's fun," Leah said, sounding defensive of her aunt. "She plays Hide and Seek with us." Leah was the older of the five-year-old girls—by three minutes—and made sure the world knew it by always being first to speak her mind.

"I know, sweetie," Amy said to her daughter, while still looking at Emma, "but your auntie needs some grownup fun too." She sat and leaned forward across the table toward Emma. "When's the last time you've been out on a date?"

"Does taking Charlie out for a walk, count?" Emma murmured under her breath, but thankfully Laney was asking her mom for the butter to spread on her roll, so Emma's words were drowned out. Still, Emma was tired of this same conversation, practically every time she came for dinner now. She debated back, as she usually did. "Dating isn't everything, Amy. Just because you are meant for the husband, two kids, white picket fence life, doesn't mean everyone is.

"And who says you're not?" Amy asked, buttering a roll for both of her daughters.

"I do! I say I'm not." As Emma spoke, she slapped scoops of food onto her plate as though her argument was with the mashed potatoes. "This is *my* life, not yours, not Mom or Dad's. I say I'm happy, just as I am. Why does nobody ever believe me?"

"Oh, Emma. You're lonely. Anyone can see it written all over your face. You're just trying to put up a front so you don't get hurt."

Just then, as if Amy needed any more ammunition, Conner

arrived at the table. Emma sat up straighter, determined to argue her points—and she had several of them.

"Sure, I'm lonely, with Mr. McGuire passing away last week, and now Meredith Rothstein getting ready to leave us at Heart & Home after being with us for only a year. Life can be lonely. Haven't you ever noticed that, Amy?" Emma took a bite, but Amy wasn't going to let it go.

"Surrounded by aging widows and death all the time, though, it's no surprise—"

"They're wonderful people—some of the kindest I've ever had the pleasure of knowing!" Now Amy was being ridiculous, and Emma was going to make sure she knew it. Thankfully, Connor kept his head down, concerning himself only with the food. He knew better than to get in the middle of a sister discussion, especially one concerning matters of the heart.

"I'm sure they are," Amy replied. She had yet to dish out any of her own food. "We just think you need some *living* in your life. Right, Connor?" Connor only barely nodded. Emma shook her head and continued shoveling in food so she could take a moment to calm down before unleashing her rant. Amy finally reached for the roast beef. "At least think about it, okay, Ems?"

Emma hated the way her older sister always acted like she knew best, even though they had completely different lives. Emma had tried dating. It always left her feeling much, much lonelier, and Amy was right about one thing: Emma already faced enough loneliness in her life.

Emma ate in silence for the next while, lost in her thoughts and mulling over her sister's comments. Sure, she would love to meet that special someone, but admitting that to Amy would be like opening the floodgate to non-stop matchmaking. Her two nieces giggled and shared about their day at school, and Emma wished she could be as carefree as the girls again, not concerning herself with Heart & Home's difficult finances, residents leaving, or what her sister thought she should do with her spare time.

"So can you, Auntie?" Emma was brought back to the conversation at the supper table and looked at both girls who were anticipating an answer from her to a question she had obviously missed.

"I'm sorry, sweetie. My mind was elsewhere. What is it that you want me to do?"

Leah sighed and rolled her eyes at having to start her story and question for her aunt from the beginning. "Okay, Auntie, but can you please put your listening ears on now?" The adults at the table stifled a laugh at the young girl using a phrase that had obviously been used on her numerous times. Emma pretended to pull listening ears from her back pockets and secure them onto her head. "Ready and listening." She winked at her two nieces.

"Laney and I need to make our Valentine cards for our class party. Mom is helping us make the cookies."

"Hearts with pink frosting and purple sprinkles," Laney added her two cents' worth. She was by far the quieter of the two girls. In fact, she reminded Emma of herself when she was younger.

"So can you help us with our Valentine cards? We need help with the letters because we have *a lot* to write out 'cause Mrs. Sanders says if we plan on sending out cards, we have to make sure to include everyone so no one has a hurt heart."

Emma loved how excited Leah and Laney were for school parties and she knew they had been counting down until Valentine's Day on the calendar in the kitchen. However, to Emma, Valentine's Day was just one more reminder, a commercialized, in-your-face kind of reminder, that she had a habit of finding Mr. Wrong instead of Mr. Right.

"Sure, girls. You can count on me. Let's get the supplies together next week and we can begin." It had been a Hathaway family tradition to make Valentine cards ever since Emma and Amy were girls, and they had since passed this tradition down to Leah and Laney. Emma made a mental note to stop by the dollar store with them to pick up glitter and glue. She finished her meal quickly and started to clear dishes away from the table. Emma was glad her sister had given their argument a break for a few minutes, but knowing Amy, the reprieve wouldn't last long.

"Thanks for dinner. Come on, girls! Who wants to have a Suds Party in the kitchen?"

"I do! I do!" both girls said at once. They followed Emma toward the kitchen.

"You're running away from this conversation again, Emma," her sister called after her. "I can clean up later."

It was part of their unspoken agreement that when Amy cooked, which was most of the time, Emma would clean up. So Amy's words were simply a sign that she planned to argue this point until she got Emma to concede. It wasn't fair, the way her sister had so much staying power for an argument. Part of the reason she'd moved to Juniper Falls was to get away from that pushy city mentality.

"I know you can, Amy," Emma said, forcing calmness into her voice. "But it wouldn't be *fun* for you. Everybody's idea of fun is different."

With that, she let the door to the kitchen swing closed behind her and turned to her nieces with a bright smile. Who could be lonely when you were around these two sweet little girls?

# 6

## JAKE

Jake hadn't returned to Heart & Home with the intention of arguing with his grandmother, but he'd left his own home early yesterday morning, been up packing the house most of the night, and again this morning, and the lack of sleep and much-needed caffeine, combined with simply being in this town, was making him irritable.

"It's taking me forever to pack up everything in the house. I'm sure that's why it's not showing well, with the boxes everywhere. Plus, I've run out of empties again."

They were in Heart & Home's sunroom. Today, it was more populated with seniors sitting around the room working at puzzles, watching TV, or reading. Jake had been trying to keep his voice down, but he didn't realize until his grandmother spoke how loud he had probably been.

"Yes, I guess we have accumulated things over time. That's what happens when one has lived in the same house for many years."

"Yeah, the junk piles up." He sat at the table across from his grandmother, trying to be less conspicuous. He glanced around to catch the eye of anyone who might be watching their conversation to warn them off, but thankfully the seniors were minding their own business. He knew the harsh tone to his grandmother was not necessary, as age had softened her considerably, but his use of sarcasm was easier than coming to terms with the fact that he was having a hard time with the influx of emotions he was experiencing since arriving yesterday.

"No, Jake," his grandmother retorted. "Memories are made."

Jake shifted, the chair suddenly feeling a lot less comfortable. "Some memories are best left packed away, and some are not worth holding onto at all."

"Oh, Jake, I wish you would remember the good times."

His grandmother shook her head. But for Jake, his mind clouded over with the memories of all the times he fell short of his grandparents' unrealistic expectations, acting out with failed grades, fights in school, and rebellion against their strict rules. Were those the "good times" she had been referring to? However, Jake could tell that he had already pushed his grandmother too far by the look in her eyes. He had not meant to hurt her. Jake knew it must have been hard to have a kid suddenly dropped into your life when it was supposed to be filled with travelling the world and enjoying retirement together. Of course, his grandparents had a right to feel he ruined their plans during their golden years. But he was trying to make up for it by taking care of her in the best way possible now.

"See the piano?" She had a nostalgic smile on her face as she pointed to an upright piano in the corner of the sunroom.

Jake started to nod, but then recognition hit. "Wait, is that ours?"

"Remember our times singing together? When your grandfather passed, I donated it to Heart & Home."

"Donated it?" Unintentionally, his voice got loud again. "Why would you do that? They should have paid you for it."

His grandmother slammed her fist against the arm of her wheelchair as strongly as she was able. "You are not understanding, Jake! I had to make a lot of decisions all on my own after your grandpa died and what I chose to do with my own belongings is of no business of yours! I'm sorry if they don't all live up to your big city expectations where money talks, but life is more than money. When will you get that through your stubborn mind?"

Jake bowed his head. He knew everyone must be staring now. "I'm sorry, Grandma," he said into the stillness. When she got worked up, she sounded broken, not like the strong woman who'd raised him.

"Well, why don't you humour an old lady and play something on the piano? You know how much hearing you play means to me. It's been years."

It hadn't been his choice to take piano lessons, and he'd never admitted it to his grandmother, but playing was something he really did miss. It had been an escape for him at times—from the troubles at school, disagreements with his grandparents, and even the occasional girl trouble. There was something about tickling out a tune and getting lost in a song that was soothing. If he had only known she wanted to get rid of the piano, he would have loved to have it. The truth was, he'd never have fit the piano into his tiny apartment in the city anyways, so maybe it was best that it was here getting used and bringing peace and soothing to others.

"Go on," his grandmother coaxed, knowing he'd need the extra push.

He reluctantly went to the piano and ran his fingers lightly along the top of the keys, as if petting them. They felt more familiar than he expected after such a long hiatus from playing. He stepped over the bench and sat, letting his fingers rest in front of him until his grandmother had wheeled over to sit next to him. He glanced over. There was an old piano song book beside the bench. Still feeling badly about their argument, he thumbed through the different songs and came across the perfect one.

Placing his foot on the pedal, he began to play "Let Me Call You Sweetheart" and was instantly taken back to a good memory —the first one he'd had in a long while. One he had forgotten about. This was their song; his grandparents', but he hadn't always known it.

In high school, Jake had been asked to accompany the school choir for the local music festival. Begrudgingly, he'd agreed—for extra credit. That night, he'd brought the music home to practice for the next day's performance. His grandfather had been helping his grandmother finish doing up the dishes. Once, Jake glanced up from his playing and looked into the kitchen. There were his grandparents, dancing around the room as he played. Tea towel in hand, his grandfather led his grandmother confidently, gazing into her eyes, singing the words as if a special love song was written just for her. She'd been looking up at him like a love-sick teenager. Too engrossed in each other, they had not even noticed their audience. By the time Jake had finished playing through the piece a couple of times and gotten up from the piano, both were back at the kitchen sink finishing the dishes and discussing the weather like nothing had happened. Jake never mentioned the dancing to them, but it had given him a glimpse of a couple that he rarely saw and a feeling that warmed him inside.

He was through the first verse when others around the room started to migrate over, and his grandmother said, "Wait, wait! You have to sing too."

Jake shook his head and laughed, a lightness coming over him. It had been a long time since he'd let music wash away some of his stress and worry. He couldn't believe he was about to do this, but he opened his mouth and began to sing along. By the end of the next verse, his grandmother and even a few of the other seniors chimed in with him.

"Let me hear you whisper
That you love me too.
Keep the love light glowing
In your eyes so true…"

By the end of the chorus, everyone in the room joined in, obviously a crowd favorite of the generation: "Let me call you sweetheart, I'm in love with you."

Jake brought the song to a close and was grinning from ear to ear when he turned and saw that Pam from the front counter and that pretty Nurse Hathaway had also joined the singalong.

He didn't know why, but for some reason their presence made him feel shy about his playing, especially when they started whispering to one another.

One of the elderly ladies called out, "Another one!" taking his attention.

"I wish I could, but unfortunately, I have a lot of packing to do." He smiled at his grandmother, so she would know he wasn't feeling as agitated about it anymore.

"Wait!" Nurse Hathaway said, suddenly serious and rushing over to him. "Meredith isn't leaving so soon…?"

"No, no." Jake stood from the piano bench and turned toward Nurse Hathaway. "I was talking about my grandparents' old house. It looks like we may have to run an Open House to sell it, and with being so busy at my job in the city, I guess there's still a fair bit to sort through and pack." Jake felt the need to explain himself to her somehow. He knew yesterday he had made a terrible first impression, and it hadn't been his intention. At the same time, he wondered why he even cared about any impression she had of him since he'd never see her again once he got his grandmother transferred.

His grandmother made a show of pushing out of her wheelchair. "I'll help."

That was just like the grandmother he grew up with, trying to do anything and everything herself, making him feel incapable in the process. But here, at least, he had an obvious argument. "No, Grandma. I appreciate it, but I think you'd better stay here. Remember, the house is not wheelchair accessible." She settled back into her chair. He assured her, "Don't worry, I've planned for a long night ahead of me."

"Well, I mean…I could help." Jake looked up, surprised at the voice of Nurse Hathaway. He stood there with his mouth open but not answering for far too long, so she added, "If you want? And if Meredith is all right with it, of course."

"You?" he stammered out. It's not that he wouldn't love having a good-looking woman like her to keep him company. But she didn't even know him. Why would she offer?

"I'm off work in a few hours." she said with a friendly shrug.

"Of course, dear. You'll be able to make sure the fragile pieces aren't tossed about," his grandmother said with a twinkle in her eye.

His thoughts launched off his tongue without his permission. "Why would you help? You don't even know me."

She twisted her face into a smirk. He couldn't tell if it was demeaning or if she was just having fun. "That's what small-town folks do, Mr. Rothstein."

"Well, I would appreciate the extra hands. I'd be more than happy to financially compensate you for your time." His voice sounded too serious, too businesslike, which was such a contrast to hers. He added, "Please, call me Jake."

Her smirk grew. "Okay, I'll do that. And no need for financial compensation. Small-town folk lend helping hands without expecting anything in return...Jake." She held out a hand to shake, as if she was trying to meet his business performance and raise him. "Emma," she said. They shook, but just as quickly she backed away. "There are some empty boxes in the storage room, I'll load them into my car and meet you there later."

Jake scrunched his forehead, wondering if there was some sort of Juniper Falls angel suddenly looking after his every need. He shook off the thought and said, "Let me write down the address."

"It's just around the corner from where I live." Another smirk. "Juniper Falls is not that big. We will see you soon."

"We?"

"Of course. Charlie comes too. We're kind of a package deal."

"Charlie?" Jake felt a pang of jealousy. Who was Charlie? Anyway, if she brought this Charlie it would be another pair of hands helping pack up. Not a competition.

"You've already met him." Emma gave a wink and whistled out to the yellow lab who had been snoozing in the sunshine by the patio doors where one of the residents had been working on a paint-by-numbers. Charlie yawned, gave a stretch, and sauntered toward where Emma and Jake were standing.

"Come on, Charlie. Let's go find some boxes."

Emma walked away with Jake staring after her.

"Wasn't that kind of Emma, offering to help?" his grandmother asked, but he was still stunned in place, not really comprehending what just happened. "Jake? Are you listening to me?"

He forced himself to clue back in to the conversation with his grandmother. "Huh? Oh yeah, sure, kind. Yes, she certainly is."

"You will be nice to her, won't you, Jake?"

Jake finally looked away from where Emma had disappeared through the door several long seconds ago. "Of course, Grandma. I will be on my best behavior." He kissed his grandmother on the head, something he had never done before, and added, "I promise."

# 7

## EMMA

Emma carried a load of boxes toward her car. As she passed the administration counter, Pam had something to say about Emma's plans.

"You're serious about going to that house to pack with him, aren't you?"

Emma paused, resting the boxes on the counter. "I told you, I plan to have a word with young Mr. Rothstein—Jake—before he just forces his grandmother to sign herself out of Heart & Home. After all, what did you say about the flies and honey? Simply following your suggestion," she sing-songed.

She would at least start with the honey approach. If that didn't work, she had other tricks.

"Right. Young and *handsome* Mr. Rothstein. Is that what you're thinking, after watching him play piano with the residents?"

Emma's face warmed. It was true that for a second there she'd admitted to herself that it was possible this new guy hanging around did indeed have a heart. It was also true that she'd noticed how handsome he was, especially when he let his guard down while singing with the residents earlier. To cover up these two errant thoughts, she waved a hand in front of her face and forced a curt tone. "Oh, please. You're as bad as my sister. If I was in the market for a man, which I am not, Jake Rothstein would be the last one I would choose." Thankfully her words sounded believable, even to her own ears. She would want someone caring and dedicated, like Patrick the paramedic, not that she was interested.

Just then, Mr. Willoughby walked through the front doors and toward Pam. On instinct, Emma took a step back, removing the boxes from the counter as though she'd done something wrong, always unsettled by the owner of Heart & Home. Even though he towered above both ladies with his presence, he was a kind man with a gentle spirit. Despite that, if it had filtered down to the staff, he must be stressed about the financial future of the facility. She did not want to give him any reason to be frustrated with her helping a resident's family pack up to move them away from Heart & Home.

"Any messages for me, Pam?" Mr. Willoughby asked as he leaned down to give Charlie a treat from the bowl on the counter where Pam kept dog treats for the residents to feed their beloved mascot. The dog inhaled the treat and showed his appreciation by lying down at Mr. Willoughby's feet.

"Here's the mail and the list of supplies we need." Pam glanced at Emma for the briefest of seconds. "And there's some paperwork here I'll need your signature on for the release of a resident who's considering moving to another facility."

"Another one?" Mr. Willoughby shook his head. "I'm going to have to make cuts around here somewhere, and I doubt trimming the supply budget is going to be enough."

Emma knew exactly what that meant: personnel cuts. He had been talking about giving Emma a promotion to head day nurse for over three months. That only meant one thing: if they'd gone this long without one, there was certainly no room in the budget for new positions. Could they even afford all of the current employees? The thought hadn't even crossed her mind until now, now that she could hear firsthand and witness the concerned look on her employer's face. She couldn't even imagine her days without the residents of Heart & Home. They were her family and her friends.

Mr. Willoughby walked off with his papers in hand. Pam and

Emma exchanged a long look before Emma strode for the door, an air of determination in her step.

---

Walking up to the two-story colonial house, Emma balanced a half-pepperoni, half-veggie pizza in one hand and several empty boxes in the other. Charlie followed behind with the wafting scent of pizza providing the motivation for him to stick close to his owner. Emma passed this house daily on her morning runs with Charlie. Meredith had told her about the house she had lived in months ago, and even though Emma would never admit as much to her, if she could have a dream house, this would be it. The porch alone would have put it in the running as something she always said was a must-have when she bought a house. Emma could imagine just sitting for hours, rocking back and forth, while watching the sunrise in the morning and star gazing at night. But she quickly pushed those dreams out of her head because the odds of her actually being able to afford a down payment on any house seemed like they were quickly diminishing. Setting the empty boxes against the edge of the porch railing, Emma reached over and rang the doorbell.

Mere seconds later, Jake swung the front door open, nearly knocking over the pizza and stack of boxes. He seemed as caught off guard as Emma. No longer was she wearing her nurse scrubs, she had changed into faded skinny jeans and a dark purple hoodie, her brown hair now framing her face rather than tied back professionally. For a second, though, it looked like he didn't recognize her.

Jake finally blinked and cleared his throat. "Thanks for coming." He looked down at Charlie. "Oh. I'm afraid the pooch will have to stay outside. I'm doing my best to sell this place, and I don't want to have to clean up dog hair and paw prints on top of everything else. You would not believe how quickly the cobwebs get everywhere."

In that second, Emma knew what she'd told Pam had been

exactly right: She was not in danger of having romantic feelings for any city guy, especially one who didn't like dogs.

She crouched down to talk to her best friend. "That's okay, right, boy? Not everyone is a dog person." The obedient lab curled up in a furry ball to lay on the porch. Emma was thankful for the mild February evening.

When Emma glanced up, Jake was rolling his eyes, but she didn't care. She went on talking to Charlie like she always did. "This is still part of our nice quiet neighborhood, and at least there's a fence here. I'll check on you in a little while. Now, no barking, boy." Even her sternest tone didn't sound very stern when she directed it at Charlie. Then again, Charlie didn't need harsh orders.

When she stood and faced up against Jake Rothstein, she realized if she needed to, she'd have no trouble with sternness directed toward him.

Five minutes later, Jake and Emma had found places to perch in the living room amid half-filled boxes. "Thanks for bringing pizza. You didn't have to, but I'm glad you did."

"Well, I figured you probably didn't have much here in the way of groceries and I needed to eat too." Emma thought again of that old saying: you catch more flies with honey.

Jake went to the kitchen and returned with a glass of water for Emma and one for himself. "Sorry I don't have anything else to offer you to drink."

"Water is great. Now tell me what you want me to do first. We can eat and pack at the same time, if that's alright with you."

"I've been filling those boxes with frames and albums," he began, gesturing and pointing around, "and these other ones with various knickknacks. The stuff by the door is to go to the thrift store and there's a box for the pawn shop. Why don't you start with the photos from the fireplace mantle?"

Emma fought the urge to ask if he'd checked with his grandmother about the items he was getting rid of. She reminded herself she was trying to get on his good side here, at least for long enough to make him see how much Meredith loved Heart

& Home but made a note to mention it to Meredith in a casual way.

She grabbed a few sheets of packing paper. "How long ago did you move away from Juniper Falls?" Emma asked, picking up a framed photo and dusting it off with her sleeve before wrapping it in the paper.

"How do you know I lived here?"

Emma wasn't sure what to say. Jake almost seemed upset and taken off guard at what was meant to be a simple conversation starter. She cleared her throat and tried to come up with a response that would minimize any confrontation. "I put two and two together. Meredith—your grandmother—said she lived most of her life in Juniper Falls with your grandfather before he passed. She also mentioned they had raised you."

"Yes, well, not by choice. Believe me, my grandmother let me know on many an occasion how she should have been done raising children." He stuffed knickknacks into his box, barely looking at them.

"She said that?"

"Well, not in so many words," Jake grumbled. "But I felt it. My grandparents adamantly didn't want me to turn out 'irresponsible' like my mom. After I moved out of town, Grandma softened up with her criticisms and expectations."

Emma nodded, not knowing whether she should respond or not. Meredith had spoken fondly about her life in Juniper Falls. Emma had never heard her complain about raising her grandson.

"So now I've climbed the ladder to a successful career and made my own way without having to rely on anyone. I'd call that being responsible. Yet I still seem to let her down one way or another." Jake shook his head, letting out a heavy sigh.

So that was it, or at least part of it. Jake was somehow trying to live up to his grandmother's expectations. Or what he perceived her expectations to be. Something just didn't add up for Emma. And every word Jake spoke seemed to come from a place of passionate dislike toward his years in Juniper Falls.

"What about you?" Jake asked, changing the subject. "How long have you been stuck here?"

He still sounded perturbed, and Emma didn't think there was much chance of convincing him of anything at this point. At least there wasn't if she couldn't find that sweet side of him she'd seen at the piano earlier. "I don't know if I would call it 'stuck.' I love Juniper Falls." Her words seemed to only be irking Jake more, judging by his hunched posture. Emma decided to try a more personal approach. "My parents uprooted my sister and me from our small-town life in the Midwest, right at the end of high school and moved us to Phoenix because they didn't care for the cold. They still live there. I had stayed in Phoenix for a couple of years attending college but moved to Seattle when I was accepted into UW's nursing program. My sister ended up meeting and eventually marrying her college sweetheart from Arizona State. After her husband, Connor, finished his residency program, he came back here to his hometown to set up his general family practice with my sister and their two-year-old twin daughters. Connor was working long hours establishing his practice and my sister was overwhelmed trying to care for the twins on her own. So that's where I came in. After I became an RN, I worked two years in Seattle and realized I was tired of city life." Emma neglected to say it was also in part, because of a broken relationship. "I packed up my things, relocated to Juniper Falls, and moved into the suite above my sister and brother-in-law's garage. I'm happy my nieces are being raised here. It is much better than raising kids in the big city." She was getting off track. "While settling in and helping my sister, I started working at Heart & Home and fell in love."

"In love?" Jake looked up from the vase he had been wrapping in newsprint.

"With the seniors there. And with my dog, Charlie. I adopted him from the shelter. Now this place feels like home, you know?" She doubted he knew anything about having a real home, not if he planned to uproot his grandmother and move her to an institutional place like Lexington Manor.

"Depends what you're looking for," Jake said, seemingly unbothered by her pointed question. "I think if you focus on your career first, the home and family part will follow. You can't support a family or buy a house if you're barely getting by. Once I move her, my grandmother will be closer, which will help."

His answer made Emma immediately irritable. Because maybe there was some truth to that. What if his intentions were truly to have his family closer? "Maybe," she forced out.

"You don't sound convinced." Now he had the upper hand, and he seemed to know it.

Maybe Emma really didn't know what was best for this other family. Just because Juniper Falls had been right for her, didn't mean it was right for everybody. "It's just… I guess I've never been a fan of big-city life and the rat race that comes with it. Not when there's a choice."

"Yes, well, some of us don't have that choice. The best jobs and room for advancement are in the city. Plus, my grandmother will get better care in the city. No offense."

Emma felt her blood boil at that comment. She gave her heart and soul to the residents she cared for. They weren't just a job for her there. Besides, anytime someone started or ended a statement with the words "no offense," it was always bound to be offensive. But she kept her mouth clamped shut and silently took in several slow breaths as they packed silently together. She kept her eyes trained mostly on what she was doing, but when she finally chanced a look Jake's way, he was shoving some letters he had retrieved from the old roll-top desk drawer into a briefcase. At least he was sentimental about something, Emma thought.

"I should probably be going soon as Charlie isn't used to spending too much time outside during this time of year." Emma stood up and went toward the door, frustrated that she wasn't able to get through to Meredith's stubborn grandson. "Sorry I couldn't stay longer."

"Well, I guess the dog…your dog," Jake stumbled with his words.

"Charlie, his name is Charlie."

"Right. I would be fine if Charlie came inside to lay down by the door. That is if you still wanted to stay longer?"

Emma couldn't figure Jake out. He almost seemed shy, asking

her to stay. "Sure, as long as Charlie is warm, I am happy to stay and help."

The lab was more than happy to come into the house and snooze some more as Emma continued carefully wrapping picture frames. She tried not to focus on what a waste of time this was. She figured she'd only have to come over here, pack a box or two, and help him see the errors of his ways. But that no longer seemed likely to happen. And if his motivation was truly to have his grandmother closer, and if for some reason he really was tied to living in the city, maybe there wasn't much error in his ways after all.

Jake interrupted her thoughts, seemingly reading her perfectly. "Look, I know you don't agree with my grandmother leaving Juniper Falls, but that's not your call to make. If you really care about her, I'd think you'd at least want her to see her options. See what she would get if she moved into the city near me."

What would she get? Emma thought, but what actually came out of her mouth was, "Why do you care about my support?" It seemed Jake also had an ulterior motive for letting her come over to the house to pack.

"Because she trusts you." Jake held Emma's eyes, and she hated to admit it, but for a flash, she thought she could see the man who had been at the piano earlier. "If you tell her to at least be open to the idea, she will." His voice became softer. "I promise, if I can't sell her on the new place, if she gives it some serious thought and really doesn't think it's right for her, there's nothing I can do. I'm not going to force her. I'm not an ogre."

Emma eyed him skeptically, but then forced out the response she knew she had to give. "Okay."

"Okay?" Jake sat up straighter, clearly surprised.

Emma shook her head at herself. "I can't promise anything, but I'll trust you at your word. I'll see what I can do to encourage Meredith to take a trip into Seattle with you." Emma kept her focus on the photos that lay on her lap, barely believing that rather than swaying Jake, somehow, he'd managed to sway her.

However, maybe spending some extra time with his grandmother might be just what was needed.

"While I appreciate that, I was hoping you might convince her to look closer at the photos of Lexington Manor online."

It took Emma a second to look up. It took her even longer to understand what he was saying. "Wait, you want her to make a decision about moving her whole life based on a few photographs on their website? Do you honestly feel that it would be an accurate portrayal of what her life there would be like?"

"No, I mean, that's not what I want. Of course, it's not." He was flustered. "Well, you see, the thing is...I can't fit her wheelchair into my car. I suppose I could rent a van." It sounded as though the idea of Meredith actually visiting Lexington Manor was a novel idea to him. "Is there a rental place in town?"

Emma eyed him for a long moment, deliberating. He really did seem to care. It's just that he had such narrow vision, he could only see one option. Maybe what really needed to happen was to help Jake see what he was choosing and how it would impact his grandma. Make him take a good hard look at it.

"How about this?" she finally said. "If I can convince your grandmother to make the trip—and that's a big *if* by the way—I'll look into borrowing the Heart & Home van for the weekend. If you don't mind me tagging along, that is."

Jake brightened more than she'd seen all day. "I think that's a great idea! My grandmother thinks so highly of you. Seems to me she would feel most comfortable seeing Lexington Manor with someone she trusts. You might make the transition easier, Emma."

That's what she was afraid of. But if she wanted Jake to be open to other options, she supposed she should also be open. Ultimately, she did want what was best for Meredith. "Your grandmother has to be willing first. And I'll still need to check on the van." Even as Emma said the words, she had a hard time imagining how she was going to bring this up to Pam.

"I'd pay you well, of course. I'll also pay a rental on the van. And there's an extra suite in my condo for guests. Of course, the two of you would need to stay for the night so we don't have to drive both ways in a day, which would be too hard on my grandmother, but I understand if that makes you uncomfortable. I didn't want to presume, I just thought it might be best for my grandmother to have someone to care for her properly."

Jake sounded so excited, it only made Emma's reluctance more obvious. "I'll see if I can make it work."

"Thank you, Emma. Really." There was the guy from the piano again. "I appreciate all your help. Listen, I know I came across as a little obstinate the other day…"

Emma started to lighten. "A little?" If he could see that about himself and even admit it to her, someone he barely knew, that had to mean something.

Jake smiled mischievously. "Okay, maybe more than a little."

She could play along too. "I understand. When you live in the city that long, you lose the small-town charm." The truth was, he was too charming for his own good. At least when he wanted to be.

Jake crumpled up a piece of packing paper and tossed it at Emma. She ducked just in time, and then, despite herself, smiled.

# 8

## JAKE

The alarm hadn't gone off yet, but Jake was already awake. He had never been one to sleep in. Even after only getting a few hours of shut-eye. Emma had stayed longer than he'd expected, or hoped for, to help him with sorting and packing his family's things into boxes. It was a huge help and Jake was grateful not to be alone in the house with his thoughts and ghosts of memories past. He had been apprehensive about how the evening would go, especially since there were a few moments where they wholeheartedly did not agree on the best care for his grandmother. However, they did agree on one thing: they both wanted what was best for her. That was their common ground.

Jake hauled out his gym bag from the trunk of his car. Maybe a run would clear his mind. He still had a fair bit of advertising work on his plate while he was in Juniper Falls. His boss knew he needed to be away from his desk for a few days, but Jake didn't want to get behind on work and give off the impression that he was allowing personal matters to derail his attention. He planned on getting caught up on phone calls and emails later that day.

Standing on the porch warming up and stretching, he couldn't help but notice how the neighbourhood had changed. The trees on either side of the boulevard had grown taller with their tops arching into the street, almost touching. It really did make a beautiful view to look down the street through the canopy of branches, even without their leaves at this time of year. It was the beginning of February and already there were crocus bulbs peeking out from the flower beds. His grandmother loved her spring flowers and had talked about each individual type of bloom arriving yearly. So he knew daffodil and tulip bulbs would not be far behind.

Jake began with a slow jog down the street, not really knowing the specifics of his running route, but one thing was for certain: it needed to end with him finding a decent cup of coffee. The instant coffee that had been left in his grandmother's cupboard was fit neither for man nor beast. Big-city coffee options had definitely made him a bit of a coffee snob.

Fortunately, there was no rain, yet Jake zipped his jacket up further as there was an early morning chill in the air. Until his body warmed up, he would try to keep as warm as possible so his muscles wouldn't seize up on him. Running outdoors was not the norm for Jake anymore. His building had a full-sized gym with free weights and elliptical trainers. He had forgotten how good it felt to run on the asphalt and soon lost himself in the steady rhythm of his feet. Past the ball diamonds and over the footpath crossing the stream, Jake rounded the corner by the gazebo and made his way up to Main Street.

If memory served him correctly, there was a coffee shop beside the used bookstore. It was still too early for most of the stores to be open, so Jake hoped the coffee shop was an exception. Surely the people of Juniper Falls also had caffeine addictions and needed their early morning fix.

And he was right. Stopping outside the coffee shop's front window, Jake did a final stretch just so he wouldn't feel too sore tomorrow, after not having run for the past several days. He looked at the name above the door. *Java Junction*. It suited the tiny shop on the corner. Jake pushed through the door and immediately his nose was met with the aroma of freshly ground beans. He went up to the burgundy counter to place his order with the spunky, wide-eyed barista who looked like maybe she was on a bit of a caffeine high as she bounced from the cash register to the bean grinder.

Black coffee. That was the way a real coffee connoisseur enjoyed a cup. It had taken Jake a couple of years to lose the habit of loading up on cream and sugar for his cup. Taking your coffee black was an acquired taste. But once it grew on him, he loved being able to taste the different roast flavors.

"Here's your coffee," the barista said, less than two minutes later. "Hope you enjoy our special Valentine blend." She presented him with his coffee and seemed to be waiting for Jake to notice the added touch of foam art in the design of a heart. But a look of disappointment set in on her face as she was quick to notice his frown.

"Is something wrong with your order?" She bit her lower lip and looked like she was ready to burst into tears at the slightest hint of his dissatisfaction. Jake quickly spoke to try to soothe over her concern and avoid any outburst of unwanted emotions.

"Well…" He tried to choose his words carefully. "It does look lovely, however, I had ordered my coffee black."

"Oh no! I did it again! My boss says I'm always too quick to take customers' orders and I get caught up in my creative flair. Sometimes I forget the specific details. I'm so sorry. I guess because everyone had been ordering our Valentine special, I got carried away making them." She took a breath, but barely. "I'll make you another one. I can always drink this one on my break." If this poor girl kept drinking her coffee mistakes, Jake mused to himself, by noon she would be bouncing off the walls.

"No, it's fine, really. I don't mind drinking it this way." Jake looked down at his cup and furrowed his brow at the words coming from his mouth. Normally, he had high expectations of customer service and would not think twice about having someone redo an order to his specifications. What was this town doing to him?

"Jake!"

Looking over in the direction where he heard his name, Jake saw his old school buddy sitting with a cup of coffee and newspaper in hand waving him over. It was too early to be sociable, and he hadn't yet had a sip of his coffee, but he wanted to give the poor barista a break before she started apologizing again, so Jake made his way over to Paul.

"How are you enjoying our coffee shop? Not as fancy as some of the big city Seattle ones you're used to, I'm sure, but it still makes a good cup of joe." Coming from anyone else, Jake would feel Paul's comment was a shot against him and city life. However, he could tell his friend was sincere.

He took a sip. "Not too bad. Just need to clarify the order next time." He looked down at the now-deformed heart-shaped foam in his cup.

Paul laughed. "That's Megan. She means well but couldn't get an order right if her life depended on it." There was something about the girl that reminded Jake of himself. He made a mental note next time he was in *Java Junction* to give her a decent tip for his coffee, even if it was wrong.

"So, any idea how much longer you're in town? I was serious the other day about getting together. You remember Jennie from our grad class?"

Jake nodded. Jennie had had a not-particularly-subtle crush on Paul through most of high school.

"We got married almost three years ago, now. I mentioned to her that you were in town and we would love to have you over for a home-cooked meal one night. Think you will be around next week? I'm working days, so any evening is open."

"Well, I'm just in the process of packing up more of my grandmother's house and I'll be taking her into Seattle for the weekend to check out a new place I hope she'll be open to moving into. You know, the convenience of having her closer, and all." Again, Jake found himself justifying his actions.

"So maybe Monday night? You'll be bringing her back, so you'll be in the area anyway, right?" Paul didn't give up easily. He had been Jake's first friend when he came to live in Juniper Falls as a boy. Jake had thought he'd just be visiting Juniper Falls for the summer, but when September had rolled around, and his mom hadn't come back to get him, his grandpa sat him down and explained that he'd be starting school in the small town. No word about why his mom wouldn't be back in time for school, or how long he might be staying. As much as he had loved his summer with his grandparents, he hadn't known what to think of the fact that he wasn't moving on to the next home his mom had set up for them, wherever that may be, and when he started school, he mostly kept to himself—having learned from moving around a lot that it was easier not to make connections or friendships—thinking it would soon be over.

That plan had been short-lived since, on one of the first days of school, a big-eared, dark-haired boy had come over to where he'd been watching ants march off with some lunch crumbs and begun rattling off ant facts to him. Even though Jake hadn't said a word in reply, Paul kept coming up to him every day to talk. Finally, Jake had succumbed and responded back to the strange insect facts being spewed at him. When Jake learned he would be staying in Juniper Falls into the New Year, and maybe even longer, he was crushed. But it was Paul who responded by saying, "Now we can be best friends." And they were, until Jake left Juniper Falls and never looked back.

Jake certainly owed Paul at least a dinner.

"Sure. That sounds good," he said now, pulling out his phone to take down Paul's address. "Thank Jennie for me." After all, maybe a home-cooked meal would be nice for a change. By Monday, he would probably be sick of take-out food.

"Looking forward to it, Jake. It's been way too long." The two old friends shook hands and Jake left the coffee shop with his now-lukewarm coffee.

Rounding the corner, a large blur of golden fur leaped up onto Jake, bringing him to a crashing halt. Coffee spilled all over the front of his jacket. Before he had a chance to focus his eyes on what had jumped on him, he heard a familiar voice.

"Oh my goodness! Charlie! No! Down, Charlie! Now!" There was Emma, face flushed, running up to Jake at the sight of Charlie now licking coffee off the soaked jacket.

"Jake! I am so, so sorry. Charlie is a squirrel chaser and he caught sight of this one black squirrel and took off from me like a shot." She let out a couple of hard breaths before she could continue. "Obviously I need to work on my short distance sprinting. Or figure out a way to rid Charlie of his squirrel fascination."

Jake just stood there slightly shocked and a little dazed over what had just happened. Yet here he was, for the second time this morning, wanting to gloss over someone's error so as not to hurt any feelings. Two nights in Juniper Falls and he was already losing his edge. Jake looked into Emma's eyes. He could tell she wasn't sure what more to do or say. Charlie, by now, had his fill of the coffee and foam off Jake's jacket and was in the process of licking the remains off the sidewalk.

The sight was ridiculous, and Jake started to laugh. He couldn't help it. It felt good just letting go and laughing. Emma looked questioningly at him, as if to get permission to laugh along too. Charlie lifted his head from the sidewalk with a snout full of coffee foam. That did it, Emma could not contain herself any longer. Jake liked the look of Emma laughing. Her eyes crinkled in the corners and she looked so alive.

"Can I buy you another cup of coffee?" Emma composed herself and put Charlie back on his leash.

Jake looked down at himself and chuckled. "Thanks, but I'll take a rain check on that coffee. If that's okay with you? I'm going to go home to shower and then head over to the realtor's office to check on the progress of the Open House, but I might need to schedule it for next week. Who knows, maybe by some miracle she might have a lead on a potential buyer."

"Sounds good." She called back as Charlie was pulling Emma away again on another squirrel hunt. "Sorry again."

He waved away her apology. "Hey, thanks again for all your help last night. It made a big difference."

Emma had already been dragged part way down the street so it was unlikely she could hear Jake's words of appreciation. "Chat with you later!" she called back over her shoulder.

Jake threw the empty coffee cup in the garbage and jogged the remainder of the way home. In Seattle, if he would have experienced a morning like he did today, he would have been in a foul mood for the entire day. Jake did not do *unexpected* well.

However, today was different. He actually caught himself humming while he headed home.

*Home.* He had used that word while talking to Emma earlier as well. Jake couldn't remember the last time he had referred to where he was currently staying as his home.

# 9

## EMMA

That evening, Emma sat on a bar stool in the kitchen with her elbows on the counter and face resting in her hands while she watched Amy bake. Cookies by the dozen were cooling on racks, covering every available counter space. Emma reached over and picked up a gingersnap cookie, taking a bite. Crispy on the outside, soft and chewy in the middle. Just the way she liked it. "I love having all this fresh baking at my fingertips, but it is so hard to stop at just one. Or five," she sighed with fake melancholy.

"It's not my baking, it's your lack of willpower *toward* my baking." Amy playfully swatted Emma's hand away from snatching another cookie off the rack.

"True. Can I take a few of these in to work for the residents tomorrow morning?" Emma knew how much they all loved Amy's baking and thought Meredith might enjoy a special treat.

"If you promise you won't eat them all on your break, help yourself. I don't want to be the one enabling your cookie addiction." Amy continued mixing batter for a batch of chocolate zucchini muffins that was next on her baking agenda.

Emma had been deciding whether or not to share with her sister how she spent the last evening helping Jake pack up his grandmother's house. She wanted to talk over her feelings and frustrations with someone and Amy was always her "go to" person. But then she also knew it would most likely get her sister all antsy about what she would most likely perceive as a romantic opportunity. Emma decided to bite the bullet and fill her in on meeting Jake at Heart & Home, and then literally running into him with Charlie at *Java Junction*, though she deliberately left out the trip into Seattle with Jake and his grandmother. Even though Emma would need Amy's help with Charlie, she was still processing her decision, not sure what to think about how easily she'd agreed to accompany Meredith and her grandson.

"Honestly, Emma, you surprise me sometimes. All this with some random guy?"

Emma sighed. "What do you mean?"

"Here you go accepting an invitation to drive with a stranger you just met into Seattle, and then stay in his condo overnight. I've been trying to get you on a blind date for the last year with Danny from the clinic and you refuse to budge."

"Wait, but how did you know about my trip with Jake? I never said a thing to you about it!" Emma had been hoping to get ahead of this with her sister, spin it in the right way so as to avoid this exact response. But somehow her sister knew about the whole trip before she'd had a chance to open her mouth. Small towns. She loved them most of the time, but not all the time. "And Jake is not some random guy, Amy. He's Meredith Rothstein's grandson, and I'm only going to help out. It's not even confirmed yet! Who even told you about it?"

Amy shrugged. "Pam was talking to Tanya at the clinic this morning. Then Connor overheard Tanya talking to Rhonda about how handsome this Jake is."

"Okay, first of all, I'm accompanying his grandmother as her caretaker, and staying in a separate suite from Jake. And secondly, I have absolutely no interest in a guy from the city, especially Jake Rothstein. I'm not going down *that* road again." Emma busied herself, tidying magazines and crayons on the counter to avoid looking Amy in the eye. Her sister should know better than to think Emma would get herself mixed up with another smooth-talking city guy. "No interest at all. Got it? And you can let Connor know to tell Tanya and Rhonda and even Pam that if they want to gossip about me, they should at least get their facts straight."

"Okay, okay. Don't get all worked up. You know how word can spread in this town, especially when it involves a good-looking and mysterious stranger with a troubled past." Emma rolled her eyes at what was sounding like the synopsis for a romance novel, but it was no use as her sister was on a roll now. "I'm just worried about you getting hurt again."

Emma looked up at her sister. "I won't. Because I'm not interested."

"Well if you're not interested in Jake, that means you'll go out with Danny, right? Give him a chance? He's got a great personality and a steady job with benefits."

"Wow, way to sell him, sis." Emma cocked an eyebrow. "Next you'll say he has straight teeth."

"Well…" Amy pulled a tray of mini muffins out of the oven. "He does."

"Amy!"

Connor came in, loosening his tie as he entered the room. He gave Amy a kiss and popped a freshly baked mini muffin into his mouth. "What did I miss?" He looked between his wife and her sister.

"Nothing much." Amy scooped fresh batter into the muffin tray. "That city guy is a no-go. But Emma was about to agree to go on a date with Danny."

Emma glared at her sister and then glanced at Connor, hoping for some compassion, but he turned to face her head on, beside Amy, and Emma could feel the solidarity radiating off of both of them.

Connor chimed in his two cents' worth: "He's got a great personality and a steady job with benefits."

"I know, I know. And straight teeth too. Seriously, you guys are too much. Is going on a blind date with this guy the only way to get you off my back?" She shook her head, admitting defeat. "Okay, fine. When I get back from this whole Seattle thing, I'll meet him for a coffee."

"Dinner," Amy countered.

Emma sighed, knowing it wasn't worth the fight, as her sister was a ruthless negotiator. In the end, Amy would get her way, and who knew what would happen? Maybe Emma would enjoy the food at least.

"You know why she's pressuring you to date, don't you?" Connor asked, teasingly. "She wants you married off. Amy has plans for your room above the garage." He popped another mini muffin into his mouth, and talked as he chewed. "But if you ask me, she just wants a place to escape from the rest of us. You know, like a she-shed."

"Not *entirely*, true." Amy smirked and winked at Emma. "But I do want you with someone who will love you the way you deserve to be loved, Emma. I hate to see you lonely." She put her hands on either side of Emma's shoulders in her classic "big sister" pose. "So, I can set up the date?"

"I guess so," Emma said reluctantly. She looked down at Charlie who had been snoozing off his long day that had started with squirrel and coffee escapades by the warmth of the gas fireplace. "But, really, all I need is this guy right here. Isn't that right, Charlie?" At the sound of his name, Charlie ambled over to where Emma was standing. She bent down and ruffled his fur. He took this as an invitation to jump up and lick Emma's face. "See? Charlie agrees too!" She giggled, and added, "Who has time for all that romance?"

Popping a second muffin into his mouth, Connor gave Amy a kiss on the cheek, and headed for the stairs. "Have fun, ladies."

## 10

## EMMA

Emma stood at the Heart & Home front counter nervously chatting with Pam. Saturdays were always busy with visitors, but they had a few minutes of lull in the crowds just before Jake was due to arrive and they would leave with Meredith for Seattle. Charlie's dog bed, bag of food, and leash were on the floor beside the counter, waiting for Amy to come by later in the afternoon. Her sister had promised Emma that she would pick up Charlie and take care of him overnight while Emma was in Seattle. She knew Charlie enjoyed overnights at her sister's place, as Leah and Laney doted on him, feeding him copious amounts of dog treats and human food that would mysteriously land into his food dish. He even tolerated being dressed up as a fairy god-dog for two adorable five-year-old princesses. Yes, Charlie would be well taken care of and loved while she was away. So there was nothing to worry about leaving him behind. It was other thoughts that occupied her mind.

Emma pressed both her hands flat onto the counter. "Tell me I'm not making a mistake doing this?"

"You're not making a mistake," Pam said in a monotone voice as she flipped through files.

When Emma had first explained the trip to Pam, she had led with her intentions for Meredith. "I figured if only Meredith could see Lexington Manor…" But now, hearing Pam's noncommittal tone, Emma doubted herself once again. "Maybe this is all wrong."

Pam took her hands and looked her in the eye. "Emma, just be professional. Don't get caught in between the two of them. It's not your issue. You are there to simply do your job."

She knew this was the truth, but she felt she needed to repeat it to herself like a mantra, over and over again. "But do you think he's being genuine? Do you think he'll be all right with her staying at Heart & Home, if that's what she truly wants?"

Pam glanced down the hall, and then looked back to Emma. "I know you want to look out for her, but just be careful, okay?" She dropped her voice to almost a whisper. "Guys like Jake Rothstein only look out for themselves. And Emma, you need to do the same."

Emma stared out the front windows of Heart & Home, waiting for Jake and beginning to doubt everything about this plan. What was she doing? Had she gotten in the middle of something that might cost her a job she loved? Across the parking lot, she caught sight of his fancy Lexus. It was too late now. She backed away and crossed the hall toward the resident rooms. "I'm going to get Mrs. Rothstein ready and help her settle into the van," Emma called out to Pam, trying to sound as professional as she could. And for the countless time that day, she reminded herself that this was her job and nothing more.

Emma approached the door and knocked gently at Meredith's room, but there was no response. She slowly opened the door, wanting to respect the elderly resident's privacy.

"Meredith?" She softly called out. Meredith sat hunched over, holding a photo in her hand, her back turned to Emma.

"Meredith? Is everything okay? Jake's here now." Meredith looked up, placed the photo back onto a shelf, and turned her wheelchair around. Emma noticed the sad look on her face and her eyes glistened with unfallen tears. She repeated the question and gently placed her hand on the woman's shoulder. "Everything okay?"

Meredith composed herself and the strong, confident woman that Emma was familiar with returned. She straightened. "Yes.

Just thinking about all the things in the room I will need to pack for my move to Lexington Manor."

"This is just a trip to look at the place, Meredith. You may not even like it when you get there, so no need to worry about packing yet. And if the time comes when you decide to move, I will definitely help you pack up your things. I promise," Emma tried to reassure her.

"I know. But I just don't want to disappoint Jake. He's worked so hard to get me a place there." Meredith looked back at the photo sitting on the shelf. It was of a young Jake with her late husband, Henry. Jake was holding a toy boat in his hands and his grandfather had his arm protectively around the young boy. It looked like a loving moment between grandparent and grandchild. Emma was confused. What happened to give Jake such a negative opinion of his grandparents and upbringing? Things just did not make any sense. Maybe the trip this weekend would give her a chance to talk to him more about his years living in Juniper Falls, and his relationship with his grandparents. However, Pam's words of warning played in Emma's mind and she reminded herself to keep some distance, not just for the sake of her job, but for her heart.

Emma picked up Meredith's packed overnight bag and grabbed a sweater from the closet, just in case Meredith needed an extra layer of warmth during their travels. This time of year it was always best to dress in multiple layers, as the rain could make anyone quite chilled. She double checked that all the medication Meredith needed was also packed. Trying to keep things light and cheery for her travel companion, Emma joked, "Time for our road trip. I've brought snacks and music. Let's just hope Jake doesn't attempt to car dance!" That caused Meredith's face to break out in a smile, losing some of the sadness and worry for the time being. The elderly woman reached up and grabbed Emma's hand, and the young nurse was reminded of the reason she was going along to Seattle in the first place. For Meredith, her friend. Forget Jake. He was a big boy. He could take care of himself.

# 11

## JAKE

As Jake crossed from the parking lot, he appraised the Heart & Home van parked right out front. If his business associates could only see him now, trading in his Lexus for a senior's transportation van. At least it was for the short term, and soon he would have the comfort of his car back again. There certainly would not be any concern for speeding tickets while driving this vehicle. He laughed to himself, just hoping the van had a hands-free option in case he needed to be in contact with work while on the road. Jake was unsure how his grandmother or Emma would take to him making work calls on the drive, so he had already decided he would try to keep them to a minimum. The last thing he wanted was to start the trip off on the wrong foot with either of them. He could tell when he was outnumbered.

Traffic would be minimal and thankfully the forecast called for sunny skies, so there wouldn't be any rain to slow them down. Door-to-door, it should take them a little over three hours, providing they didn't have to stop too many times along the way. And the benefit to driving this time of year was there was usually little to no construction. Construction in Seattle could put traffic in gridlock and the bottleneck would have a chain reaction with the other feeder routes, making driving a nightmare.

As Jake walked into the lobby, the elderly resident they called

"Geezer" was apparently also appraising the van through the windows.

"I'm coming too," he said to the windows, as if the van was about to leave without him. "Wait for me!"

Jake chuckled and decided to play along. "Sorry, buddy, but I'm only breaking one person outta this joint today."

The old guy nodded. "Okay, but how about you take me sailing one day?" Jake looked at him, shocked at what he had suggested, but then shook it off, chalking it up to senior ramblings. There was no way this stranger could possibly know about Jake's sailing.

The nurse trailing Geezer—there seemed to always be a nurse trailing him—finally caught up and placed a hand on his walker. "The only place you're going is to the sunroom. Time for exercise."

"How about I exercise my right to get out of here?" Geezer nudged the nurse. "You and me, we hijack that van out there and take it for a spin?" The nurse looked flustered like she was unsure of how to respond. Jake had a feeling it gave the old guy great pleasure to wreak such havoc and keep everyone on their toes. For a moment, he wondered how he would act when he was in his senior years, and then caught himself, chuckling at the scenario. He hoped he would still have as much spunk as this gentleman obviously did.

Just then, Emma wheeled Jake's grandmother into the lobby. "Nurse Johansson," she said. "Please help Geezer back to the sunroom. I think there's an extra-large piece of chocolate cake waiting for him." Emma winked pointedly at Geezer, which caught his attention.

Geezer shook a finger at the poor nurse in charge of him. "Now why didn't you say that to begin with? Let's go, hurry up before Doris eats my piece!"

As Geezer and the nurse headed off, Jake sidled up to Emma. He had to ask. "His name's not really Geezer, is it?"

She smiled, and the warmth of her expression immediately disarmed him. "It might as well be. It's a nickname from his late wife. It's all he'll answer to."

Jake liked that. He also liked how well Emma seemed to know exactly what to say to each of the residents. Hopefully that would be no different as they ventured out with his grandmother. Sometimes Jake just lacked the words or tact needed on occasion. He appreciated Emma's approach and the gentle nature she demonstrated to the elderly and furry creatures alike. Somehow, she took the rough edges off him when he was around her too.

As though she could feel him thinking about her, Emma cleared her throat, which brought Jake back to the agenda at hand.

"Morning, Grandma!" he said in the peppiest voice he could muster. He kissed her cheek, something he was new at, but that she seemed to like. "Ready to go?" His grandmother reached up and patted his cheek and nodded.

But before they could start for the door, a pretty redhead breezed through it, and straight for them. It looked to Jake like she was on a mission.

"Amy!" Emma said, clearly surprised and looking somewhat flustered. "I didn't think you would be coming by until later. Charlie is still in the sunroom helping Stanley in a game of checkers against Hank."

"I was just in the area and thought I should pop by." Jake noticed Emma turning a slight shade of pink. It was clear she was uncomfortable at this woman's presence. The way she was staring at the woman who had arrived looked like she was trying to have a conversation with her using only her eyes. And if Jake was to interpret it correctly, Emma's wide eyes were saying "leave now" to the guest. This was a different side to Emma that Jake had not seen before, and he wondered what else he would learn about her during this trip.

This Amy person stood right in front of Jake, surveying him from his brown leather Santoni shoes up to his jet-black wavy hair. "This is him? This is *the infamous* Jake Rothstein that has everyone in town talking?" Amy now looked to Emma with raised eyebrows and Emma returned a look that seemed to plead with her to stop the direction of this conversation. To Jake, Emma looked like she was wavering between being mortified and absolutely furious at the lady who was now staring straight into his eyes awaiting his response. Was this someone from Heart & Home who was upset they were using the van for the purpose of checking out another facility? He certainly didn't want to ruffle any feathers, especially with needing them to sign the release papers for his grandmother. He wanted the transition to go smoothly, for her sake and for his.

He cleared his throat and tried to keep an even tone to his voice. "Yes. I guess that would be me. And you are—?"

"I am here to check out the man my baby sister is about to go away with for the weekend after meeting him only three days ago. Someone I've never met. So I came to meet you," the woman—Emma's sister—said matter-of-factly.

Jake felt his grandmother watching this whole exchange, and his face warmed from it. However, when he chanced a glance her way, his grandmother looked rather amused. A man who normally had a comment for everything, Jake didn't know how to respond and found himself at a loss for words.

Thankfully, Emma was quick to recover from the shock of the situation and inserted herself into the conversation. "Jake, this is my sister, Amy, who apparently still thinks of me as a baby. She was *just* leaving."

"Not before I say hello," Amy said sweetly. "That would be rude." She turned to face Jake straight on and thrust out a hand. "I hope I can count on you to take care of my little sister. Respectfully."

Jake shook her hand, feeling a little like she was a dad with a shotgun meeting his daughter's date for the first time. "Of course," he said, not able to come up with any other possible response.

"Amy!" Emma said, exasperated.

Amy held up both hands. "Okay, okay, I'll go." A smile slowly replaced the protective stare coming from the older sister. "Nice to meet you, Jake."

"Likewise, Amy." Jake couldn't blame her for being concerned. The entire situation did sound a little unusual. "I'm not trying to—"

"Sorry, Jake, I was just teasing you. After all, Emma doesn't go into the city much, and I needed to make sure she is in good hands."

Emma let out a long breath at the same time she rolled her eyes. "Seriously, Amy!"

"Okay, okay. I'll back off. And for the record, it isn't the *entire* town talking about you."

"Enough, Amy." And with that, Emma put her hand on her pushy sister's shoulder to turn her around and walk in the direction of the sunroom.

"Goodbye, Mrs. Rothstein! Have fun on your trip!" Amy called over her shoulder.

Jake gave Amy his best "don't worry about a thing" smile as they walked away. The kind he often gave his clients, assuring them everything was under control. Jake pulled the wool blanket over her legs for added warmth and undid the brake on his grandmother's wheelchair. He began to wheel her down the corridor to where the van was parked, but had not gotten out of earshot from the two sisters before he heard, "No interest at all, huh? I don't believe it for a second."

This made Jake smile as he picked up his step toward the van.

## 12

## EMMA

Once Meredith settled into the middle row bucket seat behind the front passenger side and the wheelchair was secured in the back of the van, Emma made her way around to the driver's side of the van. Jake was already standing there. Simultaneously both of their hands reached for the door handle. Jake was slower and his strong hand came to a stop on hers. It seemed to linger, sending a current of excitement up her arm and into her chest. Such a small moment, yet she knew the feeling would stay in her for at least the next hour.

"Sorry," Jake said abruptly, removing his hand and leaving hers cold. His voice was lower than normal. He must have felt a connection too.

"I would be fine with you driving, but the insurance for Heart & Home requires an employee to be the driver for any off-property excursion," Emma said, hoping it didn't frustrate Jake. She knew Jake liked to be in control of situations, but so did she, and after Amy's not-so-quiet comment, Emma already felt like control was slowly slipping from her senses.

"No, that's fine. I might have to make some work phone calls anyways." Jake walked around to the other side of the van and hopped in. She was grateful for his easy response. The last thing she needed was to begin this journey with a power struggle.

Emma turned the key in the ignition and the van roared to

life. Immediately, a rap song came blaring through the speakers. Both Emma and Jake reached to turn it down brushing their hands together once more. This time, they both gave a nervous laugh, aware that Meredith was keenly watching their every move.

"Oh, my goodness! Sorry about the volume and the music selection. Colby, one of our orderlies drives a group of seniors to the farmer's market on Thursdays, and rumor has it, they have quite the rap battles in the van on the way over." Emma shook her head at the volume. Colby shouldn't be cranking up the tunes *that* loud, even for seniors with hearing difficulties.

"Rap battles? Aren't the residents a little old for that kind of music?" Jake looked confused.

This time Meredith spoke up from the back seat. "You would be surprised at what Doris and her gang listen to. I'll have to introduce you to them when we get back home."

Emma smiled to herself at hearing Meredith refer to returning home. She loved that one of her favorite residents thought of Heart & Home as her home.

Jake was flustered, caught on another word from Meredith's sentence: "There's a *gang* at Heart & Home?" Jake laughed at the thought. "Let me guess, Geezer is the leader, and you and Doris are his backup?"

"Well, not that kind of gang, Jake!" Emma looked over at Jake and could tell he was getting a kick out of teasing his grandmother.

"Good. I was worried what kind of crowd you were hanging out with for a moment, Grandma. I need to make sure that you're in a good environment for someone of your impressionable age." Jake winked at Emma. She liked this light hearted banter and hoped it would set the tone for the remainder of the trip.

The sign announcing the trio were leaving Juniper Falls soon came into view and then grew distant in the rear-view mirror and the whole trip became much more real for Emma. Here she was embarking on this journey with Meredith, who she cared about deeply, and her grandson, who filled Emma with such an array of emotions, she had yet to sort them out. She felt a heaviness weighing on her for what this trip would hold for Meredith, Jake, and for herself.

*Ding!* A light went on in the dashboard of the van, bringing Emma out of her thoughts. "Seriously? The van was supposed to be fully gassed up and ready for us." Frustration set in and she made a mental note for the second item she needed to discuss with Colby when she returned back to work Monday.

"Well, I guess we have to make a detour to get gas." Jake sounded perturbed at this unexpected stop, and Emma wondered if his light and joking tones were always so easily derailed.

"There's a little town coming up that has a gas station before we get onto the freeway," Emma said soothingly, hoping the trip didn't get derailed this easily. "We can get a coffee there too."

"Okay, but I hope it's only the gas that was neglected. The van's in good working condition, right? I just don't want to break down on the I-5. That's the last thing we need." Jake shook his head and looked out the passenger window, and then murmured to himself, but loud enough that they could all hear, "I should have just figured out a way to rent a wheelchair at Lexington and driven her in with my Lexus."

And there was a glimpse of the city boy again.

"No coffee for Jake," Meredith quipped from the back. "He's obviously too excitable already this morning." Emma could see Jake's jaws clench and brows furrowed. But instead of voicing his frustration toward his grandmother's comment, Jake gave a deep breath and seemed to let it go as he pulled out his phone. Emma breathed a sigh of relief as she pulled into the gas station.

With the van's tank filled and Meredith snoozing in the backseat, Emma got onto the freeway and drove toward Seattle.

"Thanks for the coffee." Jake sipped out of his Styrofoam cup. Emma noticed a small cringe as he swallowed the gas station brew, but he didn't say a word about the taste.

"Well, I figured it was the least I could do since my dog caused you to wear your coffee yesterday."

"It really wasn't Charlie's fault. I hadn't been watching where I was going either." Jake took another sip and this time his mouth actually puckered up like he had just sucked on a lemon.

"How's the coffee?" Emma couldn't resist asking.

"Let's just say it's been the best coffee I've had in a few days," he chuckled. Emma laughed, fully aware of how Jake had detested the instant coffee he had been drinking while at his grandmother's house.

They drove in silence for the next several miles, with the only sound being Meredith's occasional snore from the back. Emma barely recognized the landscape. It had been a long time since she had traveled into the city.

Jake broke the silence. "Hey, can I ask you a personal question?"

"Sure." Emma kept her eyes focused on the road, nervous about the question he had in mind.

"Why did you leave Seattle? I know you said your sister needed your help, but was that all? Do you ever want to go back?"

"Jake, that was more than one question," she said to give herself a moment to put together an answer.

"You don't have to answer if you are uncomfortable." Jake must have sensed her apprehension. "Sorry, I shouldn't have asked. It's not my concern."

"No, that's fine," she said, letting out a long breath. "It was complicated. The short version is that I fell in love with a guy who said all the right things I wanted to hear. We were together for a while, everyone thought we'd get married. *I* thought we'd get married. But when it came down to it, turned out we both wanted something different in life. He just realized it before I did and chose to end it with me by a text, on my birthday." Emma wasn't used to bearing her heart to someone she didn't really know that well. She felt vulnerable and kept staring straight ahead, pretending to be concentrating on the Honda ten feet ahead, instead of the fact that she had opened up to someone she barely knew.

"Wow, Emma, that's really..." Jake sounded genuinely empathetic and was about to continue when his cell phone vibrated on the console. It vibrated a second time, and he snatched it up, looking at the display and then shaking his head.

"Listen, Emma, I'm so sorry. I have to take this. It's work, and there's this client that I have to—"

Before he could finish, Emma interrupted coolly. "It's fine, take the call."

"Emma?" Meredith said softly, under Jake's loud business voice, briefing a client through his cell phone. Apparently, she had been awake during the exchange and had chosen to keep quiet.

Emma waved a casual hand back to Meredith, "I'm fine."

Meredith didn't say another word, and Emma was thankful. She concentrated on the road ahead to try and regain her equilibrium while Jake rattled on to what sounded to be a client he was trying to impress.

When Jake finished his work phone call and hung up, a stark silence came over the van.

Eventually he cleared his throat. "I'm so sorry to have had to interrupt our conversation. Now go on with what you were saying?"

But by this time, Emma had shut down her uncharacteristic desire to discuss any of the deep things of her heart, especially when he was so uncaring. When she only shook her head back at him, it was obvious by the way he pulled his head back that Jake took this rejection personally.

"Can I change lanes now?" Emma asked after a while. She still wasn't used to driving the van, and she definitely wasn't used to this kind of road busyness, now that the traffic had thickened as they closed in on the city.

"Yes, but be quick about it," he said in a cold, business-like tone. "You're going to want to exit in another three miles," he said, "so probably a good idea to get over now anyway."

Emma checked all of her mirrors as she looked for another opening. Out of pure frustration, and the mixed emotions she had been trying to process, she couldn't hold back her snippy feelings. "It's a good thing your grandmother won't have to drive in and out of this place, other than today."

"You mean other than when I move her in," Jake retorted,

with a glance over the seat to his grandmother, who was either truly sleeping again, or at least pretending to be.

She let out an impatient huff of breath, no longer willing to hide her disagreement with his plan. At the same time, she didn't want to argue while she was driving in Seattle traffic. "Am I good to change?"

"Huh?" Jake asked.

"Lanes!" Emma said. "Three miles, it has to be coming up soon, so how about we just focus on getting there safely, huh?"

"Agreed. Yes, you're good to move over." Jake slid his sunglasses from his forehead down over his eyes and Emma turned up the radio. According to her GPS, they would be arriving at Lexington Manor within the next thirty minutes. She was already counting down the hours until she would be back in Juniper Falls.

## 13

## EMMA

Emma trailed behind as Jake pushed Meredith in her wheelchair through the automatic doors into the bustling Lexington Manor complex. Large screens in the foyer advertised modern amenities such as a computer lab and a gym. Silk plants were placed every three feet along the walls with a precision that gave the place a military atmosphere, rather than a homey one.

Emma wondered why they wouldn't have real plants or some kind of water feature in such a large lobby. After all, they had the space for it, and from the looks of it, they also had the finances. Heart & Home had the koi pond out front and the residents loved sitting out there and feeding the fish. The artwork hanging along Lexington's walls was abstract and boring in Emma's opinion. So far, everything seemed sterile and cold. Hard chrome and glass surrounded them.

Meredith surveyed her surroundings with wide eyes. "This is, uh, quite some place." Emma couldn't tell if she was unnerved or impressed.

They arrived at a reception counter where three women were working studiously, not one of them looking up to greet their new guests. Pam never would have ignored people at her counter in Heart & Home, Emma couldn't help but think.

Emma eyed Jake, her abrasive attitude still lingering from the stressful car ride. She knew it was important for Meredith to have a peaceful day so she could make a clear-headed decision, and so she tried to push her irritation aside. However, she found herself feeling on edge simply from being in such a cold, almost-hostile environment. There did not seem to be anything soothing or homey so far.

Jake turned to the receptionists, who had yet to acknowledge the trio standing in front of them and cleared his throat. When there was still no response, he said, "Excuse me? Can somebody please help us?"

Finally, one of them finished typing something on her keyboard and looked up. The twitch to the edge of her eye showed her annoyance at the interruption. "Yes? What can I help you with?"

"We have an appointment to be shown around here today," Jake said.

The receptionist returned to her work, as she answered him, barely giving his request a second thought. "Well, you must be mistaken about the day. We only take tour guided appointments on Mondays and Wednesdays."

Jake cleared his throat again, and Emma could sense his discomfort. When he opened his mouth to speak, she could tell his calm and friendly tone came with great effort. "Yes, I spoke to someone who said they could make an exception, because I had already given a deposit, and was only available to bring my grandmother in on the weekend. We have driven several hours to come here today."

The receptionist kept her focus on what looked like a large and complicated spreadsheet on her computer screen. "Who did you speak with?"

Jake shifted his weight, angling further from Emma, and dropped his voice. "Um. I don't recall the name of the man."

The receptionist took in a long breath and let it out in a huff. "Fine. Give me ten minutes."

Jake wheeled Meredith across the reception lobby, almost knocking into a couple of elderly residents. They gave Jake the stink-eye, and he quickly skirted out of their way. He found an unobtrusive place at an adjacent wall to wait. Emma followed, looking around in awe. She'd never seen, or even imagined high ceilings like this in a nursing home, or even in a shopping mall for that matter. She may have once been at a museum with ceilings as high.

"Don't say it, Grandma," Jake said, off a raised eyebrow look Meredith was giving her grandson. "I know this isn't starting well, but please, *please*, just give this a chance."

And even though he didn't look Emma's way, she knew he was pleading with her as well.

---

After half an hour of waiting in the lobby and being ignored by the three receptionists, Meredith, Jake, and Emma were finally ushered to a hallway with several chairs in a waiting area. A tall man in a tailored suit strode toward them. There was something about his approach that reminded Emma of a car salesman at a high-end dealership.

"Mr. Rothstein?"

Jake practically jumped out of his chair to shake the man's hand.

"Andrew Perry. I'm an administrator on staff."

Hmmm two first names, Emma mused. This was not boding well. Her father said to never trust a man with two first names.

The man continued. "I'm afraid our regular sales team doesn't work on weekends, but I can give you a quick tour of the place, if you'd like?"

"Sales team?" Emma asked under her breath, but her words must have been louder than intended, because Mr. Perry looked over at her.

Thankfully, Jake answered, taking the man's attention. "That would be fantastic. This is my grandmother, Meredith Rothstein. We're interested to see what you have available here for her."

The administrator barely glanced at Meredith. "Sure, sure," he told Jake, and then quickly turned his eyes back to Emma. "And you are…?"

"Emma Hathaway. I'm a nurse at Mrs. Rothstein's current assisted-living complex."

He extended his hand, so she reached out to shake his. He held on tightly, for longer than seemed appropriate, but she felt awkward at the thought of yanking her hand free.

"Welcome here. Pleasure to meet you." he said, cupping his other hand over their grasped ones, as if he knew of her intention to try to get free. "And you're a nurse, you say? Did you know we're always looking for competent nurses here at Lexington Manor?"

Emma flicked her eyes again at the high ceilings. "Oh, well, thank you. But I'm happy where I am." Emma finally pulled her hand away, but the administrator kept his gaze set on her until he caught Jake's stare.

"Right," he said, straightening to his full height, which towered over Meredith in her wheelchair. "Why don't I start by showing you the accommodations wing?"

After weaving their way through what seemed like a maze of hallways, the administrator stood back and proudly held out an arm to show a tiny resident's room. Emma could swear it was smaller than their supplies closets at Heart & Home. The one shelf unit overflowed with books, clothes, and toiletries. There was nowhere else to put them, as besides that, there was only enough space for a small bed. She thought of Heart & Home's residents and how they were able to personalize each room with special keepsakes and photos. There was no room here for anything sentimental, and the walls appeared to be made of some kind of brushed metal, which wouldn't allow for hangings of any kind.

"I don't think my wheelchair will even fit in there." Meredith said, concern etched in her voice.

Mr. Perry laughed a hearty laugh. "Oh, not to worry about that. All residents are issued state-of-the-art wheelchairs, much sleeker in design than the one you're using. With a little practice, I promise you'll be able to maneuver it in alongside your bed in no time."

Emma looked to Jake, but he was only nodding at the administrator.

"And all the rooms are the same?" Jake asked. "I see this one is occupied."

"Oh, yes." Mr. Perry reached up to run his finger along the trim above the door. When it came back clean, he seemed satisfied and went on. "As you know, we have a long waiting list, so the rooms are never vacant for more than a day or two, but they have all been designed to be identical."

Emma wondered if that sounded as boring to Meredith as it did to Emma.

"They're all fully equipped with call buttons, adjustable beds, and of course the large screen wall-mounted televisions," the administrator went on. "Some residents love to spend all day in their rooms watching our long list of options on the movie channel. They can even sign out iPads to play games on if they run out of programs to watch."

"All day?" Emma blurted, unable to keep in her words. "Alone in their rooms?"

Mr. Perry must have caught on to her tone, because he cleared his throat uncomfortably. "Well, we certainly don't encourage that. Here, let me show you the full schedule of options available to our residents."

The administrator reached into his inside jacket pocket and retrieved his phone. After a flurry of finger scrolling, he pulled up a schedule which he proudly held out toward his potential clients. "We bring in experts for our residents to learn foreign languages, the meditation class is always a popular option, and our Michelin starred chef often teaches demonstrations. Last week it was samplings of the finest froie gras."

Meredith wrinkled up her nose. "Froie what?"

Mr. Perry either didn't hear her or chose to ignore, Meredith. Emma hoped it wasn't the latter as he continued.

"Our IT team also teaches classes on getting our residents using social media and other apps for helping them engage with others online."

Meredith did not look impressed with any of it. But this time it was Emma interrupting with a poorly attempted stifle of a giggle. "Sorry. I was just thinking of some of our residents and could only imagine the mischief they'd cook up if they got on Tinder."

Jake looked over at her with raised eyebrows. The administrator did not look amused either, causing Emma's face to flush with her failed attempt at humor. She tried to recover with a change of topic. "What about tea time? I know that's our resident's favorite time to visit with each other."

"And don't forget Elinor's fresh baked raisin oatmeal cookies," Meredith piped in, "Remember Jake how I would bake cookies for you when you came home from school?"

Jake smiled and patted his grandmother's shoulder. But once again, Mr. Perry addressed Jake over Meredith's head. "We have talented baristas that can brew up a mean dalgona whipped coffee. All our baking is delivered to us daily from a gourmet bakery. Since we have a variety of dietary needs, we offer a wide range of cheese and fruit platters for snack times."

"I just take my tea with a teaspoon of sugar and two splashes of milk." Meredith looked a little overwhelmed with all the information, so Emma thought she should step in.

"Should we continue our tour?" she asked. Jake must have sensed the same thing as he gently guided his grandmother's wheelchair out of the room.

Next, Mr. Perry proceeded to lead them through another complicated maze of hallways. He finally stopped at a modern-looking gym. Emma had thought the advertisement on the screen in the front lobby must have been touched up, because the gym had appeared so sleek and large, but it looked exactly the same in person. Except here, one senior moved the bar on a state-of-the-art looking weight machine. A personal trainer looked on and offered guidance. The gym was otherwise empty.

"Wow, this all looks very modern," Emma said, speaking her thoughts again as soon as they came to her, "but it seems like it barely gets used."

"Oh, no," Mr. Perry replied. "Believe me, it is well used. Our trainer, Jarrod, is booked solid for all the hours he's here. Our residents often relax alone on weekends after all the activities that we offer during the week,"

"Just one on one? When are the group classes?"

Emma knew Meredith loved the group classes they ran at Heart & Home, filled with lively music and creative techniques to keep the seniors moving, even the ones in wheelchairs.

The detail-oriented administrator ran his hand over the nearest piece of equipment. This time the movement didn't seem to be looking for dust as much as bursting with pride. "We have found that especially later in years, our residents have such individual needs, so we book one-on-one appointments to address those unique concerns. Each resident meets with the physiotherapist and develops a personal exercise program to use with our trainer. We have found group classes were a waste of the residents' time."

"Hmph. That doesn't sound like much fun," Meredith told him.

Those were Emma's feelings exactly, so she looked straight at Mr. Perry with raised eyebrows, looking forward to hearing his response.

But he completely ignored Meredith's comment, and this time Emma could tell by his deep breath and tightened jaw, it was purposeful. He went on with his bragging. "We also have dieticians right on site. Their offices are difficult for me to show you, as all appointments are private. They create personalized meal plans for each resident that will optimize their health.

"Let me guess," Emma said. "They're all one-on-one?"

Mr. Perry didn't seem to take note of Emma's sarcasm. "Absolutely! All very personalized," he said with enthusiasm.

As they walked past a nearly empty games room with Emma now wheeling Meredith, they stopped to look inside at the one senior citizen playing solitaire. It seemed a perfect picture to illustrate the whole place, actually.

The administrator pointed through a window to explain the sculpted back garden, which was apparently only for looking, not for strolling. He had Jake's attention, but Emma had lost interest in his relentless boasting, so she wheeled Meredith closer to the senior resident.

"What do you think, Mrs. Rothstein?" Emma whispered loudly in a conspiratorial voice. She always called her Meredith in the privacy of Heart & Home, but she wouldn't take that liberty somewhere like this. "Think this gentleman will deal us in? I wonder if he knows how to play 5-card stud." She winked at Meredith.

But the senior glanced up at them with a terse expression, then collected the cards together into a pile, and pushed them their way. "I'm finished with them," he grumbled. "All yours."

The man clearly had no sense of humor. Emma felt badly, and quickly backed Meredith away, telling the gentleman that they were sorry to have interrupted him.

"Actually, Nurse Hathaway," Meredith played along with Emma's game of formalities. "I feel a little tired and could use some personalized attention to get me back to my personal ride. Personally, I think I've seen enough for today." Emma grinned back conspiratorially.

Jake just shook his head, not amused with their antics or their making fun of the place he wanted to sink a whole lot of money into.

And Andrew Perry did not clue in to the humor directed at him and his facility in the least.

## 14

## JAKE

Jake wheeled his grandmother into his small bachelor suite condo, equally excited and nervous to finally have her here. He had invited his grandparents to visit once before his grandpa had passed. He had even offered to drive to Juniper Falls and pick them up. His grandmother had grumbled about the long drive and the traffic, and just generally not being a city person, and so he had told them not to bother. But the rejection had hurt. He had wanted them to see what he'd achieved and how far he had come.

He regretted that he'd never been able to show his grandpa what he had made of himself. But he could still show his grandmother, and truth be told, she was probably the one who needed to see the proof of it.

It was only a half dozen steps from the apartment door to the living room, and it took his grandmother exactly that long to find something to criticize. "This can't be it. Where's the rest of your apartment?"

Jake parked her wheelchair next to the couch and started tidying his already tidy apartment. "I know it's small, but the guest suite down the hall where you'll be staying is bigger. After all, it's just me living here, Grandma. I don't need much space." He felt Emma's eyes on him too but didn't look up from the books he was aligning on his bookshelf. "Besides, do you have any idea how much a decent sized place in the city costs?"

"Exactly why I don't think you should move me into the city," his grandmother grumbled. "Why pay more for less space? Who wants to live in a cell?"

Jake tried not to take his grandmother's response to heart. He knew she was tired from the long day. Yet her words still stung of disappointment to him and made it obvious she was not sold on living in Seattle.

With the press of a button, Jake opened the blinds, revealing ceiling-to-floor windows and a view of the city's waterfront. He hoped this would entice his grandmother into seeing a positive aspect of his apartment. Dusk now fell over the city and lights illuminated the horizon. It was, to Jake, a breathtaking sight.

"Oh dear, look at how high up you are, Jake! Too bad you couldn't have found an apartment a little closer to the ground floor. You know, being so high is very dangerous in an emergency." Jake's jaw clenched and he resigned himself to give up on trying to impress his grandmother for the night. It was as if she purposely scouted out any negative aspects to living here.

"I, for one, am starving," Emma said, in an obvious ploy to break the tension. Jake was thankful, until she said, "Let me go rustle something up for us in the kitchen."

Emma had seemed to shake off the frustration with Jake from earlier in the van. She seemed good at that—letting things go—and he could probably learn something from her. He regretted taking the phone call after she opened her heart out to him, but there had been no other choice. Jake knew if the client had not made contact with him, then the head office would be his next phone call, and Jake could not risk another associate stepping in and scooping up the job he had worked so hard on landing since last spring.

Jake was thankful that Emma was trying to give him and his grandmother some space in his small apartment to discuss Lexington Manor. At the same time, he was fully aware of the contents—or lack thereof—in his fridge. "I don't think you will find anything worth eating in there. We can order some—"

Emma waved a casual hand. "Don't worry about it. I can be pretty creative in the kitchen. Not as good as my sister, mind you, but I've been known to put together something edible from time to time. I'm happy to do it." With that, she pushed open the kitchen door.

"Wait, I don't..." Jake trailed off as she disappeared behind the door. He took a second deliberating, but then turned back to his grandmother. Emma would figure out the lack of food quickly enough, and he should use this brief moment to help his grandmother understand. Plus, for the moment, he wouldn't have to worry about offending Emma.

"So, Grandma, did you hear what they said about physiotherapists, right on site, twenty-four hours a day at Lexington Manor? I know you love the cozy feel of Heart & Home, but this place could really help you with your hip."

"Harrumph." She scowled and readjusted her right leg, only proving his point. "You should ask how much extra they charge for that. I'll bet it's a pretty penny, and my hip is doing just fine. It's not as though I'm ever going to do jumping jacks again, no matter how many physiotherapists you sic on me." Not giving him time to argue, she changed the subject. "I don't like you living way up here in this lonely building, Jake."

"Lonely? Grandma, there are hundreds of other people living in this building." He ignored the fact that work kept him so busy, that when he returned home, he just relaxed in his apartment. He had not made any attempt to meet his neighbours, not even to hang out in the lobby or recreation room.

"Sure, and which one of them would notice if something happened to you? Which one of them would know if you woke up too sick to make it to the phone one day? Or you could get mugged on the street and left unconscious. Who would know? I worry about you alone in the city, Jake."

Jake heard a note of softness leak into her voice. He couldn't help himself. Even though his grandmother's sentiments were hard-won, they always brought a softness out in Jake. "That's a problem with being single, Grandma. Not a problem with living in an apartment."

"Still..." She raised an eyebrow at him. "You admit it's a problem."

He wasn't going to win this argument tonight and simply bent over and kissed the top of his grandmother's head. Then he made his way to the kitchen to check on his other guest.

Jake stood behind Emma in the tiny kitchen as she gazed into his nearly empty fridge. "Having trouble?" The closeness of his voice seemed to startle her, and she stepped back. She stumbled slightly, catching herself off balance. Jake instinctively reached out to prevent her from falling backwards. Her head leaned back into his chest. He could smell the scent of strawberries from her shampoo and he breathed in deeply. His lips were a mere inch from the top of her head and his arms steadied her by the shoulders.

Emma regained her balance, standing up and holding onto the open fridge door. She leaned her head inside once again, as though some new food may have appeared in the last ten seconds. To Jake it looked like she was trying to cool her flushed face and regain her composure. "I admit, I can't seem to come up with a single meal to make from this," she said, gesturing at the small condiments and half-empty jars. "And I doubt you have much in your pantry either."

Jake rubbed his neck, embarrassed. It had been months since he'd had a young woman in his apartment, even longer since he'd been in such close proximity to someone so attractive, and this is what he had to prove his independence and manliness to her? "Yeah, I guess I haven't been grocery shopping in a while."

"Like since last year?" She nudged him playfully in the ribs with her elbow. "Don't worry, I know what it's like to live alone. Cooking for one often doesn't seem worth it, does it?"

"I thought you lived with your sister?" He was still in close behind her with the fridge door open, and he knew he should move away. He just couldn't bring himself to do it quite yet. A part of him was waiting for her to back into his arms once more so he could feel her softness against him.

Emma made the decision for him, closing the fridge, and moving along the counter, away from him. "Above their garage, actually. Ultimately, I'm on my own in a place not much bigger than this, though they're kind enough to invite me for dinner a few times per week. Other days, I stick around and eat at Heart & Home, so I'm probably not on my own for meals as much as you are." She ran a hand along the empty countertop, as if to highlight how empty his place was, in so many ways. But when she looked back and met his eyes, he swore it was a look of understanding she met him with. She held his eyes for a beat, then two. He was losing himself in those deep green eyes when she broke the hold and cleared her throat.

"Where are your menus? Let's order something in."

Jake opened up a drawer where a pile of takeout menus spilled out. He grabbed a handful and fanned them out over the counter. "Take your pick."

She laughed at the chaos spread out before them. "You know there are apps for this?" Jake found himself laughing along.

Maybe the day had not gone exactly as he planned, especially while touring Lexington Manor. He knew both his grandmother and Emma were disappointed with what they were shown. However, he would try his best over the next twenty-four hours to plead his case and win them over.

15

EMMA

An hour later, Emma, Jake, and Meredith sat around the small living room, eating the Thai takeout food that Meredith had selected on TV trays. Jake had claimed the restaurant to be the city's best and most authentic. Both Jake and Meredith chose a mild flavored dish with cashews. Emma loved spicy curry dishes. Juniper Falls didn't have any Thai food places, so this was a treat for her. However, she tried not to let on to Jake how much she loved the food, because she did not want to give him any ammunition for his arguments on the benefits of city living. Besides, with their own dieticians, Meredith probably wouldn't be able to order takeout anyway.

For the most part, their dinner conversation was light-hearted. Meredith had filled Jake in on Doris and her so called gang, sharing some of the crazy stories that happened at Heart & Home—some of which Emma was hearing for the first time. Those seniors sure weren't slowing down in their old age. Emma loved that they still had such spunk and only hoped she and Amy would be like them in their later years. However, Jake hadn't let up on trying to convince Meredith about moving into Lexington Manor, and kept getting comments in here and there about the benefits. Emma was surprised, though, when he turned his attention on her.

"You should think about applying at Lexington Manor, Emma. It would look good on your resume." Emma had no problem sloughing off his suggestion, until he made it more personal. "You could move out of your sister's place. I bet they have a great employee benefit package, too. And there's an apartment for rent just down the hall."

Emma squirmed in her seat on the leather couch. "I really can't picture myself working somewhere like that." She looked around the small, but very polished apartment. "Or living somewhere so...sleek and modern."

Jake wasn't to be deterred. "You might find more familiarity than you expect. Just imagine, you could still work with my grandmother each day, keeping each other company." He gestured with his chopsticks toward her as he spoke. "And, of course, I'd be happy to invite you for dinner, so you wouldn't miss the invitations from your sister too much. I promise to keep my fridge more stocked in the future. The three of us could all exist in our own little sector of Seattle."

Emma wasn't sure how to respond to his suggestion. She was taken aback but at the same time did not want to offend him. Jake confused her. One minute so strong in his opinions, and the next moment he came across somewhat vulnerable in his hopefulness. Or was it that he was simply using her moving to Seattle as a ploy to convince his grandmother? His offer sounded almost...familial. Vowing to be cautious, Emma chose to respond in a way to keep things pleasant but non-committal.

"Well, I may just need to see your cooking abilities before any decision can be reached on that front." She hoped her coy smile and response would be enough to satisfy him and change the direction of the conversation.

Meredith let out a big yawn, and though Emma didn't know for sure, she suspected it was fake.

"I'm sure you two could talk all night, but Emma, if you wouldn't mind helping me get settled down the hall?"

Emma popped up from the couch. "Of course. But don't you want to finish your meal?"

Meredith shook her head. "You kids finish up the food. I think I saw a bottle of wine on the counter, didn't I, Jake? You might just want to crack that open. Could be the perfect way for you kids to end a long day."

Emma tried to catch Meredith's eye, but she was keeping her gaze away from both of them. Was she trying to set them up? Emma admitted, as she snuck a glance at Jake, that he was definitely handsome. And tall. And charming. Tonight, when she had fallen back into him in his tiny kitchen, there was a small part of her that just wanted to stay wrapped up in his arms. Those broad shoulders would make her feel safe and protected if it was another situation, like if he were a normal guy living in Juniper Falls and not a job-obsessed city guy.

Jake looked even more uncomfortable with the idea. "Uh, yeah, there might be a bottle here somewhere," he said. It was as if he felt more confident around her when his grandmother was in the room.

The last thing Emma wanted was to know Jake was spending time with her only to placate his grandmother. So she also reminded herself of why she was here in the first place—to help Meredith—and said, "Oh, you know what? It's been a long day, and I'm pretty tired myself." Emma stood and straightened her sweater, trying to somehow prove with her posture she had not just let her mind wander to Jake's tall frame and chocolate eyes. "I'll just get Meredith settled in and come back to help you clean up." She cleared her throat. "No drinks necessary."

Jake waved a casual hand. "No worries. I've got this," He said, gesturing around to his small living room. "You ladies get some rest. I look forward to talking through our options in the morning when we all have clear heads." He reached for a lanyard hanging right inside the door. "Here's the key to the suite. If there's anything you need, just let me know."

It wasn't long before Emma and Meredith had made themselves at home in the guest suite and were dressed in their pajamas. Jake was right, the suite was more spacious than his apartment. Emma helped Meredith get settled into her bed, fluffing up her pillows behind her. She brought her a glass of water along with her nightly medication.

"You've been awfully quiet, Meredith. I know the tour of Lexington Manor didn't go as you expected. Are you worried about how to make Jake understand you don't feel comfortable there?"

The elderly woman sighed, setting her glass down on the nightstand beside the glowing lamp. "No, it went fine. I just realized some things I probably should have thought of earlier."

Emma wondered how much she should be prying as she turned on a bedside lamp and switched off the overhead light before getting into her own bed. She needed to remember not to let it get personal. "How did you feel about Lexington Manor? And about living here in the city?" Emma prodded, although she was sure she knew the answers to these questions. But it could help Meredith put her thoughts and feelings in order before sharing them with Jake.

Meredith sighed again with her eyes cast downward and rubbed a corner of the sheet between her fingers as if the repetitive movement provided a comfort. "It was fine."

Emma couldn't seem to help herself from pushing. "If you didn't like it, Jake will agree to let you stay in Juniper Falls." She thought of his own words and repeated them, "He's not an ogre."

"I know. I realize it's not Jake's decision where I live. I may be old, but I handle my own affairs."

Emma let out a breath of relief. "Oh, good. I can't tell you how glad I am to hear you say that, Meredith. Jake will get over his frustrations about this, don't you worry, and I'm happy to talk with him if you like. Just give him time, and he'll find a way to come and see you more at Heart & Home."

"Oh no, I'm afraid you're misunderstanding me, dear. It's my choice of where to live. But I've chosen to move closer to my grandson."

Emma opened her mouth, but then closed it again. It took her several long seconds to ask her next question. "What? But...why?"

Meredith flipped through the pages of a book that had been

resting on her lap and pulled out a photograph that had been tucked inside. Emma could tell it was old, as it was dog-eared in the corners. There was some writing on the back, but she couldn't make it out clearly. It was of a young woman and a little boy. Even from a distance, Emma could tell the young woman was stunning, with a natural beauty. The little boy looked up at the woman with an expression of pure trust and love on his face. Emma noticed Meredith's sadness as she held the photo.

"Jake and I have a complicated past. He didn't have his mother around for most of his life, and I wasn't always there for him." She let out a heavy breath. "Now he's asking this one thing of me."

Emma slipped out of bed and moved across to sit on the edge of Meredith's bed. She looked closer at the photo in the elderly woman's hands. "This boy is Jake, isn't it? And is this his mother?"

Meredith's hands began to tremble, and she nodded. She looked frailer now than ever. Emma didn't want to push for details and sensed Meredith's need for Emma to just be there, to listen.

But as she sat there silently, Emma grew frustrated and even angry that somehow Meredith felt she owed Jake this upheaval in her life. It wasn't fair such a weight should be placed on a woman at this stage in her life. Meredith was a sweet lady, and she had a deep-seated wisdom that only came with a long presence on the earth. If Meredith seemed so sure, Emma knew this was something she must have looked at from many different angles already.

She took a breath, trying to keep her tone neutral and even. "You feel that you should move here because he wants you to?"

"He wants me closer for once in his life, and yes, that means something to me. It means a lot, so please don't try to convince me out of it. I know you want to have my best interests at heart, Emma, but this is something I need to do." The more she spoke, the more determined Meredith's words sounded. Emma didn't feel it was her place to change Meredith's mind, exactly, but she still felt like something wasn't quite right about the way her friend was making this decision. She'd known Meredith for a while now and their relationship had only gotten deeper over the past few months. She didn't feel any reason not to at least talk to Jake about it, first chance she got.

For the time being, she tried to at least lighten the mood with Meredith. "Is this why you're pushing me at your grandson? So that you don't have to move here alone? The wine was too obvious, Meredith. You need to work on being a little more subtle." Emma gave her a wink.

"Emma, I would never want you to make a choice that's not right for you. But I will really miss our times together when I move here. You have become like family to me." Emma felt the same way about Meredith and leaned over to give her a gentle hug before moving back to her own bed.

Meredith lay back into her pillow, her voice sounding tired. "I just thought it might be nice if you two got along. Maybe you'd still visit once in a while."

Emma sat up in bed to give her reassurance. "Oh, Meredith, of course I'll visit! I don't need your grandson to wine and dine me to make that happen." Emma laughed.

"You say it now, but I know how busy life can get when you're young. I just don't want to lose another friend," she added softly. "Either way, you still think I'm making the wrong decision," she declared more loudly.

Emma eyed the photo now lying on the nightstand. How could she know the years of history that had passed in their family? She was simply seeing one chapter in their story. "No, that's not necessarily true. I can understand why you may feel you have to make this choice. I'm just not sure I agree with Jake asking this of you." Meredith started to interrupt, but Emma knew she was tired and needed her rest, and truth be told, even Emma was tired of arguing over this tonight. "But I do think he's right about one thing: We'll all probably be more clear-headed about this after a good night's sleep. If you still want to move to the city, the least I can do is help you look for better options than *that*."

With that, Emma reached between their beds and switched off the lamp. Before long, she could hear the gentle snores of her roommate. Emma lay awake staring up at the ceiling. Counting sheep wouldn't help her fall asleep easily tonight. But she did know she could count on Jake to see he was not offering much of a choice for his grandmother.

If Meredith moved into Lexington Manor, it would be out of obligation, not desire.

# 16

## EMMA

Morning came quickly. While Emma spent a lot of hours working at Heart & Home, and was very comfortable with the residents, she was used to waking up in her own bed. She was not used to having a roommate. Once she opened her eyes and caught sight of the guest suite in the early morning light, she couldn't seem to relax enough to get back to sleep. She sighed, pulled the warm duvet off, and stepped onto the cold hardwood floor and tiptoed into the kitchen. The light was streaming through the large windows as she—or Jake—had forgotten to close the blinds before they had turned in last night. It really was a stunning view and she could see all the way to the waterfront. Small fishing boats dotted the harbor and large barges were off in the distance. Looking closely, she could even make out a Seattle ferry, transporting travellers between one of the islands and the mainland.

Emma was restless and found herself wanting to go exploring. Locating a notepad by the phone, she scrawled a message to Meredith, who was still soundly sleeping. Quietly, she placed it beside the photo on the nightstand. It would be at least an hour before Meredith would be ready to get up so she decided to take advantage of the alone time. Throwing on her leggings and a hoodie, Emma pulled her hair up into a ponytail and grabbed the keys Jake had lent her so she could get back into the building and suite. She left her phone number on the table in case he needed her and locked the door behind her, deciding to head outside to have a look around the neighborhood.

She was expecting to hate it right from the moment she stepped out of Jake's lobby, expecting noisy traffic and littered streets, but in the early Sunday morning, things were surprisingly peaceful in his neighborhood. Not only that, but next to Jake's building was a four-plex apartment with a cute little fenced garden in the front. While she truly could not see herself living somewhere like Jake's high-rise place, this little complex next door felt surprisingly homey, with various trellises and flower boxes attractively positioned around the small yard.

Last night she'd gone to sleep feeling righteously angry at Jake, but now, she wasn't sure how she felt. Maybe he had a point, and if she expected Jake to take a good look at her side of the argument, she should at least consider a job at Lexington Manor before dismissing it thoughtlessly. Not that she was seriously contemplating moving back to the city, but otherwise she wasn't any different than Jake with his negative attitude toward Juniper Falls and small-town life.

Emma strolled around the block, and even though there was more traffic than in Juniper Falls—likely more in this one block than in her entire town—there were also more shops, more flower stands, and more coffee carts. There was even a coffee bicycle right outside of Jake's building. Sunday morning here seemed rather slow paced, a coffee-and-crossword type of day. Not what she had remembered while living here in the past. Of course, back then, she was thrown into the chaos of working long hours at the hospital's ER in the heart of the city, which was far from peaceful on every level. But this area of Seattle? Maybe she could get used to it.

After making a loop of the large city block, Emma headed for the coffee bicycle.

"This is really interesting," she said to the young man running it.

He gave her a friendly smile as he nodded and proceeded to take her order. Emma knew Jake took his coffee black and strong, but she collected some cream and sugar packets for her own coffee, and tea with milk for Meredith. As the barista made up her order, he chatted to her about how he had worked in a traditional coffee shop while he put himself through school, but he much preferred the coffee bicycle.

"Oh yeah?" Emma asked. "To me, it's so unique, but what do you like about it?"

The young man handed her the order, all set up in a takeout tray. "I like that I can set up somewhere new every day. Though, I'll admit, I like this neighborhood a lot, and could see myself setting up here often."

As Emma left the bicycle cart, she decided she agreed with the barista. She headed into the building and up the elevator with her coffee tray, hoping either Jake or Meredith was awake by now.

Emma put Meredith's tea and her coffee on the hallway table and knocked softly on the door to Jake's apartment, wanting to get him his coffee while it was hot but not wanting to wake him. No answer. Either he was still sleeping or over at the suite with his grandmother. As she was about to return to the guest suite, she turned back at the squeak of a door. There stood Jake, seemingly just out of the shower, wearing only his sweatpants and still holding a towel, drying off his hair. Water droplets rolled down his bare chest. Emma couldn't help but notice how muscular he was and caught herself staring. She had not realized his body would be this defined underneath his expensive designer shirts.

Jake seemed rather amused by her admiring reaction and gave her a wicked grin. Emma looked away and held out the coffee, words escaping her for a brief moment, until she regained her composure. He seemed quite confident of himself now, not like the night before when Meredith had attempted to meddle.

"Here. Coffee...black, right?" was all she stammered out, and she took a step back and thrust out her arm with the coffee as if to keep a protective distance between them. Jake reached out to take the coffee from her, brushing her hand in the transfer, and Emma wasn't sure if it was the heat from the coffee or Jake's touch that suddenly washed through her body. She also wasn't sure if the brush of his hand against hers was deliberate or not. It seemed to Emma that he was taking great delight in seeing her flustered at the sight of him shirtless.

"Thanks," he said, taking a gulp from the cup. "Just how I like it." His intense stare, not leaving her, caused Emma to move toward the suite.

"No problem. I'd better get this to your grandmother before it gets cold," she said, grabbing the tea from the table.

"Well, once you're both ready, let me know. I thought I'd take you to this great Italian place down the street. They have a delicious brunch on Sundays with cannoli to die for."

"Sounds great to me. Thanks, Jake. I'll go check on your grandma and let you know." Emma let out a deep exhale once her back was turned, shaking the image of Jake out of her mind and collecting her emotions before she greeted his grandmother.

When Emma opened the suite door, Meredith was propped up in bed, an outstretched hand with the remote pointing toward the TV. She scrolled through channels so fast Emma's eyes could not even focus on what programs were being displayed. "Two hundred channels, and they don't get my gameshow station? I can't believe it."

Emma wondered what had been going through Meredith's mind, and if she'd had a change of heart since last night as well. "I'm sure there will be all sorts of new things to get used to in the city." The note of bitterness that had tinged her words last night was gone. It was a new day. Emma passed Meredith her tea and explained Jake's plan for brunch.

"Oh, I don't know," Meredith said. "I'm fairly tired this morning. You two go, and I'll just stay here and watch some TV, see if I can't fall asleep again for a little bit."

Emma wondered if she was playing matchmaker again to the nurse and her grandson. But Meredith did look rather tired. Emma was sure yesterday's adventure had taken a lot out of her, both physically and emotionally.

"Well, if you're sure. We won't be gone long. It won't be as much fun without you, though." She reached for the notepad.

"I'll leave you my number." Emma pushed the phone closer to Meredith's bedside. "We'll eat quickly and bring you something back. Then we can discuss how you feel about all this."

"Take your time, I'm not going anywhere." Meredith looked relieved that Emma did not try and convince her to join them. Picking up the remote, Emma looked through the guide on the television and was able to find Meredith a channel with some of her game shows to keep her occupied while they were gone. Soon the elderly woman was calling out prices to contestants on the large screen TV, all while she knit and sipped her tea. Yes, she looked quite content, Emma mused.

Emma quickly showered and got ready, and then left to go meet the handsome man waiting for her in the lobby.

"You're sure Grandma is okay, though?" Jake asked for the third time as they walked down the street toward the restaurant. Emma loved how concerned he was toward his grandmother this morning.

"She's fine. Just a little tired from the big day yesterday, I promise."

They were almost to the restaurant when they came across an outdoor marketplace. All down the block were various stands filled with fresh produce, flowers, various jars of jams, cheeses by the wheel, and a plethora of fresh seafood.

"I forgot they run this on Sundays. Usually, I'm so busy working from home on weekends, I barely leave my apartment."

"You really do work too much, Jake. What's the point of living in a place like this if you are never going to venture outside of your apartment to enjoy it?" Emma scolded lightheartedly.

"Well, it's not as much fun doing these things by myself, I guess. So you are actually admitting this is a pretty great neighborhood?" Emma detected a slight smugness to his smile. He had a point, though, Emma agreed. Going places by yourself soon became tiring without anyone to share the experiences with. Often, Juniper Falls had special activities and events going on. Emma would either take her nieces or simply choose not to go on her own. Some outings were just meant to be enjoyed with others.

"I have an idea." Jake's face brightened as he gazed around at the various stands. "What if we skip the restaurant and pick up some things from here for brunch? We can take them back to my apartment and I can cook brunch for you and my grandma. Then she's not alone for as long, and we can also pick up a few things to snack on for the trip back today."

"Now that sounds like a great plan. And it doesn't involve *me* having to cook," Emma joked.

Jake made his way to the first vendor, one that specialized in colorful vegetables. "Well, I will need a sous chef," he said.

"That I can do," she said quickly. "I don't mind cooking on my own, but it's much more enjoyable with others. Anyway, we'll be able to hit the road a little earlier back to Juniper Falls."

Jake stopped putting peppers into a cloth bag and looked up at her. "I thought you didn't work Sundays. Now who's the workaholic?" Emma wasn't sure, but she thought the look on Jake's face might be something akin to rejection, which made the next thing she had to say feel especially uncomfortable and harsh. However, she needed to be forthright with him.

"I don't have to work. It's just...well, I have this date tonight."

Jake jerked, surprising her, but he remarked without missing a beat, "Oh. Yes. Okay. Right. Well, I guess we'd better finish up here and start cooking. Can't have you missing a chance at love. After all, this is the month for romance." Jake's sarcastic jab did not sit well with Emma who was already dreading the date that evening. Truth be told, she wished she could have stayed in Seattle a few more days, something a mere twenty-four hours ago she would never have wished.

# 17

## JAKE

Jake unloaded the bag containing the artisanal bread, cheeses, and produce onto the counter and pulled out the cutting board. It had been a quiet walk back to the apartment and he wondered what was going through Emma's mind. Probably the anticipation of her big date that evening. Someone that beautiful and confident must go on plenty of dates. In fact, Jake found it hard to believe she wasn't already married, or at the very least seriously committed. He had tried not to come across as too disappointed at Emma's eagerness to leave Seattle earlier than planned, however, she really wasn't to be faulted, it was he who had failed to make his interest known. Jake had been so focused on showing his grandmother the positive aspects of being in Seattle and closer to him, he had neglected to make his personal feelings toward Emma clear.

Emma had gone over to the suite to help Meredith get dressed and pack up her things for the trip back. Jake began chopping onions while the skillet got hot. Skillfully and rhythmically, he sliced and diced, unable to remember the last time he'd had such a relaxed and enjoyable Sunday morning. He felt a twinge of guilt for ignoring work, but he would catch up tonight. Yes, he would have all evening to work and then continue packing up his grandmother's house while Emma was out on her date.

He tried to ignore the pangs of jealousy as images of her laughing with someone else at an intimate dinner began to play in his mind. Of her nudging another man or looking at him with passionate eyes, even if the passion came from annoyance. It wasn't even fair of him to feel this way: he hadn't said anything, made any moves, and couldn't give her what she needed or deserved—not unless he was willing to sacrifice the ladder of success and he wasn't going to do that any time soon.

Emma wheeled Meredith into Jake's apartment. He stopped chopping, wiping his hands on the kitchen towel, and went into the living room to help navigate his grandmother's wheelchair around the furniture.

"Morning, Grandma. Hope you slept well." Jake kissed her cheek, marvelling at how something which was once so strange, was now anticipated and almost normal, even after barely a week. Jake didn't mind. He saw how she smiled at this new interaction between them.

"I'm feeling much more rested now, Jake, thank you. Emma says you're making us brunch. What a lovely treat. Remember how you and Grandpa would make pancakes every Sunday when you were a little boy?"

Jake did remember. He would sneak into his grandparents' bedroom while his grandfather would pretend to be sleeping. When Jake had gotten close enough, his grandfather would pop open his eyes and growl, grabbing the young boy and pulling him in for a bear hug. Then, together, they both went downstairs to begin the tradition of making pancakes. Lemon juice and milk went into the batter to make them extra fluffy. His grandfather always maintained lemon juice was their secret ingredient for the recipe. Jake's grandmother could never figure out why their pancakes were always much fluffier than when she made them. His grandpa would wink and say, "Must be the talented cook's helper." Jake always beamed at his comment, no matter how many times he had said it. It felt good to remember those moments. Lately, some of those good memories had been making their way into his mind again after years of replaying all the ones where Jake felt like he'd failed and let his grandparents down, especially since his grandfather had died.

"So, how can I help?" Emma had tied an apron around her waist and waited for his instructions.

"Well, why don't you wash the mushrooms, then slice and sauté them with a bit of garlic butter so they're ready to put into the omelettes?"

"Whoa, you really can cook?" Emma said with a dramatic gasp.

Jake shook his head, laughing at her playful spirit and tossed the brown paper bag of mushrooms at her. Emma ducked and they sailed over her head landing in Meredith's lap.

"Oh no! Grandma, I'm so sorry." Jake rushed over to his grandmother, who began laughing at how worried her grandson looked. "Jake, I may be old, but I'm not that breakable."

"I guess your grandson needs to work on his aim, Meredith," Emma laughed, gathering the mushrooms that had spilled out of the bag onto the floor.

"Oh, he used to be an amazing pitcher on his baseball team when he was younger. You should have seen him. Other players were so nervous when they walked up to the plate and our Jake was pitching."

Jake looked at his grandmother with furrowed brows. "What are you talking about, Grandma? I was terrible. Grandpa told me so himself."

"Jacob Henry Rothstein! What on earth are you talking about?" Jake could not remember the last time his grandmother had used his full name. "You were fabulous. We went to all your games and you made us so very proud."

"But Grandpa told me I would never be good at pitching. That's why I quit playing the following year." Maybe his grandmother's old age was making her forget aspects of his childhood. She waved her hand, beckoning him closer. Jake knelt down beside her wheelchair.

"No Jake. That wasn't it at all. Your grandpa just did not want you to give up everything else and other opportunities for a dream he felt wasn't realistic. He saw what it did to your mo…"

His grandmother caught herself. Jake knew what the next word was going to be out of her mouth, but he chose to ignore it.

"It didn't mean you weren't good," she continued, as if she hadn't had a slip, "it just meant the chances of making it in the big leagues were slim. He knew you had so many other talents, and he did not want you to give up on them."

Jake appreciated how Emma was busily preparing the vegetables and trying to make herself invisible in his small apartment. He was surprised how strongly his grandma felt about this memory. Had he been wrong all along about his grandparents thinking he would be a failure? Or in her old age, was his grandma only wanting to remember the good times together?

---

Brunch was hearty and delicious. Conversation was tepid, though. Jake tried to effuse Lexington Manor and the benefits of living in Seattle while Emma ate with a determined silence and Meredith hummed indecisively and said she'd need to think on it a bit more.

While Jake cleaned up, Emma pulled the van up to the front of his building. Jake locked up and wheeled his grandmother down to the lobby to wait. It had started raining and there was a definite chill to the air. The doorman helped load the bags into the back of the van. Jake worked with Emma to maneuver Meredith comfortably into her seat, wrapping a shawl around her shoulders and a plaid blanket over her legs for extra warmth.

"Doing okay back there, Meredith?" Once back in the driver's seat, Emma glanced in the rear-view mirror, checking on Jake's grandma as she navigated her way out of the city. Jake was returning some work emails and text messages from his phone. Surprisingly, he had not missed much at work over the weekend.

"I would love to listen to the radio for a little while if you don't mind?" His grandmother spoke up from the back seat.

Jake put down his phone and began scanning through the various stations until he came across an oldies one he thought his grandma might enjoy. Frank Sinatra came crooning out through the speakers and Meredith clapped her hands together with the excitement of a giddy teen girl at a rock concert.

"Frank it is!"

Emma and Jake laughed at the enthusiasm coming from the back seat. Meredith snapped her fingers along with the song, gently swaying and humming along.

Jake wondered why he couldn't remember this relaxed, at ease part of his grandmother from when he lived with her. Or had that been a new development since his grandpa had died? She had been so guarded when he was young. It was as if she'd believed that any hint of unstructured time would automatically spiral out of control into a destructive path. She had been a woman that needed to be in control at all times. But now, she seemed different, almost carefree with her feelings and looked for the fun in moments. Why the change? Was this what old age brought out? It was almost a role reversal with Jake now being the serious, no-nonsense "parent" of the family.

The lively song ended and was replaced with a serenading love ballad. Meredith looked wistfully lost in a memory and began to sing along with Sinatra, "My funny valentine…"

Jake looked away, giving her privacy. He knew that his grandparents had loved each other. That was certain. And he was mindful of the fact that his grandfather's passing had been hard on his grandmother. He regretted the way he had handled it with her. But at the time, she hadn't wanted to let him in either. Their family did not talk about feelings. Feelings were messy and they did not do messy. They did things that were ordered and clear. But now there were tears in her eyes. He floundered, not sure if he should say something, or let her have the moment to herself.

Emma had noticed too and stepped in before he could decide. "What a beautiful song, Meredith. Such lovely lyrics," she said brightly.

His grandmother looked up and smiled, wiping her eyes. "The thing about living these many years is one has collected so many memories. My Henry, Jake's grandpa and I danced to this song when he kissed me for the first time. Oh, how I remember that night. My parents were strict about not letting me attend our local dances. Father always felt nothing good could come of boys and girls dancing together. One night a bunch of girls and I decided to go to the Valentine's Sock Hop in the next town over. It was a daring move, and I was so nervous to disobey my father. He thought I was going over to my friend's house to do some homework. At Sharon's, we got all gussied up to the nines and then loaded everyone into her father's old Chevy pickup truck."

"Grandma!" Jake was surprised to hear she would sneak out, this woman who had been so proper and stern in all the time he'd known her. As far as he knew, she was the one who made the rules, and then most certainly followed them. This story went against everything he had ever thought of when he imagined her younger years.

"There's a lot you don't know about me, Jake," she winked.

That seemed to peak Emma's interest. "So what happened at the dance, Meredith?"

"It was everything I had hoped for...and more. My dress was made of a soft pink chiffon that twirled whenever I turned, a perfect dress for dancing the night away. I felt absolutely beautiful that night. Our group of girls stood by the punch bowl visiting and swaying to the music. My back was to the dance floor when I felt a light tap on my shoulder and heard a voice behind me. When I turned around, there stood the most handsome young man smiling and holding out his hand, asking for a dance. He led me to the dance floor, and then held me in his arms. I never wanted him to let go. We danced every dance together that evening. He swept me off my feet and I've never danced with another man since."

Jake noticed it was now Emma with the tears in her eyes. He wondered how it was that he had never heard the story of how his grandparents met before. But then it dawned on him: he had never cared to ask.

"That was beautiful, Meredith. Thank you for sharing. The love you had with your husband was rare. I don't think love like that exists anymore." Emma reached for her sunglasses from the console and Jake wondered if it was more for trying to conceal her emotions than protect her eyes from any brightness. After all, it was still cloudy and drizzling.

"Well, don't give up, dear. Sometimes true love comes when we least expect it. Love finds you, and not the other way around. Just be open to the possibilities."

Emma had possibilities, Jake thought. In fact, she had a possibility of finding love tonight, going on her date with Mr. Small-Town. He wanted to ask about the man she was going out with, but knew it really was none of his business. That feeling of jealousy gnawed at him again.

He sat back into his seat, and instead tried to focus on this new side of his grandparents he had never known. Falling in love had always seemed like such a long and drawn-out process to Jake that was rife with expenses, wasted hours, and failed expectations. But hearing his grandmother tell her story, it sounded like it could happen so quickly—all in the blink of an eye.

# 18

## EMMA

Later that evening, Emma sat in Brambles Bistro, a new restaurant in Juniper Falls, waiting for her date to show up. In hindsight, she wished the date would have been set up for another night, but when she had agreed to it, Amy had set her up for her first available moment so that she "didn't have time to rethink or cancel it like you have before" according to her sister.

She sighed, not looking forward to the evening. Part of her even wished she would just get stood up. Emma could only imagine how her sister would be pacing at home this very moment, wondering how things were going. It would not have surprised Emma in the least if Amy were to show up at the restaurant with Connor "coincidentally" just to check up on them. Hopefully, sensible Connor would prevent that from happening. Her sister had scrutinized every ounce of her wardrobe selection from head to toe as she got ready for the date earlier that evening. In the end, her hair had gotten pulled into a loose fishtail braid and her scoop neck emerald green blouse and fitted black jeans with knee-high black boots had passed her sister's inspection. One glance in the full-length mirror and Emma herself was impressed with the outcome.

She was exhausted both physically and mentally from the time away with Meredith and Jake and did not feel like she was putting her best foot forward on this date tonight. After returning back to Heart & Home late that afternoon, Emma had first gotten Meredith settled back into her room. Jake stayed to help too. His grandmother seemed more emotional than she had been when they left. Emma had chalked it up to the memories on the ride home, as well as the long days, and the decision weighing heavily on her heart about moving closer to her grandson. No matter the outcome, Emma knew Meredith's relationship with Jake had improved with this trip.

For now, she needed to concentrate on her date for the evening. Thinking about Jake would just distract her. After all, Jake had seemed in a hurry to leave as they walked out of Meredith's room and down the hall. He had even neglected to thank her for coming along. Not that she was expecting thanks. Emma had done this trip for Meredith's sake more than she had done it to help her grandson.

Emma glanced toward the front door and noticed a tall, good looking man had arrived. He spoke to the hostess who, in turn, pointed over to the table where Emma was seated. He nodded to her, then continued in conversation with the hostess, pointing to something outside. After another minute of animated chatter, he made his way over to the table by the fireplace where Emma was seated.

"Danny?" Emma asked as he approached the table.

"Yep. Emma?" She nodded and gestured for him to have a seat. These first few minutes were the most awkward on a blind date until some common interests came to light, to ease the flow of the conversation. She knew that. This wasn't her first rodeo.

Emma smiled across the table at her date. "I've wanted to eat here ever since it opened. Thanks for suggesting it, Danny."

Danny sat up straighter, as though he took it as a personal compliment. "You'll love the food. Plus, I have a stack of 2-for-1 coupons, so I bring all my first dates here."

Emma could appreciate his desire to be frugal and save a buck or two. After all, she was also working hard at saving for a house down payment. However... "All your first dates? Didn't it just open?" she asked, feeling slightly alarmed. How many first dates could he have had in that amount of time?

"Sure," Danny said with a laugh. "If the date is a total bomb, then at least it's a good meal. Win/win, right?" He winked at her.

By the wink, she figured he must be joking. He must simply have a different sense of humor. Amy was always telling her to lighten up, so she did her best to play along. "That's an interesting way to approach dating. Sounds like you do this often?"

He put his menu down, barely looking at it. "Seems that way. I'm always getting set up on blind dates by friends and family. It's a gamble. Sometimes she's a real looker, other times..." By his even tone and demeanor, Emma realized he was serious. "But don't worry," he went on. "You are way hotter than how Connor described you."

Emma raised an eyebrow, barely believing Connor would have arranged this, let alone referred to his sister-in-law as *hot*. Then again, she had thought Amy had been the one to set this up. She probably had never actually had a conversation with Danny, only decided from a distance, "he's handsome, he's single, so he'll be perfect for my sister." "Oh, and how exactly did my brother-in-law describe me?" She braced herself for an unpleasant evening. She hoped that the food was at least, indeed, good.

Danny waved a hand. "Something about a caring personality and a real people person, blah, blah, blah. To me, those are code words for lonely and desperate cat lady." Danny laughed at his own joke. "I had to pry to get a rundown on your looks."

Emma crossed her arms and said, "I'm a dog person, actually. Remind me to thank Connor later for setting this up," she added, her voice dripping in sarcasm. "I'm really going to owe him one."

"It's all good. He told me you haven't been on a date in quite a while, so I was happy to help."

Emma's cheeks flamed at this stranger knowing this personal bit of information. Connor's explanation had her coming across as some type of charity case in the dating world. But she tried to hide her embarrassment by saying, "How very philanthropic of you."

"Hey, I have a hot nurse date." He laughed again, louder than necessary and causing others to look their way. "It's all good."

Did he really just say that? Well, if she was going to let this kind of word-vomit go, two could play at this game. "Shocks me that you haven't been snapped up off the dating market yet, Danny. Aren't I the lucky one?"

Now Danny raised his eyebrows. She thought she'd surely offended him, but then he said, "Play your cards right and I might just be willing to fold." Either he enjoyed this type of banter or really couldn't hear sarcasm.

"Hmm. Tempting." The automatic response was out before she could stop it. She felt horrified. Danny would probably make that out to be an invitation rather than a jab.

Before she could form a sentence that was as clear as purified water, he started talking again. "Saw you admiring my car when I pulled up. She's a beauty, isn't she? Classic 1967 GTO convertible. Restored her myself."

Emma had not even noticed him driving up in the car. In fact, she doubted it would even be visible from where she was sitting.

He puffed out his chest. "Stella goes with me to car shows across the country. I won't go anywhere without my girl."

"Stella?" Emma confirmed.

"Yeah, my car. Stella gets quite jealous when I date. There was this one time I was dating a gal for almost three entire weeks. A total record for me by the way. The entire time Stella kept stalling her carburetor every time we went out. She speaks her mind and has one fiery temper."

"Your...girlfriend?" she asked.

"No. Stella." Danny looked perturbed that Emma didn't understand his car's feelings, but continued on with his explanation, "That relationship came to an end, and fast."

"Your girlfriend broke up with you over Stella?" Now Emma was just plain confused.

"No, of course not. I dumped *her*. Every girl has to pass the Stella approval test."

So now, not only was she out with a date-happy egomaniac,

he was also turning out to be weirdly obsessive and delusional about his car. "I see." Emma honestly did not even know what to say next. But she needed to put some space between her and her date.

"Can you excuse me for a moment? I forgot I needed to check in at work on something."

Danny pulled his phone out. "Hurry back. I've got dozens of photos from every step in her restoration I want to show you. It will help you bond with Stella later."

Emma left the table and strode so fast toward the restrooms, she almost tripped over her heels. In fact, she was in such a hurry, she didn't see Jake until he caught her by the arm. "Emma?"

"Jake! What are you doing here?" She couldn't believe how happy she was to see a friendly, normal face.

"Picking up take-out. You mentioned this place was new and had great reviews, so I thought I'd try it myself." Jake looked around the room. "How's your date going?"

Emma leaned in closer. She could smell Jake's musky cologne drawing her in further. "Well, let's just say it's a little crowded with all four of us at the table."

"He brought other people along on your date?" By the raised eyebrows, Emma could tell he was surprised, but he also looked slightly smug.

"No, he brought his ego and Stella. His car. I was just about to fake a work emergency."

Jake raised his eyebrows. "Isn't that a little cold-hearted, Emma?" Emma didn't know how to properly explain how bad this guy was, but then Jake winked with a smile.

She let out a quiet laugh. "You got me." Emma resisted the urge to take a deep yoga breath of that enticing cologne, trying not to envision him as shirtless as he'd been that morning.

"Listen, there's enough food here for two, and I could really use some extra hands packing." He dropped his voice conspiratorially. "You could say it was an emergency with a friend. We're friends, right?"

Emma smiled, because even after all of her initial distrust of Jake and his motives, she really was starting to think of him as a friend. "Give me two minutes to grab my coat and let Romeo down gently."

Jake backed away and headed for the counter. "Meet me out front." He turned back. "And Emma?"

Emma stopped in her dreaded trek back to the table. "Yes?"

"Try not to break his heart." Jake smiled.

# 19

## JAKE

The wind and rain had picked up by the time Emma followed Jake out of the restaurant. It was typical in February to get some winter storms like this one, and Jake was thankful they had made it back to Juniper Falls before it had become miserable. Emma pulled in behind his car in the driveway of his grandmother's house. Jake met her at the driver's door holding out an umbrella. Exiting the car quickly so as to protect their food from getting soaked, they both ran up the steps to the front door of the two-story house together. They sheltered under the porch from the pelting rain while Jake fumbled with the key in the front lock.

"Sorry, it's an old lock. I need to get it changed." The key finally clicked into place and he opened the door to let Emma inside. She shook off the rain from her jacket before entering the house. Jake had left the gas fireplace running while he slipped out for the food, so the room was pleasantly warm, a reprieve from the bitterness outside.

"Thanks for giving me a reason to escape my date tonight," Emma said as she carried the bag of takeout into the kitchen. She began opening the containers while Jake found a couple of disposable plates and forks to use. Most of the kitchen had been packed up, but he had kept a few necessities out while he was still staying there.

"My pleasure, but from the sounds of it, you probably

would have come up with another reason to end the evening early even if I hadn't been there. Tell me, Emma, do you usually go on such interesting dates?" Jake carried their plates into the living room and put them on the coffee table. Emma pulled out a couple of the throw cushions that were sticking out of a packing box and tossed them on the floor. The pair casually plunked themselves down on the cushions and began to eat. It felt so natural, like they had been doing this for a long time. It was comfortable, but also exciting, having her sit so close to him.

"No, not at all. To be honest, I don't date much, though this was a first in terms of a date being so peculiar. Most likely that'll be the last of any blind dates for me."

"I'm sure Stella will be relieved to hear that you will not be any threat to her."

With that comment, Emma gave Jake a playful shove. "You are not going to let me live this down, are you?" Her mouth crinkled in a sultry grin and her green eyes shone with the fire burning in front of them.

"Not at least for a little while." Their conversation felt flirtatious and Jake was suddenly thankful he was the one on the receiving end of Emma's attention this evening. Her blind date probably couldn't appreciate her witty banter anyway, by the sounds of him.

"How about after we eat, I help you with packing a few more boxes?"

Jake had a long list of things to accomplish, but he would rather just sit together exactly as they were doing now. He didn't know how to say that. As he was trying to come up with a way, the lights flickered and no sooner had Jake looked up and said, "Uh-oh," than everything went dark.

Emma gave a slight gasp and reflexively put her hand out to get her bearings. It landed right on his leg.

He leaned over and put his arm around her in the dark. "Guess the power went out with this storm." He kept his arm protectively around her and she made no attempt to move for the moment. They sat, listening to the howling wind, and hearing the rain pelting against the window, letting their eyes adjust to the firelight flickering before them.

Jake broke the silence, his voice quiet. "Listen, I wanted to thank you for coming to Seattle this weekend to help with my grandmother. It meant a lot to me." Sharing his feelings in the dark was much less intimidating for him. It was somehow easier to be vulnerable. And he sensed Emma felt the same way.

"Thank you for trusting me to come along, Jake." He felt her head ease down to rest on his shoulder.

There was a loud crash outside in the backyard, which brought Jake to his feet and the moment to an end. Emma followed him into the kitchen to look through the back window. He used the light from his phone to see if they could discover the source of the sudden noise. Shining it around the corner of the yard, it appeared the noise had simply been the recycling cans blowing over and into the fence gate.

Jake dug through a few of the open kitchen boxes, as he remembered seeing a couple of used candles, and he knew a packet of matches were in the emergency bin under the sink. There was no telling how long the power outage would last, and he didn't want to run the risk of the battery on his phone dying out.

"Well, I guess our packing will be by candlelight." Emma took one of the lit candles back into the living room and Jake joined her with a couple of boxes that still needed to be sorted through. Emma lifted the flaps and took a peek into the first box holding the candle closer. She let out a squeal of excitement.

"Oh, Jake, look! It's filled with old vinyl albums." She flipped through the upright collection. "There's Bing Crosby, Dean Martin, Ella Fitzgerald, all of the singers your grandmother was talking about today in the van. I bet she would love to keep some of these in her room." She paused, sitting back from the box. "The only trouble is, though, Heart & Home doesn't have a record player."

"Maybe not, but I bet they have a phonograph." Jake laughed at his own joke as he looked over Emma's shoulder while she flipped through more albums.

"Not funny, Jake Rothstein. Seriously, though, Heart & Home may be old fashioned, but the residents have fun together and it's like a family there."

He knew how her heart was connected to that place and decided he shouldn't really tease her about it. Maybe he was a bit jealous that she could care about something so much and have such a passion for her job. Not for money, power, or prestige, but for making a difference in the lives of others. Plus, he could tell how excited she was about this find for his grandmother's sake.

"Sorry, you're right," he said. "Hey, I think there's actually a record player stacked in the donation pile by the front door." As Jake walked uneasily over toward the door, the power flickered back to life.

Jake immediately spotted the case containing the record player and brought it over to Emma. It was a model that contained its own speaker, so he wouldn't even need any other components to set it up for his grandmother.

"Not sure if this thing even works anymore, but let's take a look." He popped open the lid and plugged it into the outlet beside him. The turntable started to go around. Emma handed Jake the album *Best Big Bands of Swing*. Setting the needle gently on the grooves, the sound of slightly crackling music filled the living room. Emma clapped as gleefully as his grandmother had earlier in the van when she heard Frank Sinatra's music play.

Feeling caught up in the moment, Jake jumped to his feet and put out his hand to Emma. She looked a little flustered and taken aback at first.

"Oh! But I have no idea how to swing dance. Don't tell me *you* do?" Her surprise made Jake grin shyly.

"Another one of the classes my grandparents signed me up to take when I was young. It actually paid off during my college years. Impressed the girls." He winked, trying to overcome his shyness, and pulled her up to join him.

Jake was surprised with how willing Emma was to let him lead her around the living room, twirling her back and forth into and out of his arms. She moved gracefully for someone who had not much swing dance experience, and the nostalgic movements made him giddy with energy. It made for a tight dance space with all the boxes piled around, but he made it work. He couldn't remember the last time he'd had so much fun. The song ended and they both stopped to catch their breath. A slower, more melancholy song came on. Looking into each other's eyes, Jake pulled Emma closer toward him. It felt natural to fall into each other's arms and sway to the rhythm. Her head rested against his chest and the moment seemed so right. Just the two of them.

"*Dream a little dream of me...*" the record player crooned. Lost in the music, Jake hummed along. Emma lifted her head, looked up into his eyes and he melted. Was she even aware of the power she had over him? Leaning in closer to her, he could feel her pulling closer too. His mouth, mere inches away from her slightly parted lips.

Was she okay with this?

Was *he* okay with this?

A sudden loud ringing phone startled them both back to reality and out of the magical moment.

Jake immediately straightened, but it turned out the ringing was coming from Emma's phone. She scrambled away from him, grabbed for it, and looked down at the screen. "It's my sister. I'm sorry, I have to take this. She's probably wondering why I'm not home yet. Sorry, Jake." She walked over toward the kitchen, but Jake could hear Emma's end of the conversation carry through into the living room.

"Yes, I'm fine, Amy...No, it didn't go well...Look, I'll be home soon, okay? We'll talk then." Emma ended the phone conversation and walked back to where Jake was trying to occupy himself by sorting through some stacks of photos and letters in an effort to calm his racing heart and bury the smack of rejection that had hit him when she pulled away.

Emma grabbed her coat from where it hung on the post of the bannister. "Guess I should probably get going. Sorry, Jake. I wasn't really much help to you tonight, was I? What if I came by tomorrow evening after work? We could at least load up some boxes to take them to the thrift store."

Jake would like nothing more than to continue from where

they had been interrupted be it tonight or tomorrow night, but he remembered he had dinner plans with Paul and Jennie tomorrow night. Paul had even texted him earlier to give a reminder, along with the house address. It was obvious he was looking forward to the visit and Jake knew he couldn't back out without hurting his old friend. Paul had been there for him through some difficult years, and showing up for supper was the least Jake could do after he ignored Paul's efforts to connect with him once high school was over.

"Actually, I have dinner plans at an old high school friend's house tomorrow night. But...any chance you would like to come along? I mean, don't feel obligated or anything. It's just that his wife is really nice, and I think you would enjoy yourself, but I completely understand if you don't want to..." Jake knew he was babbling but he could not seem to stop talking in circles.

"Are you sure it's okay with them?" she asked, nibbling her lip.

Jake couldn't imagine Paul saying no, but to put Emma's mind at rest, he said, "I'll double-check with him and let you know if there's any problem. But if it's okay with them, is it okay with you? I should be able to let you know by tomorrow morning." He met her eyes, feeling like he was pleading, but he couldn't help himself. He needed to know when he would see her again. Truth be told, he wanted to simply ask her to stay right now.

"I would like to." Emma responded as she buttoned up her coat. "However, if anyone starts talking about showing car restoration photos, I'm out of there." She winked, and he let out a loud laugh at her joke.

Emma opened the front door and ran down the steps out into the rain toward her car. Jake followed behind her and stood under the overhang calling out, "By the way, you look really beautiful tonight."

He wasn't sure if she even heard him over the noise of the wind through the trees, but Jake stood, watching Emma leave until her car disappeared down the street.

Already he was counting down until he would see her again.

## 20

## EMMA

Monday morning, Emma took Charlie out for an early morning run to see if it would help her sort through all the emotions swimming around in her mind. The storm had continued through the night, but today the sun was shining. There was a freshness in the air. Spring was just around the corner. Emma wondered what the new season would bring for Meredith, Jake, Heart & Home, and herself.

So many unanswered questions. Not so long ago, her life had seemed laid out clearly, as well planned as the blueprint of a house, with a steady job she loved, surrounded by friends and family, and Charlie by her side. But now, so much seemed uncertain. She looked down at Charlie. Well, one thing was certain. She smiled and thought again of Lexington Manor, where they would most certainly not allow her to bring in her best friend.

Had she been seriously considering that anyway? Maybe she had, but only for a brief moment. Charlie tugged on his leash, bringing her back to the present, and she picked up her jogging pace.

After Emma had showered and dressed in her scrubs for work, she walked down from her suite and through the back door into the kitchen. Amy was getting the girls ready for school. Emma had snuck in last night and sent Amy a quick text to say she was home but too tired to chat. Truth be told, Emma had used Amy's phone call as a welcome excuse to be able to take a moment and process the emotional charge that was building between her and Jake. As she drove closer to home, she realized how much she wanted to return to that charge and how little she wanted to talk with her sister, the one person who could always see right through her.

But now she was here. They were both wide awake. She knew it was time to face the music with Amy

"Auntie! Auntie!" Leah and Laney simultaneously called out. She gave her nieces big hugs, kissing the top of each blonde head.

"Don't forget, you promised to go shopping with us this week for supplies to make our Valentine's Day cards." Laney handed Emma a sticky note. On it was written a specific shopping list.

"I would *never* forget!" Emma exclaimed in a dramatically shocked voice as she tucked the note into her back pocket.

"So?" Amy said, whipping around to face Emma. "What exactly happened last night? Connor got a text from Danny saying something about Stella intimidating you and there was a friend who needed your help, so you bailed on your date? Who is Stella, and what friend was he talking about? With the terrible storm and not knowing what was going on, I was on pins and needles all evening until I saw your car pull into the driveway."

"Coffee first." Emma headed straight for the coffee pot near the stove and poured herself a cup. The great thing about having a foodie for a sister was that she had every kind of syrup and creamer available. Emma took a minute to fix hers up just right —caramel creamer with caramel syrup—and took a sip before turning back to her sister and leaning against the counter. "Next time you and Connor want to set me up, do me a favor? Don't."

"Why? What happened?" Amy looked truly shocked.

"You haven't met this guy, have you?"

"Well, no, not officially. I've seen him plenty around the clinic, though. He seems nice enough."

"You should have a conversation with him sometime. Consider that next time someone seems perfect and is single for over a year, there might be something else going on." Emma crossed her arms, trying to show her sister she was serious about not interfering in her dating life in the future.

Just then, Connor came into the kitchen. The girls ran out to get their backpacks ready for school.

"Sorry, the date not go over well, Emma?" Connor looked a little sheepish. He probably knew exactly what type of guy Danny was all along but felt the need to get Amy off his back from nagging him and help set her up on a date.

"Look, all the guy wanted to talk about was himself and his car. Thanks for your help and I appreciate your intentions, but I am just not interested in dating right now."

"Yeah, Stella is kind of a priority in Danny's life," Connor chuckled.

"Stella? Who is this Stella?" Amy asked, sounding peeved.

"His car," Emma and Connor said at the same time.

"Connor! You knew?" Emma's eyes widened, and when she saw the smirk on Connor's face, she swatted him on the chest.

"Connor!" Amy shouted, horrified, "I finally get Emma to go out and she just needed one date to go well so that…" She trailed off, and then changed tactics, turning back to Emma. "Okay. We'll back off. For now. And I'm sorry you had to go through that." She shot her husband another steely glare. "So what did you end up doing for the rest of the evening? I heard you come in after midnight."

"Well, *Mom and Dad*, if you must know, I ran into Jake and decided to go over to his grandmother's place to help him pack more of his boxes."

The twins returned to the kitchen just as Amy and Connor gave each other a look.

"Who's Jake?" Leah asked.

Laney, the real eavesdropper in the family, said, "I think he was Auntie's second date!"

Emma shook her head and laughed, but for some reason, that's all the rebuttal she could formulate.

When she got to work, Emma tidied the recreation room and helped residents while she waited till it was time to bring the medicine cart around during mid-morning teatime. She kept an eye on Doris, who was sitting with two members of her gang, Geezer and Beatrice. All three seniors were working on a 500-piece puzzle of a lighthouse. Every so often, when a puzzle piece would fall onto the floor, Charlie was quick to pick it up with his mouth and gently place it into one of the three resident's outstretched hands.

Since the storm the night before, pails had been placed around the sunroom, as such heavy rain occasionally proved too much for the roof and several leaks had appeared. Mr. Willoughby, the head of Heart & Home, had done an earlier walk through with a couple of maintenance workers. Emma noticed he wasn't his usual chatty self with the residents. Mr. Willoughby's brows were furrowed, and he discussed getting quotes to replace the roof of the sunroom. Emma felt bad for her boss. She also knew this added burden did not bode well for Heart & Home's current financial position or her potential promotion.

Doris kept sneaking looks at Emma and then whispering to her cohorts. Emma sensed they were planning something. She had told Meredith about her awful date last night, sending the woman into peals of laughter, and was sure the story had run through the home like wildfire. She was extra glad she'd left out the details about her dinner and evening with Jake.

Emma worked her way around the room, only catching a few phrases from their conversation, despite the fact that they all tended to speak more loudly than necessary: "...needs a man... have it all...here all the time...must be lonely...guess it's up to us now..."

Doris, the most hearing-impaired and therefore loudest of them all, slapped a puzzle piece onto the table and declared in a conspiratorial whisper, "Heart & Home is a safe place for Emma. We are her family here, and family looks after family. I think I may just have an idea of what we can do."

Geezer and Beatrice leaned in closer to Doris and they kept

her quieter as she began to explain whatever she had planned. Nods of agreement followed, along with quick glances directed her way. Something was up.

Emma sighed, but her next task took her to a different room. She hoped the old folks didn't get too involved or invested in anything regarding her. With any luck, they'd forget about their "secret plans" by lunch.

---

Emma began to doubt her conviction later when she returned to find that the gang of three seniors had now been joined by Stan around a card table playing what they believed to be a covert game of poker. The nurses were all aware of their undercover poker games, but turned a blind eye as long as there weren't any high stakes. Charlie lay his head on Geezer's lap. Emma stayed by the doorway inconspicuously keeping an eye on their potential scheming and shenanigans.

"Where's Meredith?" Geezer asked since she was a regular player with them. Emma noticed their friend had been absent from a couple of the seniors' activities ever since she had taken the trip into Seattle.

Beatrice shrugged. "Not interested in playing." Beatrice shuffled the cards, making a mess of them, and then took her time to align them again. "I think she's got a lot on her mind since coming back from Seattle. Feeling a little depressed about the fact that her grandson is trying to talk her into leaving here, though she'd never admit as much."

Doris reached for the cards. She was better at shuffling than Beatrice, but not by much. "Playing cards just doesn't seem right without her."

"Well, we'd better get used to it." Geezer sighed. "She was the best dealer and bluffer around."

"She's not dead, Geezer," Beatrice said, taking the cards back and dealing them, and causing Emma to smile. "She's just down the hall in her room. Come on now, we need to finish this hand before Stan falls asleep."

Doris laughed. "Too late." She nudged the dog under the table with her foot. "Charlie, you know what to do."

Charlie leapt up, eager to please, and lunged for Stan, giving him a sloppy lick on the face.

Stan stirred, but didn't open his eyes. "Not tonight, Nora, I'm too tired."

The rest of the seniors giggled, and Charlie went in for a second lick. Finally, his eyes opened.

"Huh? What?" He looked around at all of his friends laughing at him, and then, without looking at his cards, he pushed them to the center of the table. "I fold."

Across the room, a door opened with another resident and Emma sighed to herself, knowing that she could now easily be seen from where they were seated.

Sure enough, Doris whipped her head around and spotted Emma by the doorway. "Incoming!" she said in an urgent whisper.

The seniors scrambled to slide all of the poker chips to the side of the table where Charlie jumped up and covered the chips with his paws.

Geezer, not missing a beat, held up his hand of cards, cleared his throat, and said, "Got any 2s?" in a loud voice.

"Go Fish, Geezer," Doris replied, making a show of shaking her head.

Emma entered further into the room with raised eyebrows. "You're not fooling anyone, Doris." She looked around at all of them. "And bringing in my Charlie as an accomplice? Shame on you all."

As she walked over, the squad played innocent and continued with their Go Fish game. Emma surreptitiously pushed a few chips that had fallen over to Charlie who swept them under himself. "Of course, if you had been playing poker, I hope you now know that as long as you're not endangering yourself or others, none of the staff are here to enforce every single rule."

The seniors grinned at each other. Doris asked, "Any special plans after your shift, Emma? I hope you're not planning on just hanging around at Heart & Home again. Not that we don't love having you around, but a beautiful young lady your age should be painting the town red or whatever you kids call it nowadays."

"Getting her groove on," Stan said, doing a little jig in his seat. Everyone looked at him. "What? I like to keep up with the times. Can't fault a guy for being hip."

Emma chuckled and decided to play along. "I'd always rather be here where the action is." She winked at them as a group. "But if you must know, I'm actually cutting out early and Nurse Johanssen is covering the rest of my shift."

"Ooooh! Tell us more!" Beatrice leaned in closer with her good ear, looking like she did not want to miss out on any juicy gossip.

Emma leaned in closer to the group as if she was letting them in on her secret plans. "I have an afternoon date with two five-year-olds who are anxious to make Valentine's cards with their aunt." The seniors' faces dropped with what seemed like disappointment.

In truth, she did have a social engagement planned for this evening, with Jake's friends. He hadn't been by today, but he had left her a message that their dinner was on and where she should meet him. He'd also said how much he was looking forward to seeing her. But in the interest of not feeding the wildfire that had blazed around Heart & Home about her date with Danny, she decided to keep the details of tonight to herself. "I hope to be just like you folks one day—with good friends, playing poker in secret, and laughing together."

"I hope instead, you're off with the love of your life, traveling the world together," Doris said.

Emma waved Doris off, even as her cheeks warmed. "I'm not interested in any of that."

"With that attitude about marriage," Stan said, "It's no wonder it's taken a good long while to find a man."

"Sure, sure," Geezer said, clearly not believing her.

"What's the point?" Emma argued. "In the end, we all end up on our own. Having good friends is key." She looked around the table with raised eyebrows, in way of congratulating them. "Come on, Charlie. I think you've had enough of their bad influence." She started to walk off with Charlie trailing behind her, but then said over her shoulder, "Nurse Johansson is coming around with snacks soon, so if you don't want to get caught with anything that's not approved, I'd start getting packed up." She winked again and led Charlie out of the room.

She was sure that in their hearts, the seniors knew it really wasn't against the rules to play poker as long as no money exchanged hands, but it made them feel wild to think they were living on the edge a little.

## 21

## EMMA

Emma found herself in the middle of a glue and glitter explosion. She had been crafting and creating with her nieces ever since they returned from shopping for supplies to make classroom valentines. It was hard to imagine how two small girls were able to make such a big mess in such a short amount of time. Emma wondered how she was going to get all the purple glitter off of herself before meeting Jake to go to his friends' place for dinner.

Dinner with his friends. Emma was shocked when he had first asked her to join him, but on her way home that night, she convinced herself it was probably nothing. He'd reassured her in a message that his friend Paul was more than happy to welcome a plus one. Emma chalked the invitation up to the fact Jake was probably only interested in not being the third wheel and bringing her along was convenient. After all, they had become more comfortable with each other the past several days, and he surely wasn't interested in forming any new relationships since he wanted to cut ties with the town. True, the conversation between them flowed more smoothly now. But Emma needed to remind herself this was a short-term friendship. Any spark felt the other night was simply both of them getting caught up in a sentimental moment. Jake would be going back to Seattle soon to focus on his career, to the life that he had established, and he still intended to bring his grandmother with him.

Giggles from her nieces brought Emma's attention back to her responsibilities at hand. Even poor Charlie had not escaped the invasion of the glitter, with purple and silver sparkles all over his coat. He, however, didn't seem to mind. Leah had made a pink tissue paper crown to adorn his furry head. Charlie was a good sport. And *he* wasn't going out tonight.

"Everyone on my list has a card now. What about your list, Laney?" Leah looked over at her sister's cards. Each girl had a neatly stacked pile of cards ready to hand out next week for their classroom Valentine's Day party.

"My cards are done too." Laney stuffed her cards into a large plastic baggie, ready to take to school. "That was a big job, thanks for helping, Auntie."

Emma smiled. "When I was your age, each student would decorate an empty shoebox to be a Valentine mailbox. Then all week, we brought cards to deliver to each box. Sometimes there would even be a card signed '*Your Secret Admirer*' and it was so exciting to get one."

"What's a secret admirer?" Laney asked.

"Someone who did not want you to know that it was him or her that sent the card. It was a secret." Emma spoke in a hushed tone to indicate the excitement of such a secret. She remembered the parties from her childhood, and she loved sharing the love and excitement with her two nieces.

"But why wouldn't that person want you to know?" Leah looked confused.

Emma smiled. "Well, it could be because they had a crush, and the one person was too shy to tell the other person."

"Ooooooh, that's so romantic!" Laney swooned, the eternal little lovebird. But her sister was more of the practical thinker.

"Then how would that person ever know if the other person had a crush too?"

Emma could tell Leah wasn't quite sold on the idea of a secret admirer. She picked up a pinch of glitter in her hand and, opening up her palm, she gently blew the glitter into the air. Both girls squealed. "Well, sometimes with love, magic just takes over."

Emma only wished she could believe her own words. She could use some magic of her own right now, not in her love life so much, but with her career and the unknown future of the assisted living facility she loved so much.

"Who are you giving all your cards to, Auntie?" A pile of cut out hearts lay beside Emma's purse. While the girls had been decorating their cards, she had made some of her own for the residents of Heart & Home. Thinking it could be her last Valentine's with the residents there—for one reason or another—she wanted to make it a special one. She had written a personalized note to each of the seniors she looked after.

"These are for the residents where I work. They are not only the people I care for, but they're also my friends. Sometimes we can take those around us for granted and I just want to make sure they know how special they are to me." Emma had also picked up some extra card making supplies, as she thought some of the residents may enjoy making cards of their own this week when she was working. "Valentine's day is for all kinds of love. For family, friends, even pets," she said, ruffling Charlie's fur and sending a spray of glitter to the floor.

Laney looked through the names on Emma's cards. "I don't see one here for that guy named Jake. Don't you think he would like a card too?"

"No, I don't think he would care for one." Emma laughed at the thought of Jake receiving a Valentine's card from her. He was not the sentimental type. She had seen how he just shoved some handwritten letters away when he found them in his grandmother's house on that first night she was over helping him. Emma would not have been surprised if he had simply thrown them away without even reading them first. No, Jake would not be an eager recipient of a Valentine's card.

Just then, Amy walked into the kitchen and froze, seeing the chaos all over her counters. Emma and the girls stopped their conversation and froze as if being caught with their hands in the cookie jar. Wide-eyed with disbelief that her kitchen could get this messy, Amy put her hands on her hips and shook her head.

"Don't worry Amy, we'll get this clean, won't we girls!" The girls knew what would melt their mother's heart and immediately threw their arms around her, giving the biggest, glitteriest hugs.

"We love you, Mommy!" Laney cried, batting her eyes innocently.

"There's even a card for you, and one for Daddy." Leah chimed in for good measure.

It did the trick. Amy was putty in their glitter-covered, sticky little hands, and could not stay upset. Her face softened and she returned the hugs.

Now that is magical love, Emma thought with a smile.

"Girls, let's get this mess cleaned up. I have to try and wash this glitter out of my hair before I leave," Emma said as she began to dust off her hands over the counter.

Amy didn't miss a beat. "What's tonight? Don't tell me you are going on another date?"

"Of course not. Just a supper thing with some friends," she replied, carefully keeping her eyes on the counter as she began sweeping all the glitter into a pile. It wasn't that she was lying to her sister, per se. It was more like an omission of the specific details.

"It's with Jaaaaaaaaake!" sang a voice from behind her. Emma turned around to see Leah with Charlie's front paws on her shoulders swaying back and forth to imaginary music. Some days, Charlie seemed to have a better social life than she did. But then Emma was reminded of her dancing the other night with Jake. She sighed, lost in her own little day-dream moment. Her mouth gave way to a grin as she remembered twirling around the room in his arms.

This look of dreaminess was not lost on her sister. "Emma? Emma? So are you, or aren't you?" Amy asked, sounding agitated.

"What? Oh, sorry, I wasn't listening."

"Are you or are you not interested romantically in Jake Rothstein?"

"Absolutely not. No, no, no. Jake is not a dateable guy. I'm just helping him out while hopefully convincing him to let his grandmother stay at Heart & Home."

"Well, does he know that? I just don't want to see anyone's

heart get broken. Especially your heart, Emma. I think there's more here than what you care to admit, whether to me or to yourself." Amy walked around the counter and put her arm protectively around her little sister.

"I know, I know. Don't worry, it's all under control. Believe me, Jake knows as well as I do that his life is in Seattle and mine is here, in Juniper Falls."

Emma turned around, hearing giggles from her nieces behind her. Both girls looked suspiciously guilty as they shoved something behind their backs.

"What are you two up to now?" Emma put her hands on her hips trying to look stern. But it was no use, the girls both saw through the facade and it just led to more giggles.

"It's the month of love, Auntie," grinned a toothless Laney.

"Somethings are just meant to be a *secret*." Leah added and both girls looked at each other dissolving into another fit of giggles and rushing out of the room. Whatever they had been holding behind their backs was now gone.

Emma glanced at the clock on the stove and realized she was going to be late to meet Jake at seven if she didn't hurry.

## 22

## JAKE

The night air was crisp, but a pleasant reprieve from the rain. Jake nervously sat waiting for Emma on a bench inside the gazebo near the park, holding two cups of hot chocolate. He had asked Emma to meet him here so he could chat with her before going to Paul and Jennie's place for supper, hoping it would be a little less intimidating for her if they arrived together. Also, Jake felt he owed Emma a further explanation as to who the people were that she would be meeting, just so she was prepared for what the evening held. Especially if Paul brought up any of their antics from back in the day since Emma didn't know much about his youth. Besides, the house was around the corner from the park and it was a pleasant night for walking.

From across the street, he saw Emma rounding the corner to meet him. She looked classy in an off-white pea coat and knee-high leather boots. Her brown hair flowed gracefully in the breeze. Her pace quickened when she saw him sitting, waiting for her.

"I'm so sorry, Jake. There was a little incident with two five-year-olds and a boatload of glitter. I think I'll be picking sparkles out of my hair for the next month." She nervously ran a hand through her locks.

Jake chuckled and handed her the drink. "Here's what is

*supposed* to be a hot chocolate. It smells like it is, but I can't promise."

Emma took a sip. "It is. Thanks! Was Megan working?" The girl from Java Junction had a reputation for mixed up beverage orders in general, but her heart was in the right place. She was just overenthusiastic.

Jake nodded and laughed. "She's a sweet girl, just gets a little confused sometimes. Thanks again for joining me tonight," he said, as they began walking. "Yet another time that the kind Nurse Hathaway comes to my aid."

"If you remember, it was the charming Jake Rothstein who came to *my* rescue the other night and saved me from my awful date. Call us even." She gave a little grin and looked up at him.

"Well, I'm warning you. You may hear a few stories about me tonight, stories that will make you wish you had stayed far away from me."

Emma stopped walking and looked concerned. "Why? What are you talking about, Jake?"

"Let's just say I went through a rebellious stage in high school. Not my best years, and I haven't seen Paul and Jennie much since then. I just wanted to give you fair warning that tonight may be filled with high school stories, and not my best moments."

Emma put a gloved hand on his arm. "Oh Jake, is that all? Everyone has those embarrassing stories, and we have all grown and changed since high school. Believe me, I am definitely not the same person now than I was back then. I'm not even the same person I was a year or two ago."

"I appreciate you saying that, but I just wanted to prepare you for the dark side of Jake Rothstein."

"Consider me prepared. And maybe a little relieved. It's nice to know that underneath your well-put-together exterior, lies a bit of a rebel." Emma nudged his arm companionably. "So let's get going. I'm excited to learn more about your wild side." She proceeded to walk ahead, and Jake quickened his steps to catch up to her.

Walking up to the house several minutes later, Jake noticed

the wooden carved sign: *Welcome to the Sanders', Love Lives Here.* Jake took a deep breath before ringing the bell. Emma must have sensed his hesitation because she reached over for his hand. She gave it a quick squeeze, as if to say, "Don't worry, I'm here with you," which was exactly what he needed.

Just then, Paul opened the door and pulled Jake into what he referred to as a bro hug. "Here he is! So glad you could make it, Jake. And Emma, so nice to meet you." Paul stuck out a hand to Emma, shaking it and pulling her inside at the same time.

From around the corner, came Jennie. "Welcome, you two. Here, let me take that for you." In an instant, she had gathered their coats and the empty hot chocolate cups, whisking them out of sight. Jake remembered Jennie as an enthusiastic cheerleader in high school, and she obviously still maintained that energy over a decade later. Paul took Jake's coat and gestured the two of them inside.

"Paul, dear, don't forget to offer them drinks!" Jennie called from what Jake presumed was the kitchen.

"Supper will be ready soon, but please, have a drink. We have some white wine chilling as well as a local brew. Let's have a seat and catch up." Paul led them into the living room. It was modernly decorated in smooth and sleek styles of a neutral palette. Calming and soothing, the atmosphere was just what Jake needed to put him at ease. He took a seat beside Emma on the couch, their legs brushing against each other.

"You have a beautiful home," Emma commented as she looked around the room.

"Jennie loves to decorate. She watches all those home improvement, fixer-upper shows on HGTV. When we bought it a few years ago, it was basically an empty shell, void of any personality." At the mention of her name, Jennie popped back into the living room and took a seat on the arm of her husband's chair.

"The only trouble is trying to find the time. Each room is a project all of its own. I teach Kindergarten, and those little ones keep me hopping. By the end of the day, I don't have much energy left for home improvement projects."

"Wait a minute. Now I know why your name sounds so familiar; you're Mrs. Sanders! You teach my nieces, Leah and Laney. No wonder you're tired after a day of teaching!" Emma and Jennie started a conversation about her nieces, and Emma shared the story of the glitter fiasco. Jake relaxed into the couch and began to enjoy the evening, his worries about this becoming a high-pressure date quickly melting off of him.

The four sat down to enjoy a pot roast meal, complete with all the trimmings. The conversation flowed effortlessly from one topic to the next. Jake and Emma were entertained with Paul's stories of working on the police force and Jennie's busy Kindergarten classroom.

"So Emma, tell us what it's like to work at Heart & Home?" Paul asked his supper guest. Jake felt a sense of pride listening to Emma share about her love and passion for working with the residents at the home. Emma had everyone in tears of laughter, sharing stories about the residents' poker games, rap singing battles, and Geezer's attempts to fool the nurses into giving him extra servings of chocolate pudding for nighttime snacks.

"The other day in the staffroom, I overheard one of my colleagues saying that Heart & Home was struggling financially. His uncle lives there. Will that affect your job, Emma?" Jennie looked concerned. Emma shifted uncomfortably in her seat.

Jake was surprised at this news. Emma had not mentioned anything to him regarding the financial struggles of the facility. Part of him felt genuinely bad for her, the staff, and the residents, especially if they would have to make budget cuts to personnel staffing, or worse, close the facility. Yet, there was a small, guilty part of him that was hoping it might increase the odds of Emma moving into the city to be closer to his grandmother and himself.

"I'm not sure what will happen, but we are all a little concerned about the residents and our jobs." Emma's eyes showed her worry. "I know the owner, Mr. Willoughby, is looking at some possible options and cuts."

Jake suspected the plan to pull his grandmother out of Heart & Home would only contribute to the problem. But he couldn't let that be the deciding factor for him. He had to look at what was best for his grandmother, best for their family.

"I know when our school has been short with budget or needed extra money for a project, we planned a fundraiser, and it was amazing how the community pulled together for the children. Maybe you could do a fundraiser for Heart & Home?"

That made a lot of sense. Jake watched for Emma's reaction. She went from gloomy to excited in a matter of seconds. It was as if Jake could actually see a little cartoon light bulb light up above her head. She obviously had an idea brewing.

"A dance! A Valentine's Day Dance. We usually plan something special for the seniors around Valentine's Day, but this year it could be bigger, to include the community. We could sell tickets and hold a raffle or a silent auction."

"That sounds fantastic, Emma. I'll talk to my officers, but I'm sure they will be more than willing to help and contribute in any way you need," Paul said. "We haven't had a community dance in years. I bet it will be well attended."

"Thanks, Paul. And Jennie, maybe your class would be willing to make some decorations we could use? I know for a fact there are two twins who would be more than happy to put the glitter to good use again."

Jake found himself getting caught up in the excited energy too. "Well, count on me for any advertising, Emma. I can make posters and take them around town, and design the tickets to sell."

Emma looked over at Jake with the widest eyes he'd ever seen on anyone. It looked like disbelief, which made him feel a little uncomfortable for jumping on the bandwagon so quickly. Maybe he'd overstepped the boundary between them.

But his worries were quickly put to rest when she leaned over and threw her arms around him. "Thanks, Jake! I know how busy you are with work and packing. This means so much."

Jake's smile could not have gotten any wider that evening. Paul and Jennie seemed to pick up on the spark between their guests and shared a wink. Jake felt his cheeks flame, but for once, he didn't fight off the feeling. So what if they could see how much Emma affected him?

After dessert and coffee, Jake and Emma decided they should head back to their cars. Emma wanted to get to work early tomorrow morning to meet with Mr. Willoughby and run the idea of a fundraiser past him and then get back to them about further planning. It would be tight to make it all happen in just over a week, but Emma looked so hopeful that Jake would do whatever he could to assist.

"Thank you both so much for a wonderful evening," Emma said at the door, and Jake echoed her sentiments by initiating a hug with both of their hosts. "And for the great fundraising idea. I can't wait to get to work," Emma added.

They left the Sanders' house with a promise to connect again the next day. Jake knew his time in Juniper Falls would be wrapping up soon, but after tonight, he hoped to stay in touch with his old friends and one new one.

The pair began their walk down the quiet street toward the gazebo where their cars had been parked.

"I thought I'd pop by Heart & Home to visit my grandmother tomorrow. If you have time for a coffee after, we could discuss design ideas for the posters, if you get approval for the dance."

"Really?" She barely waited for Jake's nod, before saying, "That would be so great. Thank you." Emma chattered non-stop about the possibilities for the dance.

Jake smiled and listened to her plans wholeheartedly. She really was amazing, he mused. As they walked, their hands brushed against one another, and as natural as if they'd done it a thousand times, Jake intertwined his fingers with Emma's. Not missing a beat, she continued talking excitedly about her plans, while giving Jake's hand a slight squeeze.

Arriving at the gazebo, Jake found himself wishing their walk could have lasted longer. Emma reached into her purse fumbling to find her car keys. "I know they're in here somewhere." Finally digging to the bottom there was a jingle and her hand emerged holding the keys. She raised them up victoriously. "Here they are!"

Emma leaned in and gave Jake a quick hug. "Thanks for tonight. The company was great, and now I have hope for Heart & Home."

"Thanks for coming along, Emma," Jake said, and he meant it. The evening would not have been nearly as wonderful without her by his side.

Watching her drive off, Jake turned to leave when he noticed something lying at his feet. It must have slipped out of Emma's purse when she was trying to find her keys. He bent over to pick up a purple card. Turning it over, he saw his name in what looked like a child's printing. When he opened it, glitter flew up and into the air with the slight breeze. There was a message underneath the glitter:

*Bee Min! Luv, Yor Secrit Admirr*

Jake smiled, feeling his heart clench as though he was a boy in grade school all over again. Either Emma needed to work on her spelling and penmanship, or she was having a little help from her nieces around matters of the heart. He blew out the remainder of the glitter before tucking the card into his inside jacket pocket.

Jake hadn't thought about the idea of a secret admirer in years. It brought on a sense of nostalgia, and as Jake drove home, he found himself whistling a familiar, nostalgic tune...*Let me call you sweetheart, I'm in love with you...*

As he whistled, he came up with an idea for the perfect theme for the Valentine's Day dance. He could hardly wait to share it with Emma tomorrow.

## 23

## EMMA

Emma sat in Mr. Willoughby's office, sharing her fundraising plan for Heart & Home with as much enthusiasm as she could muster. In fact, she had stayed up most of the night putting together a proposal for the event and calling potential sponsors. The owner listened intently to what she suggested, taking notes and nodding—in agreement, she hoped—to what she was offering. No doubt it was a huge undertaking, and especially with the tight time frame.

"And are you sure your sister doesn't mind doing the catering for free, minus the cost of the food? That's extremely generous of her."

"Amy's plan is to develop a catering business and thought letting the community see what she could offer would be a win/win. Her services, free of charge for Heart & Home, and we advertise her catering business on a banner at the dance. Plus, Martin's Grocery is willing to donate many of the ingredients and the produce. From what I can tell already, the entire community wants to help out, Mr. Willoughby. Heart & Home means so much to everyone in Juniper Falls." Emma could tell the owner was moved by such kindness and community generosity. He also seemed impressed with Emma's initiative.

Despite that, he seemed hesitant to charge admission. "Heart and Home has hosted or sponsored community events in the past, Emma, as you know, which enabled the residents here to maintain their relationships in the community. But those have always been free, to ensure the continued well-being of the people here. I'm concerned that charging for an event will be seen as profiteering."

"Sir," Emma responded, "I understand your concerns, but this is not a way to increase a budget or save money. We're doing this to help keep their family members and friends nearby, in a safe environment, where they will be well-cared for. I think the community recognizes the value of keeping our people in town where they can maintain relationships in a way they would be unable to do if we closed and they needed to be transferred elsewhere."

"Look, Emma, if we can all pull this off, I would like to give you more responsibilities around Heart & Home. The residents and staff all love you and don't think I haven't noticed that you go above and beyond in your work."

Emma rose from her chair with a warmth in her chest from his words. "Thanks for your support, Mr. Willoughby. I'll keep you updated on everything."

"Please, call me Dennis." Emma felt surprised and honored at this offer. She hadn't heard anyone around Heart & Home call him by his first name. "And Emma, thank you. Heart & Home isn't just a business to me and my family. It is so much more. It's heartening to see that others feel the same way."

Emma left the office and made her way to the lobby. She was a little late for her shift and Pam would be anxious to hear how the meeting went. However, when she made it to the counter, Pam didn't even seem to notice Emma's approach. She was too busy with the tech guy who had come by to teach her how to run a new accounting program on her computer. A giggle escaped Pam's mouth and she twirled a strand of her hair around her fingers that had slipped out of her bun. Was the always-proper office administrator flirting with Andy the tech guy? Yes, in fact, she was.

Pam batted her eyelashes and was asking for him to show her the steps of the program one more time. Emma hung back and watched the two of them. Andy, with his dark rimmed glasses that were too big for his skinny face, kept having to use his index finger to push them back up on his nose. He rarely smiled, but today he had a new confidence as he led Pam through the navigation of the program one more time.

Was Pam also wearing a hint of make-up? Emma grinned. This was just too sweet. Love was in the air at Heart & Home. She hated to interrupt, but she needed Pam to print off a couple of patient schedules for her shift. Emma cleared her throat gently, so as not to startle them both.

"Oh, Emma! How did the meeting go? What did Mr. Willoughby think?" Pam seemed flustered, swatting back her stray hair. Andy moved back from Pam's workstation, looking awkward again.

"I better be going but let me know if you have any more trouble, Pam." He slung his computer bag over his shoulder and headed back down the hall with his head down so as not to have to make contact with anyone walking his way.

"Isn't he adorably awkward?" Pam gushed the second Andy was out of earshot. Emma was glad for Pam. Andy seemed like a sweet man. He would frequently go into residents' rooms and help with any technical problems with their televisions, iPads, or hearing aids, even though it wasn't his job. Last month, he had even brought in his old video gaming system and installed it on the TV in the sunroom, trying to teach Geezer to play Super Mario. Watching them play was entertainment in and of itself for the residents. Yes, Andy was one of the good ones.

Emma filled Pam in about the meeting and her plans. Pam was more than willing to put together a spreadsheet with everyone's tasks and timelines, including a transporting schedule for the Heart & Home residents to the community hall for the dance. Tomorrow, Emma would work with some of the residents making Valentine's Day cards and beginning some of the decorations. She only hoped the seniors would be more careful with glitter, glue, and scissors than her nieces had been. But right now, Emma put a pause on planning to check in with Meredith, who she had heard left breakfast early to go back to her room.

Meredith's room door was slightly ajar, so Emma knocked gently, just in case she was napping. She didn't want to disturb her. However, she heard a welcome bark from Charlie on the other side of the door. "Come on in," Meredith said.

Emma opened the door to find Charlie lying his head on Meredith's lap while she was knitting. Both dog and resident looked rather gloomy. Emma pulled a chair up beside her friend.

"Everything okay, Meredith?" Emma could see the photo albums were out on Meredith's bed. She had a feeling she knew what was troubling her.

"I'm going to miss this place. Not just Heart & Home, but Juniper Falls. I've lived here my whole life, Emma." Meredith reached out and patted Charlie's head. Her hand seemed shaky. The dog nuzzled into her. Charlie sensed he was needed and was more than willing to give his unconditional love.

"Have you talked to Jake, lately?" Emma knew Jake still had his heart set on moving his grandma, but maybe if he could see how sad she was right now, he might soften.

"Truth be told, Emma, at first I thought Jake wanted me to move closer to him so he could keep an eye out for me. But over the last week, I sense it is also because he needs me. He may not realize it yet, but he's lonely, Emma. I can see it in his eyes, but he just has that Rothstein stubbornness that makes it difficult to share matters of the heart."

Emma knew what Meredith meant, as she had also come to see brief glimpses of him dropping his defenses and letting Emma in.

"Jake doesn't understand. What we did, his grandfather and I, it was all for him. We tried to give him the life he deserved, but at the same time not let him go down the same path as his mother. It wasn't his fault that she left. We pushed her to get her life sorted out, for Jake's sake. But in retrospect, maybe we pushed too hard. She chose a different path, one not fit for raising a child and she didn't want anything to do with any of us anymore. And we were left suddenly taking care of a young child again. I think that made us harder on Jake. We were scared he would follow her lead. We loved him so much, Emma. And I still do. I want to be there for him. I'm just sad to leave everything here, everything familiar to me. But I know it's worth it to be there for my grandson. He's all I have left."

The tears flowed freely now, not only from Meredith, but from Emma too. Emma reached over and grabbed the Kleenex box from the side table, handing a tissue to her friend and grabbing one for herself. Charlie kept looking from woman to woman not sure who to console.

"A fine pair we are, Meredith Rothstein. Look at us, two single women a week before Valentine's Day, and we're sitting here sobbing together over a man."

That got the elderly lady smiling. They both dabbed at their tears. Emma had wanted to share her plans for the Valentine's Day dance with Meredith but knew this wasn't the time. She would fill her in later.

"Emma, you are a pretty special young woman. And I know for a fact Jake thinks so, too. Please do me a favor and don't give up on him." Meredith grabbed both of Emma's hands in her own. "Will you promise me that?"

Startled, Emma whispered, "I promise," even though she wasn't quite sure what that meant. Jake would soon be gone back to Seattle, and would she even see him again?

But for the moment, he was still in Juniper Falls, and she needed to talk to him. She left Charlie to keep Meredith company while she went to find Jake.

Emma didn't have to walk very far to find him. Jake was just coming through the main doors. He looked stylish in a navy cable knit sweater and a pair of chinos, but the thing Emma noticed most about Jake Rothstein's looks today was that he appeared happy. *Happy.* In fact, he was grinning from ear to ear.

Jake waved a red folder in his hand as he approached Emma, "I have a theme idea for your Valentine's fundraising dance."

"No formalities or greetings, huh? Right to business?" Emma teased.

"Oh, sorry. Hey there. How's your morning going? That better?" He looked rather sheepish at his lack of manners.

"I'm just kidding, Jake. I'm glad you're so enthusiastic. So, what's the theme you came up with? I thought our theme *was* Valentine's Day."

"Yes, but not just *any* Valentine's Day. A dance set in the big band swing era. Just like how my grandmother described her dances to us." His already large grin grew. "What do you think? All the old crooners' songs? An old-time dance. We could call it Sweetheart Serenade?" Jake proceeded to open up the folder on the counter and spread out what he had clearly been working on through most of the night.

*Heart & Home's Valentine's Day Fundraiser "Sweetheart Serenade."*

He had designed several examples of posters with the facility's logos advertising the dance. Emma was amazed at his creativity and how he captured exactly what they were trying to accomplish.

"These are fabulous, Jake! Any one of these are bound to grab people's attention."

Jake blushed at the compliments of his designs. Emma could tell he was not used to his work being gushed over like this. He seemed embarrassed, yet proud that she liked what he had created.

He cleared his throat. "Thanks. Once we finalize everything, I can take them to the printer's this afternoon, along with the tickets. Did you get approval from the boss?"

Emma nodded. "Yes, Mr. Willoughby is behind us all the way."

Jake gathered his papers and closed the folder. "I'll just go spend a little time with my grandma. I phoned her this morning, but she seemed a little down. Hope she's not coming down with the flu or anything. She got her flu shot, right?"

Emma glanced back toward Meredith's room, unsure of how much to say after he had just been so helpful for their upcoming event. "Yes, she did. All the residents and staff get their annual flu shot. But listen, Jake, I don't think it's the flu that's got her down. Just talk to her, okay? Listen to what she has to say. Everything is a little overwhelming for her right now. I'm sure she could use a listening ear."

Jake's forehead creased from her comments, and Emma worried she had said too much. Here she was again, getting in the middle of things.

"Oh, okay. Well, I'll go check on her. Thanks, Emma." His demeanor had changed, and Emma felt like she was the one who had taken a pin and popped his balloon. She hadn't meant to deflate his good mood, but at the same time it was important that Meredith and her grandson talk about their feelings.

Sooner rather than later.

24

EMMA

As tea was being served the next day, Emma walked into the sunroom with a bin of craft supplies. Mr. Willoughby had given her permission to share the news of the fundraising dance with the seniors. Word had quickly spread among the residents that Heart & Home was in financial trouble. The room was in a rather glum state Emma noticed as she made her way to the front table to set down the supplies and make the announcement.

Never one to mince her words, Doris motioned for Emma to come over to her table. She was sitting with Geezer, Beatrice, and Stan.

"Look, Heart & Home needs to come clean with what's going on. We have a right to know if they are going to close. So spill the beans, Emma."

Emma looked down and shook her head. "I'm sorry, Doris. No one was trying to keep anything from any of you, I promise. We didn't want to worry anyone needlessly." Emma went up to the front of the room where all eyes were on her.

"Listen everyone, I know there are probably many different rumors flying around about the future of Heart & Home, but I want you all to know that we have a plan. It involves getting the entire community behind our facility, and we need your help too. We're organizing a fundraiser for Valentine's Day." Her voice became more excited as she spoke. "So dust off those dancing shoes and find yourself a sweetheart, because Heart & Home is planning a swinging community dance! Now, who wants to make some Valentine's cards for all of our guests?"

Emma was excited and began to pass out the materials to begin crafting the cards. Suddenly, she noticed Doris bolt upright in her chair and start whispering furtively to her gang. Emma suspected they were probably kicking their plans up a notch to find her a date for the dance, but she smiled anyway. What harm could come from four well-meaning elderly friends?

It did not take too long into the activity for Emma to come to the realization that seniors and five-year olds are equally as enthusiastic and messy with the use of glitter. Poor, napping Stan awoke to find himself covered in sparkles.

By the time the afternoon was over, the residents had a large pile of cards they planned to hand out to guests at the dance. Spirits were lifted and plans had been put in motion.

---

Emma had a spring in her step as she walked home with Charlie after her shift ended that day, excited to share with Amy all about the day's events. However, Emma was rather shocked as she walked into the back door of her sister's house. The normally pristine kitchen looked as disastrous tonight as it had two days ago, but instead of glitter and scraps of paper, the counters and table were covered in index cards, baking supplies, cookbooks, and sheaves of paper haphazardly balanced on each other. Leah and Laney were perched on stools up at the counter, contentedly dipping French fries into mounds of ketchup on their plates. A grease-stained paper bag lay on the counter. Amy rarely let her daughters partake in the world of fast food. It was obvious her sister was feeling the time crunch to be ready for next week.

"Honestly, Emma, I've got it covered," Amy insisted, catching a look of Emma's shocked-silent face.

Emma tied a floral apron around her waist, ready to lend a helping hand to her sister however she could. She looked around at the various sticky notes of lists on cupboards and counters. "I know you do."

Her sister was highly organized, but Emma also knew how catering the fundraiser was putting extra pressure on Amy, and she felt a little guilty about it.

Emma located a black hair elastic out of her bag on the chair and pulled her hair up, ready to get to work. "Look, I may not be great at actually cooking, but I can prep. Just bark out the orders, and I've got you covered."

Charlie lifted his head from laying on the rug and gave a little bark. Both sisters burst out laughing, a humorous reprieve from the stress they both were feeling.

"Well, since you're willing…" Amy handed Emma a whisk and a candy thermometer. "I could use the extra set of hands. Once my catering business gets off the ground, then I can afford to hire some help. But right now, free labor works just great." Amy pointed to a pot on the stove. "Just keep checking on the fudge and let me know when it hits 237°F."

"Who said anything about free? I fully intend to sample as I go." Emma winked. "You can pay me in calories." She grabbed a handful of chocolate chips and popped them into her mouth pointedly.

"Emma, I think it's really great how you've spearheaded this entire fundraiser, and I honestly hope it makes a difference. I don't want to be the pessimist here, but have you considered what you will do if it doesn't work? It's already Wednesday and Valentine's Day is next week."

Emma didn't consider Amy a pessimist, more like a realist, and losing her job, losing Heart & Home, well, it was a real possibility. "Believe me, I've been thinking a lot about it. In my heart of hearts, I want this to work, for everyone, but if it doesn't, well, I guess I'll cross that bridge when I come to it."

"Are you still considering applying at Lexington Manor?"

Emma had brought up the idea of moving back to Seattle with her sister a few days ago, before coming up with the plan to save Heart & Home. "I'm not sure. I'm torn," she told her sister honestly. There were so many things to consider, first and foremost what she would do with Charlie if she worked at Lexington Manor all day every day.

"Just, whatever you do, don't do it for others. Make this decision for yourself, Emma. Mrs. Rothstein would not expect you to pick up the life you have in Juniper Falls just for her, no matter how cute or single her grandson happens to be. And honestly, it wouldn't be right to uproot your entire life just to be with her for the last few years of hers."

"Well, that's a first. Normally, you're the one who's pushing me out the door and into the arms of any single guy." Emma continued to whisk the fudge with more vigor, as the temperature was rising, and it was now starting to bubble.

"After the last dating fiasco I sent you on, I've had a change of heart. All I've ever wanted is for you to be happy, Emma. And being your big sis, I've felt a responsibility to look after you. I might have gone about it the wrong way, and I'm sorry if I've been too pushy, but it's only because I care. I'll try, and I emphasize the word *try*, to back off from now on."

Emma would believe it when she saw it. However, she loved that her sister was making an effort. The doorbell rang, which prompted Charlie to jump to his feet almost knocking down Amy, who was wiping off her flour-coated hands and making her way to answer it. Emma focused her attention on the temperature of the candy thermometer, not wanting to be the culprit responsible for burning the fudge. She could hear voices in the foyer, and Amy laughing, but didn't pay much attention to it until Leah came bouncing into the room singing, "Auntie, your boyfriend is here, your boyfriend is here! And he's super-duper cute!"

Emma almost dropped the thermometer into the fudge. *Boyfriend?* Who was at the door? Jake didn't know where she lived. It couldn't be Danny, could it? She had a flash of a memory of Danny with his puffed-out chest, blathering on about Stella. He could have easily found Connor's address, and she prayed he hadn't come to try to win her over. She glanced around to see if she could make a quick escape. But she couldn't leave the fudge. It was almost up to temperature.

So there would be no escaping out the back door and up to her apartment. Amy would kill her if she left the fudge to burn. Maybe after what Amy had said to her a few minutes ago, she would just get rid of Danny for Emma. She could only hope.

Emma leaned her body as far away from the stove as possible, without leaving the fudge unattended, to see if she could hear any hint of what her sister was saying.

"Sure, come on back into the kitchen. Emma? You have a visitor!"

*No!* Emma felt like a deer caught in the headlights. Nowhere to run. She was frantically trying to think of an excuse to make a quick exit when around the corner walked Jake. The shot of panic was quickly replaced with surprise.

"Jake? What are you doing here? Is anything wrong with your grandma?" Emma couldn't figure out why Jake Rothstein would be standing in her sister's kitchen.

"No, no, nothing's wrong at all. I just...well, I have the materials for the dance. I picked them up from the printer's and wanted to bring them by. Sorry to alarm you. I probably should have called first." He seemed uncomfortable, like he was feeling guilty about something.

"No, that's totally fine and I'm glad you came by. Thanks for picking them up," Emma reassured him, trying to hide her relief. "But how did you know where I lived?"

Jake's mouth turned up into a smirk. "Remember, Emma? Juniper Falls is not that big. Someone reminded me of that the other day." He shrugged. "Also, Pam gave me your address."

Amy walked over and took the whisk of out Emma's hand. "I've got this. Go with Jake and look over the posters. Maybe at the coffee shop?"

And she was back—Matchmaker Amy. Emma laughed inwardly at how short lived her sister's promise to back off from meddling in her love life, or lack of it, had been. Just then, the twins came bounding into the room. Emma wondered if they had been just around the corner eavesdropping. "Can we go for coffee too?" they pleaded; eyes open wide with innocence.

Amy was quick to respond to her daughters. "No, I need your

help in the kitchen. Jake and Emma have some business they're working on. Besides, you two monkeys don't drink coffee." The two girls looked as sad as if they had just been told the tooth fairy had quit. Jake looked uncomfortable at their obvious disappointment and offered, "Well, I don't mind if they come along. We can walk there, and Java Junction's hot chocolate is delicious, especially with extra whipped cream." He raised his eyebrows at them in question. The girls began jumping up and down, pleading with their mom and with Emma. Charlie heard the word "walk" and got caught up in the excitement too.

Amy sighed at the face of a united front and said, "Okay, monkeys. But listen to your Auntie Emma and don't bother them while they're working. Now go get your coats."

"I guess it's a group outing," Emma laughed, and they all headed for the front door.

———

Hot chocolates in hand, the four made their way across the street to the park with Charlie leading the way. It was a clear evening with the full moon shining down casting a glow off the pond. Twinkling lights dressed the trees throughout the park, giving a magical feel in the air. The girls led the way toward the fountain near the pond, however, Jake seemed uncomfortable with going to the brightly lit fountain. He had offered up ideas of hanging out at the gazebo, or by the play structure, but each girl had her mind already made up. Emma was curious as to the reason for his apprehension.

Laney took Leah over to the fountain to make a wish. Charlie stood protectively by both girls while they tossed the loose coins that Emma had rummaged through her purse to gather for them. There was a bench nearby, so Emma and Jake made their way over to sit down and watch the trio play by the pond.

"Your nieces are really sweet, Emma."

"Thanks, Jake. It's been great to live close by and watch them grow up. I get to see them all the time." She would miss them dearly if she moved away from Juniper Falls. As if the girls knew she was talking about them, they both turned around and waved at the same time, all toothless grins and whip cream mustaches, and then resumed their wishing at the fountain.

"So, did you come here to make wishes too when you were a young boy?" For the briefest of moments Emma saw a look of pain flash in his eyes. "I'm sorry, did I say something wrong?"

Jake seemed unsure of how to respond to her and Emma felt terrible for obviously stirring up a bad memory he had probably tried to bury.

"The longer I stay in this town, the more it seems I'm dealing with my past head on," he said eventually. He paused and stood, looking off toward the pond. "My grandfather would bring me here on weekends to sail a remote-controlled boat around the pond." Emma nodded. It was still a popular pastime for children in Juniper Falls. "One day, I had seen other kids throw coins into the pond and make wishes, so I asked my grandfather for a coin too. I was five, the same age as your nieces. I closed my eyes, tossed it into the water, and excitedly told him what I wished for."

"What had you wished for, Jake?" Emma asked the question quietly. Jake seemed very vulnerable at the moment, even more so than he had been with his grandmother.

"I wished for my mom to come back to Juniper Falls so we could all be a family." Jake looked down and cringed, as though saying the words physically hurt him. "And you know what my grandfather told me? He said it was silly to waste my money and my time on a wish that couldn't possibly come true. We went home right after that. I spent the rest of the afternoon in my room while my grandparents talked." His hand clenched and he gripped the bench. "That night I overheard them on the phone with my mom. It was clear they were arguing about me."

Emma's heart ached for the little boy whose hurts carried into his adult life. No wonder coming back here was so painful. She reached over and put her hand over top of his.

Her voice came in a whisper. "Oh, Jake."

"My mom never came back to Juniper Falls. My grandfather had been right. And I've never actually told anyone about that memory before, Emma Hathaway." He smiled. "You have a way of making me lose my edge."

She blushed.

A buzzing from Jake's jacket broke the mood and Emma turned away, focusing on the girls to give him privacy. She heard him sigh and return the phone to his pocket.

"Not important?" Emma asked.

"No, it probably is. It's work. But it can wait."

Leah and Laney ran up to Jake with Charlie hot on their trail. "Jake! Jake! Come make a wish. We have two coins left. One for you and one for Auntie. Come *on*!" Pleading, each girl grabbed one of Jake's hands, pulling him forward, and leading the way back toward the fountain. It was quite the humorous sight to see, a grown man being pulled along by two little girls, and Emma suspected it was just the kind of light moment Jake needed as a reprieve from his hurtful memories. Emma started to laugh herself.

Jake managed to turn back to Emma and call desperately, "You coming?"

She stopped laughing long enough to respond. "Most definitely. I think it's time for both of us to make some new wishes."

## 25

## JAKE

He'd been in Juniper Falls just over a week, but it had been a blur. Between packing the final boxes, spending time with his grandmother, and helping Emma with the fundraiser, Jake felt like he was running a marathon of activities. Paul and Jennie had even come over last night to help him with cleaning so the house was ready to show for the Open House. He knew he could not have done it all on his own and Jake was thankful for the help. When he first arrived in Juniper Falls, he had wanted to go undetected and leave the town and his memories behind when he left with his grandmother for good. But this was no longer the case. He had reconnected with old friends and made new ones. The Juniper Falls of his past still held plenty of painful memories, but there were now reasons in the town for him to smile.

Jake only hoped this Open House did the trick. He knew his boss was beginning to lose patience with him being away from the office for so long. His vacation time was used up and a couple of clients were chomping at the bit to move forward with advertising plans. He didn't want to lose them. And yet, it felt different lately. It was hard to explain. Work didn't encompass his life as much as it used to, there were other concerns, and he just did not have the same dedication he used to. Jake was sure that when he returned to the city, he would fall back into the familiar groove again. But his first priority was to get this house sold. He could not have it sit on the market any longer. Lexington Manor's hefty admission payment would be due the day he moved his grandma, and he needed the house sale to close before then.

"Where is she?" he muttered to himself, checking the time on his phone as he waited for the real estate agent. Jake paced back and forth in his grandmother's house, looking out the front window. He wanted to be able to visit his grandmother tonight and tell her there was an offer on the house. However, the tardy real estate agent was beginning to cause him frustration and doubt about her ability to move the house off the market.

At a quarter after ten, a beige minivan pulled up along the curb.

"Finally," he muttered after the real estate agent had gotten out of her vehicle. When he'd first hired her to help sell his grandparents' house, he thought she was friendly and pretty, and the type of person who could likely sell houses. But since then, he'd noticed her lack of returning phone calls, her late notice for showings, and her unprofessional and nearly constant gum chewing. It was almost as if selling houses was merely a hobby for her.

"It's about time!" he commented once she walked through the front door.

Just take a breath and calm down, Jake, he told himself only a second later. Being brash wasn't going to sell this house any quicker. He took a step back and tried again with a calmer tone to his voice.

"This Open House was supposed to start at ten. Where are all the people?"

Leanne, the agent, took her time placing a large basket on the kitchen counter. It was as if she was completely oblivious to Jake's urgency and impatience. Casually, she removed her coat and placed it in the front closet before turning to Jake to respond.

"Sure, ten, eleven, somewhere in there. These things often don't pick up steam until after lunch, but the weather's nice, so you never know."

Jake guessed she couldn't have been bothered to have explained this earlier, even though he had been in her office several times and had had numerous phone conversations with her in the last few days. She obviously was not a detail-oriented person. He took a deep breath and tried to calmly ask for clarification. "Never know *what*? You mean it might not pick up at all? Doesn't your agency advertise, or anything?" He thought of the many advertising campaigns he had put together for realty agencies in the city.

"Sure, sure, we put a notice up in our window and on our social media pages, but small-town folk, they mostly hear about these things through word of mouth. Sometimes when people are out on a walk, they notice the Open House sign and just pop in. More often than not, those are just the curious ones, nothing serious. But hey, traffic is traffic. And if it doesn't sell, we can always drop the price again. Spring is just around the corner, it will be easier to move then, I'm sure."

Jake shook his head in disbelief and murmured to himself, "Depending on advertising through word of mouth? Who ever heard of such a careless attitude?" He still had more frustrated energy than he knew what to do with. He looked into her basket, as if he'd find some sort of miracle in there to turn this day around. "Are those your balloons? Are they to put up around the neighborhood today?"

"Well, sure," Leanne said, as she smacked her gum. "Sometimes we put them out at the lawn sign, or at the street corner." She made no move to reach for the package of balloons, so Jake shook his head and reached for them.

"May I?" He wasn't actually interested in her answer. It was the least she could do to allow *him* to advertise *her* Open House. Thankfully she nodded, so he headed out of the house, balloons in hand.

Twenty minutes later, balloons fluttered from both corner street signs. Jake was tying the last of the balloons to a real estate sign on the front lawn when Emma approached, walking Charlie along the sidewalk.

"Looks like somebody's in a party mood," she said when she was still at too much of a distance to notice Jake's mood.

He quickly tried to wipe off his scowl as he turned to her, hiding it with a smile. "No, I'm afraid this is very much *not* a party. It's an act of desperation. If my grandmother's house doesn't bring in any interest today, I don't know what I'm going to do, Emma. We haven't even had a single actually interested buyer so far. Well, except for you. Guess you're not in the market for a house, huh?" As soon as Jake had said it, he realized his insensitivity. Emma wasn't even sure if she would have a job by next week. He saw her face fall. "I'm sorry, Emma, I wasn't thinking."

"Believe me, if I had the money, this would be my ideal home. I could picture myself sitting out on that porch every evening, rocking in my chair, staring up at the stars in the sky with Charlie by my side. Isn't that right, boy? You would love it here." Emma scratched the top of his furry head and Charlie's tail wagged in what looked like his agreement.

"I wish I didn't need the full price so badly," Jake said, softening, "because I'd love for my childhood home to go to someone like you." He met her eyes so she would know he sincerely meant it. Truly, if Emma wouldn't consider a move to the city, he would love to have her here, taking care of the house, either on a temporary or permanent basis. It was too bad it wasn't possible.

She smiled back at him, understanding in her eyes.

"Why don't you come inside?" Jake asked. "I'll show you around the rest of the place now that it's all tidied up, just for fun. After all, I couldn't have gotten everything ready without you."

"It's my day off, so Charlie and I have no where we need to be. Lead the way!" Emma followed Jake toward the house. The gate was open for visitors, so Emma looped Charlie's leash around a side post, and bent to talk to him. "Now you be a good boy, Charlie. Stay here. Your paws are all muddy and would track through the house. No chasing squirrels and no barking."

Jake had become accustomed to those around him carrying

on conversations with this dog and smiled at the false strictness Emma wore to give instructions to Charlie. He even found himself patting the dog's head and adding his own, "See you soon, Charlie!" as he led the way up the steps to the front door.

She wasn't a customer, but she was still the person he needed here most to help calm his nerves.

## 26

## EMMA

Emma followed along on a tour of the house, even though she'd already seen most of it while she had been packing. But she felt bad for Jake. He really had poured his heart into getting his grandparents' house ready to sell so he could finally have Meredith closer to him. He desperately wanted it to go to a nice young couple with their life ahead of them, but now it looked like he'd have to take the first offer he got, no matter who it was. He could not afford to be particular.

Emma had to admit, the place did show well, especially now that it was cleaned up and the boxes Jake decided to keep had been stowed away in the garage until they could be moved to a storage unit in Seattle. It was even easier to picture herself living here now, with her own small amount of furniture moved in from her sister's place, sitting among her books and knick-knacks in front of the fireplace, music playing while she worked on a knitting project. Yes, it would do Meredith good to know her house would be loved by someone like Emma. She could only imagine how hard it was for Meredith to see her house about to be sold to just anyone. It wasn't just her house, it had been her and her husband's lifelong home.

Jake led the way up the curving staircase. He stopped to show Emma the guest bathroom and talked about how he and his grandfather had updated it together with new fixtures a couple of years ago on a rare visit he'd made. Emma loved the senior-friendly high arc lever faucet they had chosen. Down the hall was his grandparents' room, which sat empty and freshly painted, another similar guest room, and finally a small bedroom with a runner of wallpaper covered in boats. Emma was surprised the wallpaper hadn't been removed when the room had been painted.

"Was this your room?" she asked.

Jake heaved out a breath, like this was a difficult subject.

"I used to love sailboats. That's why, for my birthday the year I first moved here, my grandparents put up this wallpaper and gave me a remote-controlled sailboat. It's what began our weekly outings to the park. It was something we could do together, just my grandfather and me. We would sail that boat for hours. I dreamed of sailing around the world, visiting foreign countries, and having adventures. That was back when I thought that seeing the world meant having achieved some level of success." He ran his hand along the sailboat border, lost in thought or memory.

"And what does success look like for you now, Jake?" Emma hoped he wouldn't think she was getting too personal. After all, he had opened up so much to her already.

"Truth be told, I'm not a hundred percent sure anymore. I mean, I thought a well-paying job, fancy car, and high-rise apartment with a view of the city would give me a sense of satisfaction and fulfillment. I worked hard, proved to people I had what it took. Jake Rothstein wasn't some trouble-making kid from Juniper Falls anymore, you know? Honestly, I just wanted to make my grandparents proud of me. It felt like I had disappointed them for so long and I wanted to finally have them see me as a success."

"You are successful in your achievements, Jake. But are you *happy*? Do you feel like anything is missing?" Emma had been revisiting what she wanted in her life too. She tried to picture herself living in Seattle again if she had to move. Could she be happy there? "I do, sometimes." She sighed. "It feels almost pathetic to still be figuring out what I want in life. I thought I knew, but now, with Heart & Home's difficulties and people moving...I don't want my happiness to depend on other people or things."

"Once I get my grandmother to Seattle and settled in at Lexington Manor, I think that will make me happy," Jake said confidently. "In terms of missing anything in my life, sure, there are things that would complete my life. But I guess you can't have it all. I've seen too many of my colleagues try to balance work and family life. Sooner or later, they fail and one aspect or the other falls apart."

Emma wondered out loud. "Couldn't you have it all, though? Reach for the stars and dream big, too? Plenty of people do, why can't you?"

"I'm not so sure, Emma. Look, I grew up having it drilled into my head that lofty dreams aren't realistic to hold onto, and now that I've been out in the world, I have to agree. Hard work is what pays the bills, and dreams don't put food on the table. Dreaming is for people who don't know where they're headed in life. I was taught that my entire life and I've learned that it's true."

"I think dreams are about having a balance, but still being open to possibilities and allowing yourself to have hopes. It's the dreams that keep you going, and spark the fire inside you," Emma argued. She'd said it to counter Jake, but it was like she was giving herself permission to feel this way too. She could tell that Jake was thinking about it as well.

"When you tossed your coin into the fountain the other day, what did you wish for?" she asked suddenly, now watching how he would respond.

He smiled a mischievous grin. "Emma, everyone knows if you tell someone what you wished for, it won't come true."

She laughed at his response. "Okay, fair enough. But what I'm saying is you allowed yourself to dream for a moment, didn't you? And didn't it feel good?" When she'd thrown her coin in the fountain, she'd found herself dreaming about what the future might hold. The unknown scared her but energized her at the same time. And that was what dreams did.

Jake stepped closer to Emma and looked deep into her eyes. "It did feel good."

He leaned closer, and Emma's heart beat harder in her chest. Part of her knew she should put a hand up and clarify how their future plans could possibly work together before he came any closer. But the other part of her loved being this close to Jake and wanted to be much closer.

Just then, though, they were interrupted by a screech of tires outside, followed by a high-pitched yelp. The sound barely took a second to register, and Emma was racing for the door.

"Charlie!"

# 27

## JAKE

Time seemed to pass in slow motion. Jake loaded Emma's injured dog into the backseat of his car so his head was resting on Emma's lap, and he wrapped a blanket he found in the trunk over Charlie for comfort. Jake drove as quickly as he safely could to the vet, but it felt like his car was moving through wet tar. Emma gave directions from the backseat as tears streamed down her cheeks uncontrollably. She whispered to Charlie, but Jake couldn't make out what she was saying. Charlie whimpered in response and nuzzled his head against his owner.

Jake was still in shock at the veterinary clinic and couldn't even begin to imagine how Emma must feel. Charlie lay on the vet's examination table. Emma was leaning over him, resting her head gently on his chest to listen to his laboured breathing. She kept running her hands through her hair, pulling out pieces from her once-neat ponytail. Not once had she made eye contact with Jake since the accident happened. Jake felt helpless. He kept looking at Emma's tear-stained face, but such raw emotion was foreign to him, and he wasn't sure how to respond. Did she even want him there? But how could he leave her at a time like this?

Jake stood against the wall as she explained through sobs what had happened to Charlie. The vet was a man in his sixties who seemed like he had plenty of experience with trauma and distraught pet owners. He was empathetic but professional in his approach. He nodded, reassuring her that he was hearing every word she said, and began to do an assessment of Charlie's condition. An assistant was called in to give a sedative to Charlie. It provided two purposes the vet explained: to give the dog a reprieve from the discomfort so his body could relax, and to provide the stillness needed to take accurate X-rays and bloodwork.

Once settled, two assistants wheeled the table Charlie was lying on out of the assessment room to where they could do the requisite tests.

"Can I go with him?" Emma asked in a hoarse voice.

The vet put a hand on her shoulder. "It'll only be a few minutes, and in the meantime, my receptionist will help you with the paperwork."

It seemed like either a cruel or a clever method to distract a worried owner. Jake hadn't been around much trauma in his life, and while he'd never had pets, he knew Emma thought of Charlie as family. Jake had never had much in the way of family—he'd never known his father, his mother left, and he had no cousins and few friends—but he wanted to know what to do to help now.

Emma kept looking to the door where they had taken Charlie. Jake wanted to say something helpful, but words escaped him. Anything he thought of saying, he worried about how it would be taken, and he didn't want to make anything worse. He figured that saying the wrong thing would be worse than saying nothing at all. So silence filled the room for the moment.

Finally, after an agonizing amount of time that was probably less than fifteen minutes, the door opened and the vet returned, looking over the folder in his hand. Emma looked up so fast, she knocked the papers she had been filling out and pen to the floor. Jake immediately bent to pick them up, setting them back on the counter.

Her voice quivered as she asked the questions she was obviously afraid of hearing the answers to: "Is he going to be okay? When will the test results be in? Can you help him? He was in so much pain. What can I do?"

"I'll have to do a little more testing once he is awake and we can assess his comfort level. The X-rays show that he has a broken hip. We'll need to operate as soon as possible so the broken bone doesn't begin to set incorrectly, as that would create mobility issues. There's also some soft tissue damage throughout the body that will need a combination of time to heal and physiotherapy."

"How much would a surgery like that cost, Doctor?" Jake asked. He finally felt like he could help in some small way, even if it was only being the clear-headed one in the situation.

"Do you have any insurance coverage on Charlie?" the vet asked Emma.

She shook her head, looking even more devastated, if that was possible. "When I first got him, there were so many charges I wasn't expecting: the adoption fee, the shots, deworming. I couldn't afford it."

"Bottom line, Doctor," Jake said. "How much?" For the first time, Emma looked up at him. She glared. Jake was taken aback by the hostile look she gave him.

The vet spoke in a subdued, serious tone. "I'm afraid it's an extensive procedure. If it's only the hip, it would run around $2,500, and that's only if nothing else appears during surgery," he repeated. Watching this information hit Emma, Jake was sorry he had asked. The vet went on. "Plus, you'd be looking at post-operative rehabilitative care on top of the surgical cost." Apparently, his ability to deal with emotional customers did not extend to money.

Emma covered her face with her hands and let out a low guttural wail. Jake came up behind her. She still maintained that strong energy that felt like an electric fence around her, but he couldn't help himself. He lifted a hand to touch her back and comfort her.

"Emma, listen—" he started, trying to come up with any comforting words that wouldn't be a lie.

But she spun on him so quickly, she knocked his hand off of her before he could finish. "Just go. Please just go, Jake. You've done enough."

Jake choked, mid swallow. The tone of her voice and look in

her eyes felt like a punch in the gut. "What's that supposed to mean?"

"You need to get back to your precious Open House, with the pristinely-vacuumed carpets free from dog hair, and your plans to take your grandmother away from her home, no matter what she feels about it, so just go!" As words tumbled out of her mouth, she became more erratic, almost crazed, and waved her hands repeatedly toward the door as she spoke. "The sooner you go back to your precious city life, the easier it will be on everybody. I don't *want* you here and I especially don't *need* you here. Charlie and I were just great before you came along," she cried.

Before he could get a response out, let alone grasp what she was saying, she turned to the vet and begged, "Can I please go in and sit with Charlie?"

"Of course," the vet said.

Jake opened his mouth to say something, but she didn't look back to him before disappearing through the vet's door to the exam room. He knew he should make sure she at least had a ride home. Then again, he couldn't imagine her willing to take anything from him at this point.

The worst part was, he didn't know how to shoulder any more blame, even if it was misplaced. He cared about Emma and never wanted to cause her pain. He cared about Charlie too. He didn't even know what he'd done wrong.

Jake decided his only choice was to leave before he made matters worse.

## 28

## EMMA

Emma should probably have called her sister, but she didn't know how she would explain what had happened to Charlie over the phone without breaking down and being completely unintelligible with her words. She waited with Charlie until it was time for the veterinarian clinic to close. Both the vet and his assistant assured Emma that Charlie would sleep comfortably through the night with the overnight staff and if anything came up, she would be called immediately. So Emma decided to walk —taking the long way home to try and get a hold of herself. Every time she thought she was cried out, a fresh wave of tears erupted within her. She couldn't help but feel she let Charlie down.

Not meaning to, she ended up at Heart & Home, rather than her sister's house. Emma wasn't ready to walk into her place above the garage without her beloved Charlie beside her. It would just be too painful to be there alone, and she couldn't handle questions from her sister. Even though she knew her sister was always well meaning, Emma just wasn't ready to talk about what had happened yet.

Walking up to the front doors, Emma punched in her passcode on the keypad and the doors unlocked to allow her access. She made sure they locked behind her again for safety, and to avoid the escape of any patients who liked to wander through the night. There was a clean change of clothes she always kept in her locker at work. She desperately needed to freshen up and headed for the staff washroom.

It was the first time Emma had looked in a mirror all day and she was shocked at her reflection. She was a mess. Running the cold water over her face was soothing to her puffy eyes. Emma pulled out a brush from her bag and ran it through her tangled hair, pulling it back into a neat ponytail once again. Other than the sadness in her eyes and puffiness from crying, she looked much more presentable.

The reception area was empty this time of night, and Emma welcomed the quiet. The evening staff would most likely be doing their night room checks and then completing reports before their shifts were over. Usually, Emma preferred the bustle of the days at Heart & Home, but tonight she could see the appeal to the calmness of night shifts.

Geezer peered out from around a corner and down the hallway, but Emma was too distraught and lost in her own thoughts to question whether or not he was up to anything at this late hour. Geezer often took walks in the evening up and down the hallways. It helped him to fall asleep. Emma reached for a clipboard from the front counter in an attempt for distraction and to look busy so he wouldn't come over for a chat. She'd had the day off but tried to read the notes of what she'd missed to be prepared for the next morning. Everything blurred together.

She looked up at a soft *beep*. A patient's red light from their call button was flashing above the reception desk. There were interconnected red lights throughout the building, and even though Emma knew that whichever nurse was on duty would likely see it soon, she was thankful to get her mind on something else and jumped up to check on which patient was in need of assistance.

After a quick glance at the monitor, she raced down the hallway in the direction of Stan's room, grabbing a bottle of aspirin from the medical cart along the way. Stan's family had made a joint decision to place him at Heart & Home after his last heart attack. Because of the ongoing threat, he was watched closely by the staff, and had his heart rate monitored on a daily basis.

Geezer was now moving slowly with his walker near Stan's room.

"Walter—I mean, Geezer—can you please get Nurse Johannsson?" Emma's words came out in a rush as she rounded the corner and pushed through the door into Stan's room. For the second time that day, her adrenaline rose. It was easier to control her emotions when she was in her professional role, though.

The second Emma set eyes on Stan, her cause for concern increased. Stan, dressed in striped pajamas, was slumped back in his reclining chair. His right hand was clasped to his chest. Stan reached out to Emma with his other hand, his eyes wide with panic.

Emma's nursing training kicked in, and her professional demeanor took charge. She rushed toward him with a much calmer voice than she had used this afternoon when Charlie was in distress. "It's going to be okay, Stan, I'm just calling 911." She dialed on her cell phone with one hand, while feeling for Stan's pulse with the other. His pulse was racing, which was probably a good sign, but she didn't get a chance to measure it before Stan was grasping her hand to hold it.

"It's going to be okay, Stan," she repeated, reassuring him as she opened the bottle of aspirin and put one up to his mouth. "I'm here."

Stan refused to open his mouth to take the pill as Emma gave the pertinent information to the 911 operator over speaker phone. "Please Stan, I need you to chew on this pill." He swatted at her hand and the pill went flying across the floor. Then he flopped back into his chair with closed eyes.

In the distance, Emma could hear the siren from the ambulance just as Nurse Johannsson rushed into the room. "Get me the AED, stat!" Emma ordered. She opened up Stanley's pajama top and leaned over to listen for a heartbeat. Suddenly his eyes popped open and he sprung up from his chair with a surprising amount of energy, causing Emma to stumble backwards a couple of steps.

"I'm fine! I'm fine! Don't shock me!"

"It's okay Stan, please come and sit down. I need to check your vitals." Emma coaxed him back into his chair and began hooking up the monitor that Nurse Johannsson had also wheeled in with the now unneeded AED.

"You're sure she's not going to stick those zapper things onto me?" He pointed back to the nurse who was looking out the door, waiting to direct the paramedics to the right room. Other staff worked to calm the residents who had now become aware of the emergency and had come out of their rooms to see what was happening.

"No, Stan. Your pulse seems to be racing, but your coloring is good. We still need to get you to a hospital for observation, though." Emma stood up, but Stan grabbed both her hands.

"Please don't leave. You need to stay here," he pleaded with her.

"I'm not going anywhere, especially with the tight grip you have on me." Emma reassured him.

Emma could hear the sound of the paramedics wheeling a stretcher down the hallway. Finally, Patrick pushed through Stan's door with another paramedic in tow. Emma caught a glimpse of Geezer, Beatrice, and Doris all in the hallway, trying to peek in as the door opened. Nurse Johannsson was attempting to keep the group at bay. Emma could only imagine how worried his friends must be right now. Emma wished she could go and reassure them as well, but knew Stan needed her by his side more than they did right now.

"Patrick, I'm so glad you're here," Emma said. She pulled away from Stan, and this time he let go of her hands. "I just got into Heart & Home and the alarm was going off in his room. He was clutching his heart, had a racing pulse, and then went unconscious for about 30 seconds."

Patrick reached for Stan's hand, and tried to attach a blood pressure monitor to the elderly man's finger.

Stan resisted, pulling his hand away. "Wait!" Stan said, sitting up suddenly.

Patrick and Emma stared at him with baited breath, wondering if he was feeling sharp pains again.

"I think..." Stan looked up at the ceiling, or maybe to the heavens. "I think I'm feeling...better." He attempted to stand up, but Patrick gently guided him back down into his recliner. Emma knew if Stan were to stand up, his legs could buckle under him from being weak. She went to Stan's other side to lend a hand to Patrick.

"Now, now," Patrick said. "I'm not going to give you a needle or anything invasive. I just need to check your vital signs before you get moving around. Here, you're probably more familiar with the cuff." Patrick instead pulled out a blood pressure sleeve and slid it onto Stan's arm. Stan continued to resist, even though Emma herself had used a similar blood pressure cuff on Stan a thousand times.

Emma tried to help, but Stan waved a hand. "I'm fine, really. Don't you two worry about me. It must have just been heartburn from supper tonight. You really need to talk to the cafeteria staff about that fish they serve. It can really hit a guy hard late at night. All I need is an antacid and I will be as good as new. I promise." Emma had to admit, the amount of words Stan was getting out, he did sound just fine, but there was no way he could lose consciousness because of a case of heartburn. He went on. "Now, just help me with my slippers and I'll just get out of your way. Give you kids some time alone together. To talk about things. Get to know each other more."

Emma looked confused, but not for long. Something was definitely fishy, and it wasn't just the supper that was served that night. Soon understanding dawned on her, though Patrick didn't seem to catch on as quickly. He looked perplexed at Stan's instant recovery.

"I'm just going to need you to stay sitting calmly for a minute here, Mr. Richards," Patrick said, "so I can check everything over, just to be sure. After all, I wouldn't be doing my job if I left without at least taking your vitals. We may even want to take you in for observation."

"I don't think that will be necessary now, Patrick," Emma said in a monotone. She turned to Stan. "What did you think you could accomplish here, Stan? That's what I'd like to know."

Stan looked down sheepishly. Patrick continued about his business, going through routine checks on Stan's vitals, but his face had a flush to it now.

Emma left him to his work, knowing Stan was in good hands. She marched out of the room to find Geezer, Doris, and Beatrice waiting in the hallway, listening. They stumbled away as soon as she whipped the door open. Obviously, they had found a way to lure Nurse Johannsson away from their eavesdropping.

"What are you all doing here?" She had thought Stan had been playing some kind of game with her, but as it turned out, it was it all of them. They were all in cahoots together. She shook her head, another cry almost escaping. They had no idea of what she'd been through today. Normally, Emma was able to put personal issues aside and not let them affect her at work. However, she could not handle these games right now. Faking a medical emergency and making it seem like someone with a known heart condition was close to death went far beyond a simple poker game played in the sunroom.

Doris was the first to notice the stress of the day written all over Emma's face. "Oh, Emma," she said. "He's going to be fine. Don't worry about a thing, sweetheart."

Emma turned to Doris, feeling relieved for a moment—she needed Charlie to be fine—but then she realized that Doris didn't know about Charlie yet.

"Stan's a tough old bird, but maybe you should go back in and help Patrick," Doris rambled. "I'm sure he could use an extra pair of hands, just in case Stan is giving him trouble. You and Patrick make a great team, professionally speaking, of course," Doris added with a wink and a grin.

Emma looked around at the suppressed smiles on the seniors' faces. "Really? You have got to be kidding me. What have you been up to? What did you do?"

Their lips were sealed, and they played innocent. No amount of coaxing was going to break them down, but Emma wasn't having fun. In fact, she couldn't hold herself together any longer, and broke down in tears, sputtering, "I'm at the end of my rope tonight! I can't deal with your games."

A look of guilt and shame crossed all three seniors' faces.

"I'm sorry," Beatrice said quietly. "We put him up to it." They came clean about their plan to set Emma up with Patrick. "We all hated seeing you alone. We just wanted you to be happy and in love the way we all had been at one time in our lives."

Emma wanted to have patience and understanding—they were only thinking of her, after all—but it was so difficult. She should have known they would plan something and had foolishly hoped it wouldn't be anything worrisome. As it stood, her beloved Charlie was injured, she was already short money for his surgery, her job was in jeopardy, and she had made a call for an ambulance for a prank when she wasn't even on duty, which she would probably be written up for and made to pay.

Emma silently shook her head at them, not needing them to bear her burdens, and headed back into Stan's room, to finally let Patrick be on his way. The other paramedic had already wheeled the stretcher back down the hallway to load it into the ambulance. Emma tried to figure out how to explain the situation to Patrick as she walked him back toward the lobby.

"There wasn't anything wrong with Stan, was there?" she asked, to get the conversation over with.

Patrick still looked confused by the whole thing. "No, you're right. He's fine."

"And you're probably wondering why I called you in." Emma glanced away in discomfort. Maybe, in another time in her life, this might have worked. Patrick was an attractive guy. Plus, he had a heart of gold.

"Well, it had crossed my mind, yes. His vitals weren't even elevated, so I don't see how—"

"He faked it," Emma blurted, just needing to get the truth of it out there. "He knew I would call it in due to his history and external symptoms."

"I don't understand…" Patrick was so sweet and trusting, in fact, that she seemed to be having a difficult time convincing him that they'd both been duped by a group of matchmaking seniors.

Emma sighed. "Stan is part of a group of scheming seniors who think they need to find me a date. Ridiculous." She shook her head. "I'm *so sorry* for wasting your time, Patrick. I'll somehow pay for this visit myself."

Patrick's eyebrows pulled together, but then they unfolded as a smirk grew on his face. "Well, I think it's kind of cute actually, the way they look out for you. It's obvious they care about you a great deal to go to these lengths. Not that I'm condoning them faking medical emergencies, but you must admit, they are creative." Emma was rolling her eyes, about to explain how not-cute this all seemed to her at the moment, but then Patrick went on in a thoughtful tone. "Would it really be so bad, though? Giving them what they want? Let's humor the old timers and go out on a date."

Emma's eyes popped open in surprise. "Oh. Well, no, of course it wouldn't be bad, Patrick." She fiddled with the lock to the outside door, uncomfortably. "You're so kind to offer to do that, but really—"

Patrick put his hand over Emma's and helped her turn the lock so he could leave the building. "I'm not being kind, Emma. I think it could be fun."

Emma looked down, another wave of sadness overtaking her. "Any other time, you might be right, Patrick, but I'm afraid I wouldn't be good company at the moment. My dog, Charlie, he was hit by a car today, and I don't know if he'll…" Her throat constricted and cut off her words.

Patrick touched her on the shoulder. "I'm so sorry to hear that, Emma. Please let me know if there's anything I can do. I'd be happy to be here as your friend, take you out to get your mind off of things. It doesn't have to be a 'date' date."

Emma looked up at him. His eyes were full of understanding. "Thanks, Patrick. Thanks for understanding."

"Really, Emma. Let me help in this small way. Even if I'm just someone you can talk with about all you're going through, I'm happy to do it."

The idea of being anywhere other than her job and her home, where she'd feel a constant Charlie-sized hole, actually seemed tempting. Emma reluctantly agreed, and then waved to Patrick as he drove off. She headed back inside to see the four scheming senior residents all hovering near the front counter. They diverted their eyes guiltily, not wanting to give away that they had been watching Emma and Patrick's conversation.

"You guys," she said, trying for a stern tone, but it came out more desperate, "calling in a medic, it costs Heart & Home money—money we don't have. I'd been hoping for a head day nurse position, and if the boss finds out this was all because of me..." They looked at each other with wide eyes. "I'll probably be charged for the visit and can't even pay for it out of my own pocket because Charlie needs urgent medical care that I already can't afford."

"Charlie?" they all exclaimed.

But Emma didn't have it in her to explain again. She wiped away a new bout of tears, and simply told them, "Yes, Charlie," in a voice that showed the depth of her devastation. She covered her face with her hands and let out a few more sobs. The residents all cared for her, she knew that, but she couldn't help shrugging them off when they tried to rub her shoulders in comfort. She didn't blame them, she really didn't, but she also didn't have it in her to talk anymore. Eventually, they took the hint and wandered back to their rooms.

When she looked up, expecting to find herself alone, she was surprised to see Geezer, still leaning against the counter watching her.

"We didn't know. About Charlie," he said after a long silence.

"I know you didn't." Emma sighed. "I'm sorry, Geezer. I shouldn't have lost my temper with you folks. It's just been such a long day."

Geezer waddled closer with his walker and slid a fatherly arm around Emma's shoulder. She leaned into him, not realizing how much she needed someone to take care of her right now, until she felt his comforting hug. "It's a helpless feeling when someone you love is hurting. You just want to take away their pain and you can't."

She nodded into his shoulder. The old man pulled out a checkered hanky and handed it to her. Emma graciously accepted his gesture.

"You know, Emma, even though I had to say goodbye to my Marion far too early in life, I wouldn't have traded that time with her for anything. Loved ones bring us such joy. We know how much you love Charlie and the joy he brings you and all of us here. We just want the best for you, because you give so much of yourself to everyone else. All we want is for you to be happy, my dear."

Emma sniffled into the handkerchief. "I know, thank you, Geezer. Well then, you will be pleased to know that I have agreed to a date with Patrick."

Geezer pulled back. "You what?"

"I said I'd go out with him. As friends," she added. "We're not talking about true love here. Just an evening out together."

"Maybe not yet we're not." He winked and pulled her back in for a hug. "I have a good feeling that love is just around the corner for you, Emma Hathaway. And I have a good feeling about Charlie, too."

Emma didn't exactly have a hundred percent confidence in Geezer's words, but she needed to hear them badly enough that she didn't argue.

# 29

# JAKE

After being pushed from the clinic, Jake had returned to the house. He spent the rest of the afternoon in a daze, letting the realtor field questions from some people who had stopped by. When the Open House finally ended at six, he had popped all the balloons, grabbed his computer bag, locked up, and gotten in his car to go for a drive to clear his head. An hour later, he'd found himself on the highway back to Seattle.

The apartment didn't have the same feeling of comfort and home that his grandparents' house or Emma did, but it was his. When he arrived, he felt like he hadn't been there in weeks, even though it had only been a few days. The place seemed so empty and quiet.

There was still nothing in the fridge, but he didn't have an appetite anyway. He had stopped several times along the way to pick up gas station coffee and he was sure all that caffeine with no food in his stomach would soon be burning a hole in his gut. He popped a couple of antacids to be proactive. Catching a glimpse of himself in the hallway mirror, he noticed his hair was dishevelled and his clothes were rumpled from an excruciatingly long day, but he didn't care about those either. Jake slumped into his leather couch and put his feet—shoes still on—up on his coffee table.

He was past the point of caring about much today.

Apparently, he was doing everything wrong with his grandmother, again. He'd messed up any warmth of relationship he thought he had been creating with Emma, and now, on top of everything else, it looked as though she blamed him for Charlie getting hurt.

How could everything unravel like this in one day? And the most irritating part was the way he had chosen to handle it—by running away, not facing the situation head on like he should have done. But she'd wanted him out. Wasn't the best thing for him to do—to respect her decisions?

Jake was more than disappointed in himself. Deep down, he knew that he wasn't responsible for Charlie getting hurt. He had started to warm up to her pup and would never have wanted any harm to come to him. It had probably been a squirrel that caused him to bolt. Jake had seen firsthand how crazy Charlie got for squirrels. But still, Jake couldn't shake off the guilt, not for one second. Knowing that Emma was so hurt and worried, he should have known better and not have taken her attack toward him so personally. She was speaking out of fear and worry, but even knowing that didn't make her words sting any less. Why would she ever want to see him again? All his feelings of insecurity and rejection from his childhood reared their ugly faces and he had buckled and run away again.

Then again, being back in Seattle might be a good thing, he rationalized. It took him away from Juniper Falls, away from the pain that he shouldn't have allowed himself to be open to in the first place. Besides, work was piling up; It wasn't as if he was running away to nowhere in particular. He had responsibilities. Yes, that's exactly what he needed to do: throw himself back into his work. After all, Emma didn't want to see him again, that was obvious. And he did not want to cause her any more pain than he already had. There was no fixing what had happened today.

Jake pulled his computer bag onto the couch beside him, determined to get back to his real life, the one he had made for himself and that he had been proud of. He pulled out the papers from the campaign he had been working on during bits and pieces of his spare time while he was in Juniper Falls. Out fell one of the poster layouts from the Valentine's Day dance. *Sweetheart Serenade.* Guess there would be no dance for him to attend now. How had he managed to let himself get so emotionally caught up and invested in Juniper Falls again anyway? He thought of his times with Emma at the house. How she just gave of herself to everyone around without expecting anything in return.

Stop tormenting yourself, he thought to himself. Just focus on your work and leave your heart out of it.

As Jake laid out the contents of the file, he noticed a folder missing and hoped he hadn't left it back at his grandparents' house. He searched for it with a fervor born of fixation and finally found it within one of the various compartments in his bag. Jake opened the folder, breathing a calming sigh of relief, and was startled when some envelopes slid out and onto the floor. They were unrecognizable until he picked them up and saw the handwriting and return address on the other side. These were the envelopes from the roller-top desk he'd taken from his grandmother's house that first night when Emma had been over helping him pack. He'd stuffed them away to look at later, but then he'd forgotten all about them.

Taking a closer look, a couple of the envelopes had his mother's name and return address in the top right corner. Each had been addressed to his grandparents, but he somehow knew they were about him. The rest of the envelopes were unopened for Jake's mother. *"RETURN TO SENDER"* was scribbled across them in red ink, never having been delivered.

He sat back into the couch, settling in to read each one, and figure out why his grandparents hadn't told him about these returned letters. They had spoken less and less of his mom over the years, in fact, and he had to know why. Opening the first envelope, his body tensed. Was this really the day to read them, after all that happened? He certainly was a glutton for punishment, wasn't he? But curiosity got the better of him. Even though he was pretty confident on what they would contain—his mom's angry words toward her parents—he had to read them for himself. Why they had kept her son from her and why wouldn't they let her come to see him? He hoped for possibly even a response to his grandparents' complaints at being saddled with looking after him.

His began to skim, but nothing made sense. Jake flipped back to the beginning of the first page and started again with more focus.

*Dear Mom and Dad,*
   *Thanks for your invitation, but I'll be busy over Christmas...*

This, Jake expected. It's the same way he had replied to each of his grandma's last three Christmas invitations before his grandfather had passed away. Still, the words felt so different, so cold coming from his mom. Jake continued to read.

*I wish you would stop with the guilt and the invitations and telling me how much Jake wants to see me. He's just a kid. He doesn't know what he wants, and we all know he's better off with you. As you kept saying, I need to get my life together. God, I should have had that phrase tattooed on my arm so you wouldn't waste your breath on giving me lectures. Now that I'm not saddled with a kid, I can have the freedom to be me, live my dreams. I was never meant to be a mom. You know it and I know it. Dad definitely knew it too. Why should I have to change my ways just to be "the mom Jake needs" as you put it the last time we talked? I appreciate you taking him. Honestly, I do. I'll try and send some money once in a while to help out. For now, things are a little tight. I'm in between jobs and have to move out of my place by month's end. It wouldn't be good for me to visit now. We would just start arguing again, going in circles, not getting anywhere.*
   *I'll try to send you a letter when I get to a new place.*
   *Let Jake know that he'll be fine.*

*Your daughter,*
*Olivia*

Jake sat back into the couch, not understanding, or at the very least not believing what he was reading. All those years, he'd been certain his grandparents were keeping him from going to see his mom because they were controlling and angry. It sounded like it was actually the other way around. His mom came across like the controlling and angry one.

Jake's grandparents had always, even when he was too young for it, been unflinchingly honest with him about who his parents were. His mom had moved to Oregon shortly after he was born. She returned to Juniper Falls when he was four and left shortly after. Without him. His dad hadn't even stuck around that long. There was one specific memory of a time in the first grade when Jake had come home and called his grandma "Mom." All the other kids talked about doing things with their moms. Jake badly wanted that too. He had been bothered by his grandma's quick response to correct him. His grandpa had taken him to the lake to explain why he should save that title for his real mom.

Jake opened the second letter, and as he read it—more excuses, more anger and bitterness—he felt like he was in grade school all over again, only just now learning about some basic understanding of his life.

He remembered gardening with his grandmother once when he was about ten. He had been giving her grief about having to work when all he wanted to do was go play with friends. He told her he wouldn't have to pull weeds if he ran away and lived with his mom. Instead of his grandmother getting angry with his clear disrespect, she looked sad, but quickly regained her composure and diverted away from the conversation, getting his grandfather to show him how to prune boxwood cedars evenly. What she really must have been thinking was that his mom wouldn't have wanted him around, whether he was willing to pull weeds or not.

Jake picked up one of the sealed letters that had been marked *"RETURN TO SENDER"* and pried open the glue of the envelope that, by the postmark, was from when he was in middle school.

*Dear Olivia,*

*We hope this letter finds you well. The weather has been mild and I am noticing the crocus are beginning to bloom, a sure sign that spring is around the corner.*

*Your dad and I would love to have you come for a visit. We worry about you and haven't heard from you in a long time. Jake is growing as fast as the weeds in my garden. His birthday is next month, and we would love to have his party when you could be here.*

*I have included some recent photos. He loves to play baseball now and looks so grown up in his uniform. Your dad and I are proud of how hard he is working on his pitching. There is also a newspaper clipping from the Juniper Falls Times when Jake won the award for playing piano in the festival last month. He has your father's love of music.*

*I really wish you could see him, Olivia. Your son misses you dearly. I know we have our differences, but we would put them aside if you would come home for a visit.*

*Love,*
*Mom*

An hour passed and Jake read them all, tearing open letters almost frantically as his perception of his grandparents, his childhood, his *life* fell apart around him in flutters of paper.

He had been running from and pushing away his grandparents for all these years. He thought somehow that making himself a big success in the city would have earned their approval and somehow earned him his mother back. All those years his grandparents had not been honest with him, not about his mother, but he saw now it had only been to protect him from getting hurt and feeling the sting of her abandonment. He wished they would have communicated this to him, to have harshly told him his mother wasn't coming back or even to have talked about it when he became an adult. Hiding feelings, it seemed, ran in the family. He tended to do the same thing.

Jake brewed himself a coffee. Even though he was exhausted,

he knew sleep would not come easily. Sipping the coffee, he stared out the window overlooking the lights of the city. What did Jake Rothstein truly want from his life?

Whether he was energized by the coffee or by his revelation after reading the letters, Jake wasn't sure. It was going to be a long night. There were so many thoughts swirling around in his head and he needed to sort them out the best way he knew how. He grabbed a pad of lined paper from his bag and began to write. He wrote of his feelings, questions he had, and possible directions for his life.

Finally, hours later, with bleary eyes but a clearer mind, Jake put down the pen. He now knew what needed to happen and he had a plan for it. He only hoped those in his life felt the same way. He blinked blearily, wincing at the sunlight flashing on the water. He realized with a start that it was already morning. And with the new day came new opportunities.

He reached for his phone.

His boss's receptionist picked up on the second ring, and Jake's heart beat a little faster as he prepared what he was going to say.

"Morning, Lisa, it's Jake Rothstein. Can I please speak to Mr. Thomson?"

The talkative receptionist rambled on for a few sentences about how much Mr. Thomson has been looking forward to Jake's call, and how he'd been missed at the office this week. She talked about how everyone had gone out for drinks to this new place around the corner from their office, and the mussels were to die for. Jake tried to sound engaged in the conversation, but his mind was elsewhere and eventually the receptionist had run out of things to catch him up on. The conversation became obviously one sided, and finally, Lisa put him through to his boss.

"Hi, yeah, it's Jake," he said when Mr. Thomson picked up. "I was going to come in for the meeting, but it turns out I can't make it after all."

"Jake, you've missed the last three team meetings with this family situation you've been so busy with. We've been waiting on your input." Mr. Thomson was generally a pretty understanding boss, but Jake could hear in his tone that he was almost out of patience with him. After all, behavior like this was completely out of character for Jake.

Still, he had to do what he had to do. "I'm sorry, sir, I am, but I won't be able to get in there at all today."

"You're still out of town with this family matter?" Mr. Thomson sounded like he was using all of his strength to force some extra patience and understanding.

"Well, no. I'm in Seattle, but I have to head back again as soon as possible."

"You're in Seattle, but you're not coming in? Even for our team meeting? Jake, I'm concerned. What is going on?" he asked.

"Something's come up. I've already emailed all my work over to Lisa so you can have it for the meeting." Jake had worked incredibly hard to move up in the advertising company. It was something he was truly good at. But with everything else going on in his life, this job just felt inconsequential in the big scheme of things. "I'm sorry, sir, but I need to devote my energy to other matters at present."

Mr. Thomson went silent. He could obviously not believe what he was hearing from his top associate. Jake knew he was letting down his boss, but if he didn't take this leap now, he would be letting down himself. He thanked his employer profusely for all he had done to teach Jake the ropes in advertising. And then Jake gave his resignation.

Mr. Thomson seemed confused by the sudden change but wished Jake the best after he explained the reasons behind his change of heart. Jake clicked off his phone and crossed off the first item from his to-do list. Taking a deep breath, he picked up the Lexington Manor brochure from the coffee table and dialed the number on the back.

# 30

# EMMA

On Friday, Emma visited Charlie at the veterinary hospital before and after her shift at Heart & Home. She'd given authorization to have the surgery to repair his broken hip. It had been completed and now Charlie was limited to cage rest, oxygen therapy, and intravenous fluids—a mix of painkillers, anti-inflammatories, steroids, and an antibiotic for any potential infection from the cuts. Emma was thankful her dog was being monitored constantly by a knowledgeable team, however, it broke her heart seeing him just lying in the cage staring up at her with those pitiful eyes. She couldn't explain to him that the confinement and needles were for his own good.

Saturday morning it was particularly difficult to be cheerful during her shift at work. Emma's heart was with Charlie. Usually, Charlie spent his Saturdays greeting families that came to visit the seniors. Many had questions as to why their beloved dog wasn't at the front doors of Heart & Home.

As soon as Emma's shift was done, she rushed over to the veterinary hospital, knowing it would be closed for visiting on Sunday. After she had spent time with Charlie, Dr. Franklin, the vet who had been working the day she first brought him in, called Emma into his office. When he closed the door behind her and he sat down behind his mahogany desk, Emma could tell it was news he would rather not have to share with her.

He looked down at Charlie's chart, lowering his progressives and looked up at Emma from above the rim of his glasses. "We ran another MRI and CT scan on Charlie. Emma, unfortunately, he hasn't been healing like we had hoped and I needed a further look. We discovered there are two separate areas along his spine where there's pockets of fluid building up."

Spinal fluid pressure charts and nerve diagrams flashed though her mind. "So you need to operate again?" she asked with as much calm as she could muster.

"Well, we don't have anyone locally who is trained for this type of operation. Charlie would need to be transferred to a neurology specialist in Seattle for his best chance at full recovery." Dr. Franklin handed Emma a pamphlet outlining the surgery options and potential risks.

The words seemed to blur together as Emma tried to focus and read through the tears that were now falling from her eyes. The vet handed her a tissue box conveniently located on his desk for moments such as these and patted her hand.

She made out some key words such as *"paralysis"* and *"possible fatality"* but couldn't quite process them. After a few moments of quiet, Dr. Franklin added gently, "The risks are much greater if Charlie does not have the surgery, but even with the surgery, partial or temporary paralysis is a risk." He adjusted his glasses. "I know this is a lot to take in all at once, Emma."

Emma would do anything for Charlie, but the medical costs were adding up. She had already spent what she'd been saving for a future house down payment.

"So in terms of cost, what would I need to pay for Charlie's surgery, Dr. Franklin?"

"I'm sorry to say this, Emma, but it would run in the range of around $5,000, and then there's the physical therapy and post-operative care costs depending on how his recovery progressed. I know it's hard, but you may need to think about Charlie's quality of life and consider other options."

Emma's face fell at the news. She didn't know how she could put together that much money, but at the same time, she could not bear to see Charlie in such pain. Putting the pamphlet into her bag, she quietly thanked the doctor, and she left the office, desperately needing a walk to soothe her heart's ache.

Emma looped around the same blocks, over and over, wandering town in circles. She carried Charlie's leash in her pocket, rubbing her fingers over the rough material and sniffling away tears.

Dr. Franklin said he would need a firm answer by Wednesday morning so that he could schedule the specialist for Charlie's surgery before the swelling progressed too far. Memories of Charlie running in the park, chasing squirrels and butterflies, kept playing over in her mind. She owed it to him to give him the best life. After all, he had been there for her through some pretty lonely times. But there was no way that she could get that kind of money. Her own job had an unclear future, especially with the stunt Doris' crew had pulled on Thursday night. Amy and Connor had just planned a kitchen remodel for Amy's catering business and the start-up costs for the business were more than they had anticipated. Jobs in Seattle paid more, but costs of living were also higher. But maybe the bank would give her a loan, knowing she had a higher salary and some job security.

Emma just needed someone to talk to about all of this. Her mind shot to Jake. But she pushed the thought away. She knew how she had treated him the day of Charlie's accident was wrong. She had said some terrible things. Emma had tried to go talk to him after she had calmed down and sorted out her thoughts, but he had already left town. Meredith told her he had gone back to Seattle, back to his job. He would be coming back when it was time to move her into Lexington Manor. The sorrow on the old woman's face, both for her own sake and for Emma's, had been enough to have Emma fleeing the room with an excuse to compose herself,

At the first sign of problems, he ran away, Emma thought angrily, refusing to feel anything else. No, she could not depend on Jake Rothstein for anything, especially advice about loved ones.

Lost in her thoughts, Emma had not realized where her walk

had taken her until she rounded the corner, and she froze. She was standing where Charlie had been hit by the car. Her mind flashed back to the trauma of that day and she couldn't help but let out a sob reliving the pain. Get a hold of yourself, she scolded herself. After all, she was a nurse. She was used to dealing with sad moments, especially working at Heart & Home. But this pain was hers, and that made it much more difficult to handle and impossible to compartmentalize.

Emma continued walking and as she got closer to the Rothstein house, she saw the FOR SALE sign on the front lawn had been taken down. It seemed like Jake was getting everything he ever wanted, and Emma was losing all of her heart's desires. It didn't seem fair. She sighed to herself but couldn't think about any more loss. It was already too much to bear.

Inside her purse, Emma's phone dinged. She looked down and was reminded that her "not a date" with Patrick was tonight. While she didn't feel much like being with anybody, maybe he would at least provide the listening ear she needed. Wiping her eyes, she headed back to her sister's house. Lately, Emma had been spending more time in Amy's home than in her own little apartment above the garage. It was just too lonely to be there without Charlie, every silent moment a reminder that he was in pain, lying alone in a kennel, and not with her, but tonight she didn't have much time to get upstairs and get ready.

Emma decided to at least make herself presentable for her date. Maybe she could do this one thing right.

An hour later, Emma walked down the stairs and into her sister's kitchen wearing her favorite blue dress. Her hair was curled into big waves, and she'd even applied a little mascara and lip gloss. The old saying was true: making yourself look better on the outside really could lift your spirits, if only a little.

At the sight of a mess in the kitchen and towers of vegetables in various states of preparation, a wave of guilt hit her. Her sister's once pristine kitchen now looked like a tornado had run through it. Connor stood at the counter chopping onions and Amy rushed back and forth between the stove and the island, which was covered with trays of hor d'oeuvres.

It took her one second of staring. Then two.

She had completely forgotten! Amy had asked her to lend a hand in the kitchen with final preparations for catering the dance. It was only a few days away and the weekend offered more time and hours of work without school and work schedules. There had been so much to do, and everyone had picked up the slack for Emma's lack of involvement since Charlie's accident. Even the residents had taken over making decorations and invitations all on their own.

Emma felt terrible. It wasn't fair that other people had needed to shoulder the workload for her idea. She had been a neglectful sister, a bad employee, and a poor excuse for a pet owner. The one guy she thought she might have trusted, she'd pushed away and pretty much blamed for Charlie's accident. She felt like a failure in every aspect of her life, and while she truly was happy that her sister was getting to pursue her dream, Emma felt overwhelmed with her own guilt.

Poor Patrick. She was not going to be enjoyable company for him tonight. No one can really enjoy being in someone else's pity party.

And she really should be staying to help.

"Oh, you guys," she said, and her sister and Connor finally noticed her presence. "This was stupid, planning to go out with Patrick tonight. You offered to do the food for the dance, and now I'm not even helping? I'll call and cancel right now."

Emma held up her phone to dial, but Amy snatched it from her hand and set it on the counter. "You will do no such thing. You deserve a Saturday night out after everything that's happened. And, Emma, oh my! You look gorgeous, honey. Doesn't she look gorgeous, Conner?"

"Beautiful, yes," he said half-heartedly, sounding worn. Emma felt a new wave of guilt knowing that her absence had led to him being roped him into cooking with Amy after a long week at work.

"You're going to sweep that boy off his feet, Emma," Amy said.

Emma nervously slid a curl behind her ear. "Sweeping

anybody off their feet was certainly not my intention. Do I look too fancy?" She fiddled with her dress. "I just thought getting dressed up might make me feel a little better."

Amy stroked Emma's arm. "Oh, Ems. You look perfect for your date tonight." She shared a look with Conner. "We know you're sad about Charlie, but tonight will do you some good. You'll see."

Emma looked away; she hadn't been able to bring herself to tell Amy about the costs of Charlie's treatment and Amy's hopeful encouragement just hurt. Tears formed in her eyes.

"Oh, sweetie, don't cry. Your mascara."

Emma dabbed at her eyes with a tissue. Just then, her phone vibrated on the counter, and Patrick's name flashed across the screen. Emma reached for it.

"Hello?" The one good thing about all the distractions in her life was that she didn't feel nervous in the least about taking Patrick's call.

"Emma, it's Patrick. Listen, I really hate to do this, but I'm going to have to reschedule our dinner. They just called me into work."

"Oh no. I hope nothing's wrong." There were only four full-time paramedics in Juniper Falls, and even so, they didn't normally keep very busy. However, in the case of an accident near the highway, or a house fire, or something major—then, suddenly, there weren't enough paramedics.

"No, no. It's just that Darren has been fighting a sore throat. He thought he'd feel better by tonight, but he doesn't feel well enough to be on duty all night. I really hate to cancel with such late notice like this."

"Oh, I completely understand, Patrick. Really, it's fine. In fact, it's probably for the best. I hope it's not too late of a night for you."

"I'll be fine," he said. "Hopefully we can reschedule soon. After Valentine's?"

"Okay, well, thanks for letting me know." Emma smiled as she hung up. This really was for the best. Even though it had been good for her to get dressed up, now she could stay home, help Amy, and not have to worry about keeping up a conversation or putting on a cheery face.

She turned to Amy and Connor, rubbing her hands together. "This couldn't have worked out better. Patrick got called in to cover someone's shift, so I'm all yours." She looked down at her blue dress, but decided an apron would cover it nicely, as she didn't want to waste anymore time. "Put me to work."

Amy and Conner shared another look. Emma could tell they felt bad for her, but then Conner passed Emma an armful of vegetables to cut up, and said, "Phew. I thought you'd never ask."

# 31

## JAKE

Jake left Seattle in his rear-view mirror. He had managed to tie all the loose ends up neatly over the weekend. In fact, he was surprised with how quickly things seemed to fall into place once he had made up his mind. He saw it as confirmation that the decisions he had made were the right ones.

Driving into Juniper Falls, he watched the sun disappear behind the tall cedars. The sky cast vibrant oranges, pinks, and purples as it moved from day to dusk. Approaching the town limits, Jake smiled with a fresh optimism. This was a new chapter, and he was ready to write on the blank pages.

He passed a speed limit sign as he entered the town. There it was. He eased his foot off the accelerator. Now why hadn't he seen that before? Cruising down the main drag, Jake looked at the small shops, as if seeing them for the first time. Yes, Juniper Falls had charm. He casually waved at a man and his son crossing the street. They waved back, and the man offered a nod as though he and Jake were old friends. No longer did Jake see himself as a stranger here. He belonged. And that's really what he had wanted all along—to have a home where he could belong.

Pulling into Heart & Home, Jake parked his vehicle in the guest parking lot. He walked along the pathway through the gardens with a large bouquet of red roses in his arms. Entering the front foyer, he came across Geezer who was cruising past him with the walker, while a nurse was in hot pursuit. Jake chuckled at the old man's determination. "You've got this, Geezer. She's miles behind!" The elderly man turned around and gave a big thumbs up, while the nurse who passed Jake seemed slightly out of breath and annoyed at the encouragement he was giving the old man.

Pam, the strict woman who had been harsh with Jake on his visit two weeks ago had her head down as he approached. Her hair wasn't pulled back today, and it made her look a good ten years younger. "Great to see you, Pam. Love the hair. I'm just dropping in to have a visit with my grandma. She in her room?"

Pam popped her head up from behind the desk to see who had been talking to her. She was clearly shocked to see it was Jake. She scanned every inch of him like he was a different person. And he did feel different, casually dressed in jeans and a plaid shirt, carrying the largest bouquet of roses he had ever held. But he knew the biggest difference was the look on his face, one of peace and contentment.

"Oh, Mr. Rothstein, I've got all the paperwork done for your grandmother to leave with you to Lexington Manor. I'm sure you know she only agreed if she could be here for the dance tomorrow night."

Jake was already part way down the hall, headed toward his grandma's room. He called back. "Thanks Pam, but there's been a change of plans." He left the administrator with her mouth hanging open in confusion.

The door to his grandma's room was partly closed and it was dark inside. Jake knocked lightly, hoping he wasn't waking her. "Yes?" She responded quietly.

Jake nudged opened the door and saw his grandma sitting in her chair with a dim lamp lit beside her on the end table. She was holding a photo of his grandpa, running her hands along his face. She looked so sad. Why hadn't he noticed this before? Emma had tried to tell him, but he had been too stubborn to stray from his plans and what he thought was best for her.

"Grandma?"

She looked up and let her eyes adjust to the bright

fluorescent light coming from the hallway. Jake walked in so she could make out his face, and it was then she seemed to notice the flowers in his arms. Her face lit up in surprise, and then she started to cry.

"Jake, you remembered? After all these years, you remembered!"

Jake set down the flowers gently in her lap. She buried her face in their fragrance. "Every year, the day before Valentine's Day, Grandpa would bring you two dozen long-stemmed roses. He always said that a woman as special as you deserved her own day to be shown how much she was loved. You were too important to him to wait until a day when everyone got roses. I'm sorry I missed bringing them to you last year." His eyes glistened with tears as he bent down and kissed her cheek. "Thank you, Grandma."

"Thank you for what, Jake? For coming with you to Seattle? I'm almost done packing my things, and we can leave first thing Wednesday, after the dance."

Jake reached out and held her hand, setting the photo of his grandpa carefully on the table. "No, Grandma. You aren't going anywhere. Heart & Home is where you should live. Juniper Falls is your home. You want to stay here, right?"

His grandma's face looked concerned and her brows pulled together in confusion. "But what about moving me closer to you? What about your plans?"

"They were *my* plans. And they should have been *our* plans. I'm sorry for not listening to you. I'm sorry for so many things. You tried to protect me over the years and I never understood until now what you and Grandpa gave me. You gave me your love and you gave me a home. And now it's my turn to look after you. Let's unpack these things, because you're staying here, if that's what you really want."

She squeezed his hand tightly. "Yes, Jake, that's what I really want. But promise me you will drive out here from Seattle more to see me?"

"I can't promise that to you." He saw her face fall in disappointment, but he smiled in return. "I can't promise that because I don't live in Seattle anymore. Grandma, I'm coming home."

Her face tilted up, and he watched as the realization of what he said bloomed on her face. "Well, welcome home, my dear boy. Welcome home."

Both grandson and grandmother held each other tight in an embrace that said more than words ever could.

Music drifted into the room and they both lifted their heads to listen to where it was coming from. "Oh, that's right. Everyone is meeting in the sunroom to practice for the dance tomorrow."

"Well, shall we?" And Jake wheeled his grandma's chair out the door and in the direction of the music.

The staff had pushed tables to the sides of the sunroom to make space for a makeshift dance floor. Jake noticed the record player from his grandparents' house, sitting on a table. Stan had the albums spread out and chose another one to put on the turntable. Jake guessed the elderly man had been designated DJ for the evening. *The Chattanooga Choo Choo* got the seniors moving, as the Andrews Sisters belted out the words.

Jake wheeled his grandma into the center of the room, moving her wheelchair back and forth, around and around dancing to the song. She giggled and sang along. Geezer chased a nurse around the dance floor with his walker, but rather that being upset with him, she seemed to quite enjoy the merriment. She probably felt having Geezer go in circles was far easier to deal with than chasing him down hallways. Doris swayed back and forth in the arms of one of the residents Jake did not know.

After a while, a nurse came into the sunroom and over to the record player. She lifted the arm off the turning record and the music stopped. "Sorry, everyone, but it's time to get ready for bed. We have the medicine cart coming around, so let's call it an evening and head back to our rooms." She was met with some boos and hisses from the residents, but all in good humor.

Jake helped his grandma get settled in her room. He set the roses in a vase so she could see them from her bed, and he tucked her in for the night. As he was leaving, he turned off the light.

"Jake?"

"Yes, Grandma?"

"I love you."

"Love you, too, Grandma." His voice cracked and he was glad no one was in the hallway to see him wiping the tears away from his face as he walked toward the front doors.

## 32

## EMMA

The entire town of Juniper Falls had really pulled together for the Valentine's Day fundraiser for Heart & Home. The mayor and council had waived the rental fee for the Community Hall so there was plenty of room for all of the guests to dance. Paul had his police department and the guys from the fire hall work on putting up all the decorations that Jennie's school children made, and the seniors had put together. Emma was grateful to Mr. Willoughby for giving her two paid days off from working at Heart & Home to focus on final preparations for the fundraiser.

Walking into the hall, Emma was stopped, awestruck, by what she saw. She'd led most of the setup, but seeing it complete, and with the overhead fluorescent lights turned off, gave the room an enchanted ambiance. Thousands of tiny white lights twinkled from every surface of the walls and ceiling. There were red, white, pink, and purple hearts in every nook and cranny. And there was glitter, lots of glitter. Strung across the black curtains on the stage in silver and red metallic lettering were the words, "*SWEETHEART SERENADE.*" This was, without a doubt, absolutely magical.

She had chosen a simple red A-line dress with spaghetti straps and a flowing skirt that fell just above her knees. It was a dress that was made for dancing if she only felt like it. Emma knew she needed to put her heart into tonight for the sake of the residents, and to show her appreciation to everyone that made the evening possible. The dance, decor, and the food were everything she had imagined for the evening. It was almost enough to distract her from her grief about Charlie. Almost.

Guests were beginning to arrive. Colby had been shuttling the senior residents to the community hall in the Heart & Home van. He had a couple more trips to make and then all the residents who wanted to attend would be there. Tables were set up along the side wall for those just wanting to sit and enjoy the music and all the festivities.

Emma walked over to survey the platters of food. Amy had really outdone herself. People were gushing about the sweet chili meatballs, and Amy kept having to refill the cheesecake bites even though the event wasn't in full swing yet. Everything looked spectacular—from the pinwheel sandwiches to the fruit kebab tree—and by the looks of the steady stream of people walking through the door, the whole town was turning out, happy to pay the twenty-dollar admission in support of a good cause. It was the first time Heart & Home had charged for one of their community events, and Emma didn't know if it really would be enough to keep the residence open, but she hoped, if need be, God would somehow multiply it.

"Amy, you are amazing!" she said, as soon as her sister had a spare moment. "This all looks fantastic. I knew you were talented, but you have really upped your game tonight. I just know your catering business will be successful after all this. People will be talking about it for weeks!" Emma walked around the back of the table to give her sister a hug. Without Amy, this night would have been impossible to pull off with such short notice.

"Well, having the youth centre volunteer their teens to help serve food and punch has really been a huge help." Amy looked over to see teens interacting with the seniors. Geezer was showing a group one of his card tricks, Doris stood at the punch table teaching a couple of the kids how to pour from the ladle without dripping punch everywhere, and Stan had a teen at the DJ table, deep in a conversation about rap music. Emma made a mental note to look into developing a connection between the two generations through some activities at Heart & Home and the youth centre in the future.

Pam had done her part for the fundraiser, too, by organizing a silent auction. Many local businesses had donated items, as well as a few of the seniors themselves. Meredith had numerous knit hats and sweaters she had put up for bid. Geezer loved to whittle and donated a couple of wooden carved birds to the cause. Walking down the aisle, looking at the bidding items, Emma noticed one item that stood out. It was a remote-controlled boat. She ran her hand over the hull, noticing the fine detailing, and thinking of Jake's stories of his sailboat. Yes, this would surely catch the eye of some lucky bidder.

Before long, the dance was in full swing. The senior residents were a hoot to watch. Stan played a variety of big band swing music and various oldies, but every so often he threw in a modern song for the "youngins" as he called them.

At one point, Doris and Geezer got the whole room involved in the Chicken Dance—never mind that Geezer had to somehow accomplish it around his walker. Beatrice coaxed every guy in the room to dance with her, whether he was married or not, and even Connor got dragged out onto the dance floor. Emma watched the youth and middle-aged residents of Juniper Falls dance and enjoy time with the seniors who had come before them and their loved ones.

Catching a glimpse of Pam dancing with Andy the tech guy, Emma smiled. She was pretty sure there was something starting between them. It was sweet.

Even blind-date-Danny had made it to the dance. Connor had gotten him to park Stella outside the front doors as part of the decorations, but Emma wondered if in fact it was a ploy to find a girlfriend who met Stella's approval.

Emma, in turn, made sure to give each of the male residents at least one dance, and even talked herself into smiling through all of it. She was just finishing up dancing with Stan when Doris and Mr. Willoughby walked up to the microphone.

Doris cleared her throat and the microphone squealed. She held it away from her mouth a few inches before speaking. "On behalf of all the residents at Heart & Home, we wanted to thank you all for coming to our dance," she said. As she went on, Stan and many of the other senior residents drifted toward her, standing on either side as though they were all in on this announcement. "As most of you know, this dance was planned as a fundraiser this year, and we want to thank you all for chipping in through the admission price, and also for all of the generous bids for the items at the silent auction."

Emma looked around at all the people who had come out for the evening. Far more than she had imagined. Maybe they would be able to keep Heart & Home open after all.

"I'm sure most of you thought this money was to contribute to the needs of our residents," Doris went on. "And it's true, Heart & Home does need financial help and community support. But more importantly to us, one of our own needs our help."

Emma glanced around the room, wondering what Doris was talking about. She felt her hope start to dwindle. Maybe the wonderful place she thought of as her second home wasn't going to survive after all.

Doris went on. "We're hoping what we make tonight will not only be enough to keep Heart & Home open, but also to help our dear Nurse Hathaway's dog, Charlie, to undergo an urgent veterinary surgery. Charlie is part of our family at Heart & Home. He comforts us if we are lonely, and he has even been known to participate in a game of poker once in a while."

Emma's eyes widened in disbelief. But just as quickly, her heart sank back into its despair. She made her way up to the microphone. All the senior residents smiled brightly at her, but they didn't understand.

She took the microphone. "First, I want to thank you all so very much. It means the world to me that you would care so much about me and Charlie." Her voice choked on her dog's name. She hadn't even had the heart to call Dr. Franklin back yet to inform him she wouldn't be able to come up with the money for the surgery and that... "I just—" She didn't know how to say it. She desperately did not want to hurt the seniors' feelings.

"Heart & Home is in need of all the funds that were raised. There would not be enough for Charlie's care, too."

"How much?" came a voice from the back of the hall. Everyone turned to look for the source of the voice. Emma shielded her eyes from the bright lights with her hand. The crowd seemed to part, and then Emma had a clear view to the back of the community hall.

Jake. He was standing there with Meredith beside him in her wheelchair. She was beaming from ear to ear.

Emma was confused. Wasn't Meredith supposed to be in Seattle by now? With everything else she was going through, Emma had deliberately avoided being at Heart & Home for her goodbye. She didn't think her heart could take it. Instead, Emma had written a special letter that she left for Meredith with a promise she would visit.

Looking at Jake standing there now, Emma had forgotten how strikingly handsome he was, with his dark wavy hair and chiseled cheekbones. She stared at him, unable to find the words to speak. She knew she owed him an apology for everything she had said the last time she had talked to him at the vet's clinic, but this wasn't the place or time.

"How much?" he repeated, loud enough for everyone in the room to hear. "How much to get Charlie the surgery? Would selling a Lexus be enough?"

Emma didn't know what he was talking about.

But he turned to his grandmother, placing a hand on her shoulder and kept speaking. "Or how about withdrawing a down payment from Lexington Manor. Would that be enough?" Meredith reached up and patted his hand, continuing to smile.

Emma left the mic at the stand and walked toward him, feeling like she was in a dream. "Jake, what are you talking about?" She could feel all the eyes in the room on her.

"Look, just follow me and I can explain," he said with a twinkle in his eye.

No one seemed to know what he was talking about, least of all Emma. But with that, Jake turned and walked out of the room and toward the back-double doors. Emma caught the eye of Mr.

Willoughby who looked just as confused as she was by the events taking place.

Emma only stayed dumbfounded on the spot for another second, and then she was following Jake, along with a group of the seniors and curious onlookers who were close behind. By the time she made it through the crowd of people in the community hall to the exit doors, Jake was outside, and had disappeared on the far side of a van that was pulled up to the building. Leave it to Jake Rothstein, Emma thought, to park in the No Parking Zone anytime he feels like it. But she was still too confused for the thought to have much strength.

She glanced back and saw that not only had her sister followed her out, but many of the residents and townsfolk had also left the dance to see what on earth Jake Rothstein was talking about.

Was she supposed to keep following him? And whose gigantic old white van was this?

Not giving herself any more time to question it, she pushed forward through the doors and around the van, with half the town on her heels.

And then she proceeded to let out a shocked gasp.

The side van door was wide open, and in the space, Charlie was lying in his kennel. He was groggy from pain medication, but yet he mustered up enough strength to wag his tail when he caught sight of Emma. Around the corner of the van came Dr. Franklin and his assistant.

Emma rushed up to Charlie and put her hand through the bars on the kennel to gently pet his head. "I don't underst...wha...what is going on, Jake?" Emma struggled to get a single coherent question out of her mouth, but somehow Jake knew what she really wanted to know.

"I met with Dr. Franklin this morning and he has an appointment booked with the specialist for Charlie's surgery in Seattle. But he needs your permission and signature on the surgical and transport forms before he can drive Charlie there tonight."

"But Jake...the cost." Tears were already streaming down

Emma's face as she perched in the open van beside Charlie. She ran her hands over Charlie's head and looked into his eyes.

"He's going to be okay, Emma." Jake quirked a smile.

"But how did you…it costs thousands of dollars, and—"

Jake interrupted her. "What do you think of my new—well, new to me—van?"

Emma looked down the length of the van and back up at Jake, realization now dawning on her. "Your Lexus? You sold your Lexus?" she gasped.

Jake nodded. "I admit, I do miss my car already. But I also love the idea of being able to take you and Charlie, and even my grandmother out, anytime it suits us. Besides, I got a great deal on the van."

"And Lexington Manor?" Emma asked, hardly daring to breathe.

Jake looked back to where his grandmother sat in her wheelchair, just outside the entrance to the community hall. "I was able to get my deposit back. I somehow got the feeling my grandma really likes it here in Juniper Falls." Jake met Emma's eyes. Emma stood, feeling the draw to be closer to him, and she wanted to thank him for all he'd done. "And you know what?" he added. "So do I."

Doris moved up beside Jake and Emma and asked, "What does all this mean?" She had a hopeful tone to her voice.

Meredith spoke up. "It means you have one more member to add to your gang, Doris." The residents all rallied around her, giving hugs to her and to each other.

Jake kept his eyes on Emma. "It means I'm starting to see what's important."

Taking hold of both Jake's hands, Emma looked at him in question, "Jake, I can't let you do this."

"I want to help, Emma. Please let me."

"I'll pay you back, I promise." Tears moistened the corners of her eyes, and she tried to blink them away, but that only brought them on stronger.

"I just want to see you smile again. That's the only thing I need," he said softly as he let go of her hands to tenderly wipe the tears from her face.

A soft "thank you," escaped from her lips.

"This calls for a special dance," Stan piped up. "Come on back inside, everybody. Let's get this party started!"

The townsfolk started to file back inside, but Emma held back. "I'll be there in a minute. I just have to sign some papers and send my Charlie on his way."

Jake took Emma's hands in his, reading her perfectly, as he usually did. "I will see you inside when you are done. You know, Charlie's going to be in good hands. He will be up and chasing squirrels again in no time. I have a good feeling about him."

After the crowd headed back inside, Dr. Franklin briefed Emma on the specifics of Charlie's procedure and recovery. They were using Jake's van to transport him there and he would be back in Juniper Falls in two days' time. She would be able to visit him upon his return to the clinic and would get updates after the surgery. She gave Charlie a kiss on his nose and watched them close the van door and drive away.

When the van was no longer in sight, Emma turned and headed into the hall. Her heart was full. She was just in time to hear Stan on the microphone. "This next song goes out to our very special Nurse Hathaway. Not only are we thankful to have Charlie getting the help he needs, but we're extra thankful to have Nurse Hathaway's special smile back." He placed the microphone back into its stand and pressed play on *The Way You Look Tonight*.

Emma was still looking at Stan and beaming at his special dedication when she felt a warm hand on her shoulder. She turned to see Jake's smiling face. He was holding a card in his hands.

"What's this?"

"Well apparently I have a secret admirer." Jake opened the card to show Emma. She recognized the printing and looked over to her nieces who had been standing to the side, giggling as they recognized Laney's card. She wondered how on earth the girls had arranged to send a Valentine without her knowing.

"It looks like you're cared for by many, Emma Hathaway.

That said," he tucked away the card and held out his hand, "may I have this dance?"

She placed her hand in his. After what he had done, he could have as many dances as he wanted.

Winding a hand around to the small of her back, Jake led her onto the dance floor. She could feel stares from all around the room, but she didn't care about any of that. She only cared about Jake and what he had done for her.

As she turned into him and placed a hand on his shoulder, she said, "Jake," and suddenly she was choked up again. She gave it another try. "I don't know how to thank…I'm so sorry for how…" her throat constricted around her words a second time. Her emotions were getting the better of her.

He shook his head and pulled her closer. "I know how much you care about Charlie." He didn't give her time to reply, which was good, because she finally felt like she was getting a hold of herself. "But I wanted to show you how much I care about you, Emma. If you'll let me, this is just the start of what I can do."

She laid her head on his chest, but even through her tears, she looked up so she could meet his eyes. "Oh, Jake," she said.

He leaned in closer and whispered in her ear. "You look absolutely breathtaking tonight."

Emma melted. She replayed Geezer's words to her, about how he never would have wanted to spend his life without his Marion. She thought she was starting to feel the same way about Jake.

He ran a thumb from her cheek to her jaw, and then his hand slid behind her neck to pull her in. "I could get lost in your eyes," he said.

He leaned in. She tipped her head slightly back and reached up to him.

Suddenly, the whole world stopped around them—the people, the movements, the music.

Then the lights came on and they broke apart, surprised. Mr. Willoughby was on the stage beside Stan and speaking into the microphone.

"Sorry to interrupt, folks, but has anybody seen Geezer?"

## 33

## JAKE

Whispers and murmurs filled the room as groups of people began to form to discuss the missing resident. Geezer had lived in Juniper Falls his entire life, so many knew of the elderly man and wanted to help locate him.

"In all the hubbub of Jake and Charlie arriving," Doris said as they gathered around Stan at the microphone, "he must have finally escaped."

"I'd always thought he was joking," Beatrice said, shaking her head and looking down.

"We all did, Beatrice." Emma slid a comforting arm around her. A sense of guilt filled the group, as they felt somewhat responsible for not taking his previous attempts of escaping from Heart & Home seriously.

Jake left Emma while she comforted the concerned residents. He wasn't sure what to do but he couldn't just stand there. After all, if he was going to be part of Juniper Falls, he needed to lend his hand too. Paul was over in the corner talking to a few of the residents and a couple of nurses, trying to get an understanding on where Geezer may have gone. Others had already spread out to search the building, but soon returned with no new information. The old man was not anywhere in the community hall.

"It's going to get colder and snow is in the forecast." Emma said, her voice tinged with worry as she joined Jake and the others. "We need to get out there to look for him."

She instructed Pam and Nurse Johannsson to help the residents back to the waiting Heart & Home van outside, and then she asked around for those willing to get out there and look for the missing man.

She seemed stressed, and Jake didn't want to interrupt, but he had an idea. He placed a hand on the small of her back to get her attention.

"I'm going to get a ride with Paul over to Graham Park and have a look there."

"By the fountain?" Emma asked.

Jake nodded. "The couple of times I've spoken to Geezer, he mentioned how he loved the park."

"That's such a long way for him to walk, especially at night and in this cold." Emma didn't look like she thought it was too likely that Geezer had walked all the way across town to Graham Park, and Jake didn't know if it was either, but he didn't have any better ideas.

"Thank you, Jake," Emma said. "For everything." She quickly ran to the Heart & Home van, pulling a wool blanket out that the residents used for their picnics during the summer. She handed it to Jake. "If you find him, he'll be cold."

Jake rubbed her arm. "We'll find him, Emma." She still didn't look much like she believed it, so he assured her once more, "We will."

———

Paul and Jake drove across town, keeping their eyes peeled for a man hobbling along with a walker. The entire force was out looking. Even the fire department had called in extra men to aid in the search. The town had quickly been divided into grids, with each search party having a section to check. For a small town, they were efficient, Jake thought to himself.

The truth was, if Geezer had been headed for Graham Park, there was a good chance he wouldn't have even made it there yet.

Then again, who knew how long Geezer had been missing before everyone noticed among the excitement of him bringing Charlie by.

He didn't see Geezer anywhere along the road or sidewalk, but as soon as Paul pulled into the small parking lot at Graham Park, Jake could see a hunched dark figure on the bench near the lake.

Jake got out and strode for the figure along the pathway. A few feet closer, and Geezer's walker came into view, alongside the bench. Jake let out his breath and motioned for Paul to call off the search parties. He was thankful the park was so well lit, otherwise he might have missed seeing the elderly man.

Jake wasn't sure if he was the best person to talk to Geezer. He barely knew him after all. But he strode for the bench anyway. Geezer didn't stir at his approach, even when Jake moved around the bench and sat gingerly beside him. Geezer glanced over but didn't look surprised to see who had found him.

Jake was glad that he didn't seem worried about being "caught." The last thing Jake wanted to do was chase an old man through the park and then have to force him to return to Heart & Home with him.

Jake opened his mouth several times, about to start a sentence, but then was unsure of what to say or how to phrase it. Geezer seemed like a no-nonsense kind of guy, though, and so when several minutes had passed with no word from him, Jake decided that was probably the best way to approach it: Head on.

"Heart & Home seems like such a great place. Are you unhappy there?" Jake kept his eyes trained ahead on the lineup of small remote-controlled boats along a dock by the pond. He had seen them there when he was out with Emma's nieces. It had caught him off guard with a flood of memories from time spent here.

Geezer sighed. "No, I'm not unhappy with Heart & Home." Geezer kept his eyes forward too.

"Why are you always trying to run away then?"

Geezer turned his gaze onto Jake. "I could ask the same thing of you. Do you see your life-defining moments as obstacles that hinder you, or do you allow them to let you grow, Jake?"

Jake shifted uncomfortably. It was the most astute thing anyone had ever asked him. Jake felt exposed, but he wasn't sure he disliked it. In a way, it felt refreshing. The old man saw right through him. Jake had been running his entire life. It was amazing how so many others had seen this and yet he, himself, had only just recently come to acknowledge his desire to escape facing his past. He had used his pain as an excuse to run again and again.

Before Jake could come up with any kind of response, Geezer went on. "You don't remember me, but I remember you. You used to come to this park every weekend with your grandpa. Right over there." Geezer pointed to the fountain in the pond, and it was true. That was exactly where Jake had stood with his grandpa. "This was the place where I met my Marion. First time I laid eyes on her I was smitten, and knew we were destined to be together. She had the most beautiful smile and made my rough edges seem a little smoother. She was an artist and painted the most breathtaking pictures."

Geezer's whole countenance lit up as he talked of his late wife, so Jake remained silent and let him go on.

"Her work felt so life-like, it was as if you could walk right into the scene. Marion didn't just paint what she saw, she painted with her whole heart, what she felt. Every Saturday, I would come here and sit on the bench, working up the courage to talk to her. She was so immersed in her painting, I never thought she noticed me, until one day when she put her paintbrush and canvas down, got up from the patchwork blanket she had been sitting on, and walked right up to me. She looked me straight on in the eyes, and she said, 'So, are you going to ask me out for ice cream, or just keep coming here each week to watch me paint?' From that day on, we were inseparable."

Jake took the wool blanket he had been holding and wrapped it around the old man's shoulders as Geezer continued to reminisce of his true love.

"I asked Marion to marry me, here, on Valentine's Day. Some

people don't put stock into reliving specific memories, but other people—people like us—we need to do just that."

As Geezer said the words, they felt true. It was exactly why he'd brought the roses to his grandma the day before.

Geezer went on. "It was a Tuesday, same as today. We took a walk to the park. I was a nervous wreck and fidgeted with the ring that was in my jacket pocket the entire time. I had all these self-doubts. Wondered what a woman like her could see in a man like me. Well, we got to this bench here and Marion was getting out her packet of breadcrumbs to feed the ducks. I got down on one knee before I could talk myself out of it, and when she turned around and looked down, well, there I was holding out the ring."

Jake felt his own face light up, as Geezer came to this part.

"She said 'yes' and made me the happiest man in the world. This became *our* bench. It was here where we planned our future together—a future of a house filled with children." He stopped and let out a heavy sigh. "But sadly, not all plans go the way we want them to, Jake. It was after many doctor's visits, we found out that we could not have children. A piece of Marion's heart broke with that realization, and a piece of mine as well—not necessarily over our inability to have children, but over seeing my Marion hurt in a way that I could not fix."

Jake reached over and patted the old man's knee.

"Marion threw herself into her painting. She loved coming here to watch the children and over the years, the pain lessened a little as she took joy in painting the many families that came to the park. As we got older, Marion called this bench her 'healing bench.' She said by sitting here each week, she could find peace within her pain by seeing the love around her. Jake, she loved watching you and your grandfather together. Marion saw how much he loved you. One of her most treasured paintings was one she painted several years before her illness of you and your grandfather sailing the boat on the pond. He had his arm around you, guiding you. The look on his face that Marion captured on her canvas showed great pride and love in his grandson."

That string of words opened up a well of emotions within

Jake. Even when pulling into the parking lot at Graham Park, he struggled to fully let himself relive the memories between him and his grandfather. But now he did. He had to.

There had been times when Jake felt like he fit in Juniper Falls, where he felt like he had a best friend in his grandpa. Sometimes it even felt like he had a regular parent. His grandpa had loomed over him from behind, guiding him with the remote control for their favorite boat—the green and purple one—and his grandpa told him stories of his own upbringing. They used to fish on the other side of the lake, where the river runs into it, and Jake had caught his first fish there.

Over the last few days, Jake had gained a backstory to his life's journey and a sense of belonging. He didn't need to run from memories any longer. He just needed to redefine them, to put the pieces together for the entire picture. Jake knew now that he had been selective in his memories and had used that as his escape from facing his pain.

Hearing Geezer's love for Marion gave him a longing for that kind of authentic love, to be given it and to give it back in return. Jake knew he had made decisions that were now guiding him on the right path, with his job, his grandma, and with Emma. He just needed to continue on his journey.

"Thank you, Geezer, for sharing your love of Marion with me. She sounds like she was one special woman. I can see how coming here makes you feel closer to her. And Marion was right." The old man looked up at Jake. "This is, in fact, a healing bench."

Geezer nodded with a knowing smile.

"I guess I haven't spent much time thinking about my life-defining moments," Jake continued. "Not until recently."

As if Geezer could read Jake's memories, he said, "Some of my life-defining moments happened right here, too, Jake. Right on this very bench."

Jake could tell Geezer was getting cold even with the blanket covering him. He took off his jacket and wrapped it around his friend.

"Supposed to snow on the weekend," Geezer said suddenly.

"You might not understand this, Jake, but I had to get down here before the snow. I had to have that memory the same way it was."

It made perfect sense to Jake. It was the same way Jake needed his memories. He had needed them for a while now.

"It's sad, though," Jake said. "That we have to come here to remember what's gone."

"Ehh. Remember that, and then it makes you more capable of appreciating what you have now. *Who* you have now."

"Geezer, you don't by chance still have that painting your Marion did of my grandfather and me?"

Geezer let out a low chuckle. "When Marion passed, I wanted others to share in the beauty of her work. I donated her most treasured works of art to the Juniper Falls Arts Council, and they put them on display."

"Well, I have an idea, Geezer. What if I promise to take you there to see Marion's paintings this week? And you know what? I think I might need to visit this park more often in the future. Would sure love some company from someone who knows how special it is. After all, I have the perfect van now to take new friends where they need to go."

Jake asked Geezer if he was ready to go home now. The old man nodded with tears in his eyes, not another word to be said, as if he was all talked out.

## 34

## EMMA

Even though Emma had been awake for nearly twenty hours, she still felt wide awake. It wasn't just one thing that was keeping her mind swirling, but a compilation of all the events during and after the dance. She kept surging between the moments and emotions from the evening: the adrenaline from Jake's arrival and announcement, seeing Charlie leave for surgery, dancing in Jake's arms, and then Geezer going missing. It was a day unlike any other.

After Jake and Paul dropped Geezer off, she'd spent the first hour calming herself and the rest of the residents down. Everyone was excited to see Geezer come through the doors to Heart & Home. Emma knew it made Geezer feel loved, but she could also see a weariness in his eyes. The long day had taken its toll on him. Jake had quietly tipped her off that Geezer had been missing his wife, and said he would fill her in later, but it had to do with him needing to relive a memory of proposing to his wife before the snow came. The romance of the gesture made Emma completely forget the lecture she had been about to give the old man. Instead, she made him some warm milk, wrapped Geezer up snuggly in his bed, and made sure the photo of Marion was turned so that he could see it from where he lay. Before Emma even closed the door to his room, she looked back and saw the senior's eyes close with a smile on his face.

"Sweet dreams, Geezer," she whispered, and she turned off the lights and left the room.

Hours later, she still found herself wandering the halls. Connor had left to put the girls to bed a long time ago while Amy stayed with the food and cleaned up. They told Emma to call when she needed a ride, but she assured them she would be fine to get herself home. In the worst case, she could always catch a few hours of sleep on the couch in the sunroom.

Sleeping still seemed like a far-off venture for her, though, even if the rest of the building had been lost to slumber hours ago.

Maybe a walk home was just what she needed to clear the head. Emma zipped up her down coat and put on a pair of gloves as she headed out the front doors of Heart & Home. In light of the recent events, she checked that the door locked behind her. Taking in a deep breath of the cold quiet night air, she started to stroll toward home, hoping that tiredness would hit by the time she got there.

The moon was full, casting a light like a beacon, guiding her along her path. Emma stopped to look up at the sky, blanketed with stars. She loved the fact that this sight wasn't hidden by the glare of city lights. She could hear an owl in the distance hooting his goodnight song and a faint reply echoed back. Love really was in the air, she mused and laughed out loud at her own joke. As if the universe had heard her thought, a shooting star streamed across the sky. Emma closed her eyes tight, never one to miss an opportunity to make a wish on a falling star.

Caught up in the night sky and her wish, she found that her feet had led her to a place in her heart rather than her home. She found herself a block away from Meredith's house. She knew Jake would have turned in hours ago, but she decided to stroll by and look one more time at the house that would soon have new residents. As she got closer, she tried to convince herself that she should be happy for the Rothsteins. She *was* happy for them. Meredith was now staying at Heart & Home. She could, if she wished, continue to see Jake regularly, and the relationship between grandmother and grandson would continue to grow and heal.

She just couldn't shake the thought that their house would be missed, even if she herself had never lived there.

She sighed and murmured, "Well I sure hope the new owners appreciate this place," into the night air.

"I can assure you, he does," a voice said out of the darkness.

"Jake?" Emma said, squinting toward the porch where the voice originated.

Jake emerged from the shadows on the porch. He was still in his clothing from earlier tonight, although it looked noticeably more rumpled. He walked toward her.

"The owner will love this place the way it deserves to be loved," he said.

"What—How—Do you know the new owners?" she asked. Her exhaustion must finally be catching up with her, because something was just not making sense.

"I took it off the market," he said, smiling wryly at her. "Since I decided to move back, there was no reason to sell."

"You mean—*you're* going to live here?" Excitement leaked out in her voice.

Jake nodded and moved a step closer. "I made a mistake, wanting to move my grandmother away from the home she loves, and I realized I love it too. It has grown on me the last while. Someone helped me to realize how special it actually is, and what it means to my family."

"But—" Emma started, looking at the non-wheelchair-accessible front steps, "—Meredith can't move back here. It wouldn't be safe."

"Juniper Falls," Jake said, clearing it up. "This whole town is her home. She needs the care that you can give her, and she needs the family that I can give her. And once in a while, she'll be able to visit this old place. I've already arranged to make it more wheelchair accessible." He motioned behind Emma to the house. "Who knows, maybe this white picket fence and those French doors, will even earn this place a new resident one day. You know, maybe someone who would use that porch to watch the sunrise in a rocking chair." He smirked, and she wondered if he'd read her mind about wanting to do just that.

Emma took a step closer to him, barely daring to hope.

He took this as an invitation and slid a hand around the back of her neck. "I'd wanted to do this at the dance," he whispered, and then re-thought his words. "Actually, I've wanted to do this for quite a while." And then he leaned in and his tender lips melted into hers.

Emma hadn't been kissed in so long, it took her a moment to remember how to relax into it, how to let it be. To just let herself enjoy it. But she did enjoy it. *Oh,* how she enjoyed it.

When he pulled away and stroked her face, it took her several long seconds to blink back to reality. "So why were you out here sitting in the dark all alone?" Emma asked playfully.

"The night sky was beautiful, and I just happened to find a chair that fit perfectly on the porch." Emma noticed the silhouette of a rocking chair sitting in the corner. "I'm looking for a matching one. Maybe we can do some antique shopping this Saturday and you can help me find one? After all, it's a great spot for sitting and watching the world go by. I think Charlie will agree when he returns home."

"Oh Jake, thank you! Yes, of course, I would love to help you." She threw her arms around his neck, reaching up for another one of those magical kisses.

# 35

## JAKE

If someone had told Jake a month ago that he'd be singing and playing piano on a Wednesday afternoon with his grandma and her friends in Juniper Falls, he would have told them they were crazy.

And yet, here he was—a new home, a new life.

Even a new job.

As he finished his next song, Pam walked into the sunroom carrying the latest edition of the weekly community newspaper.

"Jake!" she said, and he didn't think he was imagining her unusually peppy tone. "Our new ad came out today."

Ahh, that's why she was so excited. After a short sit-down with the staff of Heart & Home and Mr. Willoughby, Jake had convinced them that advertising works—it's just a matter of finding the *right* kind of advertising.

Jake had arranged the first three ads pro-bono, to make sure his grandmother's nursing home would keep their head above water, but after they saw the influx of not only new paying residents, but also donors, they had hired him for this latest one. This was also the one he was happiest with.

It had taken him a month or so of living here to really get a feel for the town again and their needs, but as he looked down at the ad he'd captioned, "Home is where the heart belongs," he was pretty sure he had a handle on it.

And a good thing, too, because two other local companies had hired him to handle their advertising—one of them Emma's sister's new catering business. He had no doubt her ad was going to make a splash, and he flipped through the paper until he saw the personalized ad with a giant smiling picture of Amy and a platter of food extended out in front of her. He was meeting with the owner of Java Junction next week to plan out their advertising campaign.

True to his word, Jake had taken Geezer to the gallery to see Marion's paintings. Geezer spent the afternoon reminiscing. He had a story to go along with each painting, but the one that caught Jake's eye was the little boy and his grandfather sailing the boat around the pond. The little boy was so busy with the remote control and navigating through the bulrushes that he had not seen the look on his grandfather's face. Marion had been right, a look of pride and love radiated from his smile. Indeed, a picture does say a thousand words. He was grateful and looked forward to taking his grandmother to the gallery one afternoon to visit the painting.

Paul had given Jake a homecoming gift. It seemed he remembered Jake's love of sailboats too and won the bid for the remote-controlled boat at the silent auction. Now the boat sat on a shelf displayed in Jake's home, waiting for the day when he planned to take Emma to the park, to sail the boat and to propose to her.

Charlie lay in the sunshine that streamed into the sunroom of Heart & Home. His surgery had gone even better than expected. He was now able to return for daily visits with the residents and the occasional poker game.

The residents called out, "One more!" which brought Jake back to focus on his music. He loved playing for the residents. He loved it even more because Emma was here.

Jake slid sideways on his piano bench and patted it beside him. He had already started making some pretty wonderful memories at Heart & Home, and he looked forward to what the future would bring.

Emma smiled and settled in, leaning into Jake's shoulder to sing just one more song together.

## The End

---

Don't miss out on your next favorite book!

Join the Satin Romance mailing list
www.satinromance.com/mail.html

## THANK YOU FOR READING

———

Did you enjoy this book?

We invite you to leave a review at your favorite book site, such as Goodreads, Amazon, Barnes & Noble, etc.

## DID YOU KNOW THAT LEAVING A REVIEW…

- Helps other readers find books they may enjoy.
- Gives you a chance to let your voice be heard.
- Gives authors recognition for their hard work.
- Doesn't have to be long. A sentence or two about why you liked the book will do.

## ABOUT THE AUTHOR: NIKKI BERGSTRESSER

**Nikki Bergstresser** lives in the Pacific Northwest with her husband and two teenage daughters. As well as writing romance, she is an elementary teacher and author of children's picture books. Nikki is a romantic at heart and is inspired by spending time in nature, spontaneous adventures and being surrounded by books. You can connect with Nikki on social media and follow her writing journeys at nikkibergstresser.com

www.nikkibergstresser.com

facebook.com/NBergstresser
twitter.com/NBergstresser
instagram.com/nikkibergstresser

## ABOUT THE AUTHOR: DENISE JADEN

**Denise Jaden** is the author of several cozy mysteries, young adult novels, and nonfiction books for writers, including The Mallory Beck Cozy Culinary Capers and the NaNoWriMo-popular writing guide *Fast Fiction*. She homeschools her son, dances with a Polynesian dance troupe, and works as an actress with the Vancouver Film Industry, where she can most notably be seen on Hallmark Channel's *When Calls the Heart*. She is a sought-after speaker and loves to hear from readers and writers on Twitter and Facebook—don't hesitate to drop her a note @denisejaden.

Find out more about Denise and her writing online at denisejaden.com.

www.denisejaden.com

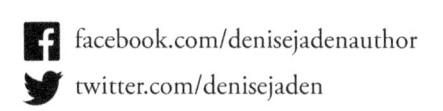

facebook.com/denisejadenauthor
twitter.com/denisejaden

Made in the USA
Monee, IL
23 October 2021